I

Will

Survive

Other titles by Graham Sclater

Ticket to Ride

Hatred is the Key

We're Gonna be Famous

Too Big to Cry

More Than a Woman

Love Shack

Cowboys and Angels

Non-Fiction

WRITE ON!

For more information on Graham Sclater and all of his books,
see his website at www.grahamsclater.com

I Will Survive

Graham Sclater

Tabitha Books

Tabitha Books

Exeter EX2 9DJ England

Tabitha books is a division of Tabitha Publishing Limited

Tabitha Books

First Published in 2020 by Tabitha Books

ISBN 978-0-9954884-3-4

Typeset in Sabon 12 by Tabitha Books
Cover design Denise Bailey

www.tabithabooks.webs.com

Acknowledgements

Ilka Volz in Hamburg, Karel at the Koopermoolen, the Amsterdam politie department, Ieva Priedite in Athens at Global Maritime Group, Barrie at Gomango Creative and the wonderful music of Pete Simensky, Barbra Streisand, Andrea Bocelli and Andy Bradford while I worked on this novel.

I would also like to thank the numerous radio presenters and media around the world who continue to support me, and lastly all the readers who have bought my previous work.

Zita whispered in Liam's ear. 'We have had fun... haven't we?'

The author in Lisbon

Graham Sclater lives in Exeter where he is a successful music publisher. Prior to returning to Devon in the late sixties he was a professional musician playing all over Europe and worked as a session musician with many name artists. His first novel *Ticket to Ride* was originally published in 2004 by Flame Books and republished by Tabitha Books in 2012. This was followed by the novella *We're Gonna Be Famous*; the historical novel *Hatred is the Key;* his psychological thrillers *More Than a Woman* and *Too Big to Cry; his* thriller *Love Shack,* set in the Red-Light District of Amsterdam, then his 2018 thriller *Cowboys and Angels,* set in Cyprus. His first non-fiction book on creative writing *WRITE ON!* was published in 2019.

Graham can regularly be seen talking in libraries, at book signings and literary events, as well as delivering creative writing sessions to passengers on cruise ships. He is currently working on his next novel, a number of television and film scripts along with his music publishing company and record label.

Graham can also be heard on regional and national radio talking about various subjects close to his heart as well as his monthly book review which is aired on radio stations around the world.

Check out his website: www.grahamsclater.com

CONTENTS

Prologue

Details of all titles written by Graham Sclater can be found on his website: www.grahamsclater.com

PROLOGUE

Living in the east end during the sixties and seventies Jimmy Patrick Reilly made the Kray twins and their cronies look like Sunday school teachers. Very much a loner, he was feared by everyone and his audacious and vicious crimes made him the envy of every would be criminal in the East End. Sentenced to a life in jail did not make his enemies safe, his far-reaching defence of his manor maintained his reputation and no one dared to openly discuss him with anyone outside of the exclusive circles. Despite exceptional rewards and deals the wall of silence was upheld. His three children - Liam, his older daughter Marie and his younger son Tommy, never went without. Several times a week anonymous cash donations were pushed through the letterbox of the family home enabling the Reilly family to maintain the life to which they had become accustomed.

Jimmy was finally released from prison in 1998 and he was at last able to take up his rightful position as head of the Reilly family.

His eldest son, Liam would never achieve a fraction of his father's notoriety and while his father had "worked" to plan every crime, Liam did not see the necessity, with the result that as a teenager he was continually in and out of remand homes and when he reached eighteen was sent to prison. He was the one person that every police officer wanted to nail but, defended and protected at arm's length by his father, he was to escape prosecution for many of his pathetic crimes no matter how violent they were.

Liam was an alcoholic and criminal and, despite being imprisoned for life, he was granted bail following the way he defended and saved the lives of two prison officers during a horrific riot which resulted in the death of several prisoners and prison officers.

Upon his release, and following yet another drunken binge, Liam accidentally set fire to the family home. Despite saving everyone and briefly being lauded a hero, his father knew the truth and forced him to leave the country. His younger brother, Tommy, who idolised Liam, stole a car and drove him to Dover where he took the first available ferry to mainland Europe, ending up in Amsterdam.

Once in the notorious city, Liam walked the short distance from the drop-off point at Centraal Station and gravitated with everyone else to the red-light district. He stopped for a coffee at the Red Cat, a run down and neglected bar alongside the Oudezijds Voorburgwal canal. While he was talking to Keeva, the petite Irish waitress, once again trouble found him. During a pitched battle on the canalside between opposing football fans, Liam was arrested and wrongly accused of stabbing to death a Dutch supporter, and arrested for murder. Keeva contacted the owner, Meener Bram De Groot, considered to be one of the most powerful villains in Amsterdam. Never one to miss an opportunity to recruit anyone that could swell his mismatched aggressive and vicious henchmen he conveniently arranged for Liam to be released on bail.

With his passport held by the police and unable to leave Holland, Liam had no option but to stay in Amsterdam.

Following a lengthy imposed discussion with De Groot, he agreed to manage the renovated Red Cat, a brothel and bar, renaming it the Love Shack. This left Liam with the greatest and most nightmarish ordeal of his life.

CHAPTER ONE

Eve of Destruction

While the residents of the Love Shack enjoyed the private New Year celebrations of 1999-2000, two motorcyclists, dressed from head to toe in black leather, pulled up unnoticed outside the dimly lit building. They each removed two Molotov cocktails from their jackets, lit them, nodded to each other and simultaneously threw them.

The flaming bottles crashed through the windows and fire immediately engulfed the building.

Within seconds thick smoke began to shroud the five storeys and narrow adjoining buildings, and fierce red and orange flames from what was the Love Shack shot high into the night sky casting huge red flames that danced in the sky illuminating the nearby buildings, clubs and bars along the canal.

The thick palls of smoke were irradiated by the continual colourful explosions of the fireworks as they shot high into the night sky.

Two brightly painted fireboats were first to get the call. Within seconds they could be heard blasting the already frenetic night air with their high-pitched ear shattering sirens, as they attempted to compete with the raging fireworks overhead, and to warn the crowded midnight tourist boats and barges choking the canals. They weaved their way in and out of the boats along the Singel, creating huge waves in their wake which almost engulfed the sightseeing boats, before turning into the Oudezijds Voorburgwal canal.

The fireboats finally arrived to what was now an unrecognisable building that just a short while earlier was the Love Shack. Within minutes the well-trained firemen fired up their pumps and with military precision aimed the hoses at the Love Shack, now beginning to burn out of control and a potential risk to the surrounding buildings.

In the hours either side of midnight thousands of Dutch people and youngsters loved this very special night and the opportunity to release their pyrotechnics. They roamed the towns and cities carrying huge stashes of fireworks in bags and backpacks, ready to detonate them anytime, anywhere and desperate to cause mayhem and pandemonium.

Brandweer Nederland - The Nederland Fire Department - was always well prepared for this extraordinary night and in Amsterdam it was no different. But on the fateful night of 31st December 1999, they weren't so well equipped and it was necessary for some of the fire tenders stationed at the Oosterdok, a massive firework display held annually in the city, to leave and offer their support. With sirens screaming and blue lights flashing, they raced across the city to assist their colleagues at the inferno that was once the Love Shack.

In 1421 and 1452, major fires ripped through the prosperous city of Amsterdam destroying many of the timber constructed buildings. Following that it was banned as the prime building material and the new buildings were constructed of brick.

Most of the 17th century buildings that circled the city's canals were generally five storeys high and narrow because taxes were charged based on the width of the building. The wider they were, the greater the tax. Consequently, most of the newly built narrow properties around the canal ring had winding staircases, making it impossible to get large items into the higher floors of the building. As a consequence, it was necessary to incorporate a steel hook, with a winch and pulley, to take everything above ground level into the building.

The fireboats were followed minutes later by the sound of high-pitched screaming sirens and alarms, raising the fear level amongst the nearest bar owners and hoteliers in the surrounding area. The first fire engines picked their way between the drunken revellers and along the road beside the Oudezijds Voorburgwal to reach the devastating fire. Following feverish activity, the additional fire crews finally pumped the water from the canal aiming their jets at the adjoining buildings.

The fire continued to burn out of control and ripped throughout the Love Shack.

The bottles of alcohol behind the bar shattered sending shards of glass into the air.

The gas canisters in the cellar exploded.

The windows blew out, sending lethal jagged slivers of glass high into the air and across the road and canal.

This was followed minutes later by the sound of a massive crack which reverberated off the buildings that fronted onto the canal. Seconds later, as if in slow motion, the brick façade of the bell gable end gave way along with the steel girder and hook, crashing away from the building. The firemen pulled back in a frenzied retreat as the burning roofing timbers, glowing roof tiles, masonry and steel crashed onto the already burning debris piled up on the street below.

This was immediately followed by the only remaining carved and painted stone gable tablet, above the door, installed in 1759 and pre-dating house numbers, when the house was constructed by the original owner, a wealthy trader.

Drunken spectators watched and swayed uncontrollably in unison as the surreal events unfolded around them until the police car sirens screamed to a halt and parked haphazardly on the opposite side of the canal. They raced to set up a cordon around the whole area and sealed off much of De Wallen and the adjoining streets.

Three more fire tenders were deployed from Schiphol airport to fight the blaze including one with a high level Magirus turntable ladder. Two helmeted firemen with masks and oxygen cylinders strapped to their backs made what seemed to be a futile attempt to aim their hoses deep into the heart of the fierce flames as they shot even higher into the colourful exploding night sky.

The fireworks continued to be seen above the city, paradoxically seeming to be celebrating the horrific events.

A helicopter whirred dangerously overhead, its searchlight creating eerie shadows around the buildings and the nearby streets.

Ambulances with their blue lights flashing and sirens wailing pulled up on the other side of the canal and the paramedics raced to remove their stretchers from the vehicles.

A few minutes later the first of several television crews arrived in their liveried vehicles and set up their cameras and satellite dishes on the same side of the canal. The first reporter stood with his back to the flames and gave his report to the camera. 'I'm standing on the side of the Oudezijds Voorburgwal as we witness the fire at the Love Shack, a popular bar here in our city.' He grinned for a brief second as he tried to hide the fact that he knew it was much more than just a bar, having visited the prostitutes on numerous occasions. He pressed at his earpiece and nodded as he listened intently to the words of his producer before continuing to speak into the camera.

'OK. We believe the Love Shack, like so many properties in De Wallen, is owned by the well-known businessman, Meener De Groot.' He paused as he pressed his earpiece and listened to his instructions before continuing. 'But at this time, I can't confirm that,' he said, obviously lying.

As he turned to face the fire the camera followed him and zoomed into the vivid orange flames interspersed with the sound of the crackling timbers as they continued to burn out of control. The reporter couldn't hide his shock from the viewers as the remaining roof timbers crashed down onto the street engulfing the firemen and engines beneath them before falling into the canal where they briefly fizzed and hissed followed by the smoke that rose as they sank into the water.

The shocked newsman tried to continue. 'We don't know the cause of the fire, yet...' He took a breath and coughed violently. 'And...' He tried to clear his throat once more. He failed and gasped before continuing in a breathless voice. 'We don't know if anyone was in the building… but if there was...' He took a huge breath and expelled the air noisily from his burning lungs. As the thick smoke blew across the canal engulfing him and his crew he strained to breathe before expelling the filthy smoke with a deep hacking cough. He pulled a handkerchief from his pocket and covered his mouth before he continued. 'According to the fire chief it is unlikely anyone could survive this horrific fire...' He coughed violently and struggled to speak. 'I'm handing back to the news desk in the studio,' he said, as the live feed was cut.

It was then that the fire chief took the decision to let the building burn out and pull back most of his men leaving just the turntable ladders in Warmoesstraat and the fire boats to concentrate on saving the adjoining buildings.

CHAPTER TWO

Somebody Help Me

Six months earlier

The telephone on the bar in the Love Shack rang.

There was no one to answer it.

The Love Shack was closed.

The bathroom mirror was covered in condensation from the hot water following Liam's long relaxing bath in his top floor flat. He generally took a shower but sometimes when he felt tired, he preferred to take a bath and add a few drops of aromatherapy oil that Zita had bought him when they were in Lanzarote. After soaking for nearly half an hour, and now feeling relaxed, he climbed out of the bath, dried himself, tied the damp towel around his waist and began to clean his teeth.

While the bath gurgled loudly as it emptied, the mirror suddenly cleared as the door opened and the cooler air from the sitting room burst into the confined space.

Liam pulled back when he saw Jaap and Luuk looking back at him in the mirror.

Jaap grabbed his left ear and at the same time pulled his left arm forcefully behind his back while Luuk grabbed his hair and right ear. Skipio pushed awkwardly past them and with the toothbrush still in Liam's mouth, grabbed at his elbow, raised it up as far as he could splitting the cold sore scab on his lip.

Liam watched powerlessly as his blood spurted onto the mirror.

Although he tried to struggle his efforts were futile.

There was no doubt that Skipio had carefully chosen his moment because Liam was now at his most vulnerable. He fought in vain trying to reach them as they pushed him hard against the edge of the wash hand basin. Skipio pushed the toothbrush deep down Liam's throat, the grotesque smile on his face confirming that he was enjoying every minute. Liam urged, vomited and screamed with pain as the toothbrush first cut his mouth, his windpipe and then pierced the vocal chords at the back of his throat. Skipio grabbed at Liam's wrist and twisted it violently, forcing him to release the toothbrush, leaving it embedded in his throat. Liam attempted to speak but the pain was excruciating and, as he struggled in vain, Skipio's henchmen inflicted even more torturous acts on him. Skipio glared at Liam's reflection, pulled a long thick cigar from his shirt pocket, chewed off the end and spat it at the mirror, all the while gauging Liam's contemptuous face. Skipio looked back at their reflection and smiled through his recently grown moustache and beard, cultivated to disguise the thick rolls of fat that had built up since he'd virtually ceased his daily strenuous training and bodybuilding. His fat neck coupled with his stance and movements made him appear more apelike than ever. Continuing his slow torture, Skipio turned on the hot and cold taps simultaneously and his moustache began to quiver with pleasure. As the water splashed over Liam's bare torso, tortuous pain crossed his already agonised face. The sweating Greek suddenly leant forward, ripped the towel from around Liam's waist and, after wiping his sweating face in the driest corner, threw it into the basin to cover the vomit. He stood back and looked at Liam's naked body, contorted with pain, as it twisted from side to side. Slowly becoming aroused he stroked Liam's tense bare

25

buttocks and thighs with his short stubby fingers, while he licked his lips as he imagined what might be. Liam was now delirious with a combination of pain and anger. Pain was no stranger to him but at least in the past he had been able to defend himself from his aggressors. Skipio lit the huge cigar and took his time to study the flame. After a deep drag he blew the thick smoke into Liam's hair. For a split second his reflection was obscured by the smoke. He patted Liam's bare buttocks while still maintaining eye contact through the smoke in the mirror. He repeatedly stabbed the cigar hard into Liam's left buttock. Liam writhed in agony, his eyes cutting into Skipio's merciless face. Skipio smirked back at him before he took another huge drag until the cigar glowed bright red. He now turned his attention to Liam's pale right buttock, repeatedly stabbing it time after time with the cigar. The Greek stood back to take in his handiwork and the raw bleeding letters on each buttock; "N" on the left and "O" on the right. Skipio threw the cigar into the bath, reached for the soap and lathered his hands before he moved close to Liam. He smiled condescendingly into the mirror before placing his fat arms around Liam's waist and grabbing his scrotum and penis in his large soapy hands. He sneered into the mirror at Liam's distorted and anguished face.

Liam made another futile effort to wrench himself free but with every movement Luuk and Jaap tightened their hold on him and kicked out at his feet forcing his legs even further apart. Skipio now removed his hands and washed them again making more lather. When he was satisfied with the thick foam in his hands he took his time to rub the thick soap into the burning flesh on Liam's buttocks. As the searing pain shot through Liam's whole body he tried to scream but the pain was excruciating as the toothbrush continued to cut deeper into his throat. Skipio dried his hands and undid his zip. He pulled out his penis and pissed onto Liam's soapy buttocks, all the while staring at him in the mirror. He knew Liam wanted to kill him but *he* was in total control. Skipio grabbed Liam's robe from behind the door and threw it over his head covering his shoulders, back and buttocks. The Greek's expression suddenly changed and he turned his attention to the chrome shower head and hose. He reached out, ripped it from the wall and smashed it across Liam's head, around his neck, back, ribs and buttocks. Skipio's relentless beating had the desired effect and Liam slumped on the wash hand basin. Skipio reached into the inside pocket of his jacket and pulled out a chrome cosh, shaped to resemble a large penis, held the scrotum shaped handle firmly in his right hand, and motioned to his cohorts to spread Liam's legs wider apart. He tore the robe from Liam's head and stood watching Liam's reaction in the mirror as he brought the cosh down hard into his open left hand. Liam didn't flinch. Skipio, enraged at Liam's reaction, walked directly behind him and pushed it hard between his open legs. The anger in Liam's eyes was murderous and intense and for the first time Skipio felt nervous. He gave a defiant smile before wiping the cosh in Liam's towel and slipping the cosh back into his pocket. The pain in Liam's throat was now almost unbearable and as he moved his tongue he could feel the furrows in the roof of his mouth where the toothbrush had scored it. But he was not prepared for what followed. Skipio reached into another jacket pocket, pulled out a handful of photographs and fanned them out before pushing them into Liam's swollen face. Liam tried hard to focus through his pained watery eyes until he could see that some of the photographs were of Zita. He shook his head as much as he could in the vice like grip of his attackers until he could see that the photographs had been taken of the two of them at Papagaya beach in Lanzarote. Skipio selected one photograph of Zita, standing naked at the water's edge carrying the spear gun and fish she had just caught. He pushed it into Liam's face, pulled it away, bent forward, opened his mouth and slid his long cigar stained tongue across it. It drove Liam crazy.

He was helpless and the torture was to continue.

Skipio reached forward and like a man possessed brushed everything off of the sink top and laid the photograph on the wet surface beside the wash basin. He grinned at Liam before pulling out a flick knife. He released the blade and brought it down between Zita's legs and slowly sliced through the photograph as far as her throat.

Liam, trying to control his breathing, exhaled a muffled scream at Skipio. 'Go to hell you bastard.' They stared at each other, the anger visibly overflowing into rage.

At that moment Liam vowed that if he survived, he would treat Skipio in the same way.

Skipio threw the rest of his photo collection into the empty bath aiming them at his still smouldering cigar, undid his zip, and pissed over them before aiming at the cigar which hissed as it continued to smoulder. He signalled to Jaap and Luuk, who both released their grip simultaneously before wantonly and blindly punching and kicking Liam until he fell forward hitting his head on the basin, cutting his chin and splitting his nose.

After stamping purposefully over his bruised and bleeding body they left.

Liam lay exhausted on the bathroom floor. He found it impossible to swallow and difficult to breathe as the cigar and singed photographs smouldered in the bath quickly filling the room with thick acrid smoke. He pulled himself up and, in excruciating pain, crawled into the sitting room and slumped awkwardly in front of the settee. While he fought desperately to breathe, unable to take the pain any longer, his body shut down and he fell unconscious.

The unexpected arrival of Zita saved his life.

She dialled 611 and called an ambulance, which fortunately arrived within a few minutes. Liam lost consciousness once again as he was lifted into the ambulance and was taken to the Sint Lucas Andreas Ziekenhuis hospital in Jan Tooropstraat.

It was dawn before the team of surgeons completed their complex operations to repair his throat, voice box, oesophagus, thyroid muscles and nerves and to repair the extensive and debilitating damage to his body. By mid-morning Liam's condition had stabilised but the damage was to leave him with an unusual voice, which was accentuated and painful, when he was upset.

Nevertheless, he was grateful to be alive.

CHAPTER THREE

Close to Midnight

New Year's Eve 1999 was suddenly much milder and, as the ice had begun to melt in the afternoon, boats were once again making their guided tours along the canals.

Skipio, De Groot's overweight Greek heavy and weightlifter, was controversially thrown out of the 1996 Olympic Games in Atlanta for using an inordinate combination of banned steroids and drugs and had spent the afternoon and evening alone in the Blue Parrot bar. He had already drunk the best part of two bottles of ouzo but was still very aware of everything going on around him. He would need to drink a third bottle before it would have had any effect on his huge body. The bar wasn't full but those present were misfits and lonely people who had no real interest in New Year's Eve. At 11:15 pm his mobile phone buzzed and a text flashed across the screen.

"Meet me at the Waalseilandsgracht Brug at midnight. You must wear fancy dress. Catwoman xxxx."

Skipio hurriedly finished the last of the ouzo and lurching apelike towards the door he left the bar without acknowledging any of his fellow drinkers and took a taxi to his filthy bedsit - *no one would live with him*. He quickly changed into the ridiculous fancy dress costume demanded by

Catwoman and continued his journey by taxi to his rendezvous at Waalseilandsgracht.

The area was dark and deserted when he dragged his huge frame out of the taxi and turned the corner. Thick mist swirled around the canal obscuring the pavements and much of the bridge. He stood briefly and squinted until he made out the bridge in the moonless sky. He shivered in the pale flowing Arabic robes and keffiyeh headdress held in place by a rope circlet - the only fancy dress he could possibly wear to accommodate his gross overweight body. He took a huge breath and sauntered excitedly towards the only light nearest to the bridge. Through the mist Catwoman seemed to be elevated in mid-air, her face obscured by her trademark mask. She wore a black ankle length coat and body-hugging black leather top and trousers which highlighted her full breasts and slim body.

As Skipio approached her she pulled back her coat and slipped her hand sensuously towards the zip of the leather top and slid it down to her naval exposing her firm breasts and hard nipples. Skipio drooled and licked his lips in anticipation as he shuffled clumsily towards her. At that moment the first of many premature fireworks lit up the dark night sky illuminating her pale body and breasts. He reached out to her and grabbed her breasts squeezing the nipples hard. She winced with pain but while the Greek was preoccupied with her body, she took the syringe out of her pocket and unnoticed, with it still hidden in the palm of her latex gloved right hand, she effortlessly flicked off the plastic cover. Simultaneously she reached beneath his keffiyeh with her other hand and walked her fingers around his huge neck until she felt his pulsing jugular vein. She squeezed it between the fingers of her left hand and after lining up her other hand, jabbed the syringe deep into the enlarged throbbing artery.

Skipio immediately slumped onto his right knee, transfixed, his body frozen by the massive dose of tranquillizer. She looked towards the shadows and nodded. Batman raced towards her carrying a tarpaulin in his latex gloved hands. He placed it beside Skipio and they rolled him onto it.

On the stroke of midnight, the skies were suddenly filled with rockets lighting up the chilled night sky. Cracks, pops and bangs filled the air reverberating off the buildings. His attackers knew that everyone in the city was looking skywards on this very special night. Catwoman removed another syringe from her coat and continued to inject directly into Skipio's carotid artery. His vacant eyes looked back at her while his whole body convulsed and out of control. His paralysed muscles and nerves reacted to the concoction of Haloperidol, Droperidol, PCP and Acepromazine - "Ace". He knew what was going on but was unable to react. Batman removed a scalpel from his pocket and slit the Arabic robes from head to toe exposing the Greek's gross body covered with thick black sweaty matted hair. They looked at each other in disgust as the fireworks continued to fill the night sky. Batman slit Skipio's huge underpants to expose his penis and testicles. Catwoman tied a tourniquet around them, to stop the blood flow, before slicing into his scrotum with the scalpel. She looked at Batman before making a deeper incision and removing his testicles. Batman prised open the Greek's mouth and she pushed them into his gaping mouth, positioning one testicle in each cheek.

Batman pushed his face hard into Skipio's vacant visage and glared into his traumatised eyes. He screamed in his high-pitched distorted voice, his vocal chords stretching painfully. 'Got ya... you bastard!'

He grabbed at the Greek's pulsating neck and pushed his gloved forefinger hard into his throat.

Batman lifted his mask to reveal the reddening, enraged and contorted face of the snarling Liam. His whole body stiffened as he began to recall, in detail, the vile torture Skipio had taken such great pleasure in meting out to him many months earlier.

CHAPTER FOUR

After Midnight

New Year's Day 2000

Liam stood rocking on the edge of the canal as he reluctantly permitted the almost unbelievably and grotesque memories to ebb away until he gradually returned to his chosen role of Batman.

Catwoman jumped off the other side of the bridge into a motor launch that they had positioned the previous day and fired up the engine. Batman now pulled a "rotje" - a banger - from his pocket and forced it into Skipio's anus before lighting it and hurriedly dragging much of the huge tarpaulin over his body.

The firework exploded causing the Greek's huge body to lift violently off the ground.

Batman watched Catwoman as she skilfully guided the motor launch beneath the bridge and let it glide towards them. She threw the rope to Batman who tied it to the bridge. She threw him a second rope which he tied tightly around Skipio's ankles and as the boat edged along the canal the Greek slipped in with a massive splash. Batman retied the boat and they ran into the shadows, stripped off, and changed into black workmen's overalls. Zita slipped Skipio's mobile phone into her pocket and then carefully placed the syringes into the pouch in her overalls and ensured they were sealed before racing back to the boat.

They jumped into the boat, piled their fancy dress costumes in the centre of the craft, and she poured petrol over them. While Liam thrust another rotje into Skipio's mouth Zita strategically placed dozens of fireworks and homemade explosives amongst the clothes. She reached out and poured the remainder of the petrol over Skipio.

They untied the boat and jumped onto the canal side and watched as it chugged along the canal dragging Skipio behind it. They raced into the shadows. Zita took several identical pairs of crumpled overalls from a black plastic bag pushed them into a nearby rubbish bin and deliberately threw several syringes behind the bin before she ran to the next bridge. She waited until the boat was directly beneath her and dropped a number of lighted fireworks into the boat. The boat continued its journey until the fireworks ignited and detonated. Skipio's head exploded, skin, hair and bone flying high in all directions and simultaneously blowing the boat high into the air.

The explosion was just one of thousands of explosions that night and went unnoticed.

Liam raced out of the shadows on his motorbike and as Zita climbed onto the pillion seat, she flicked Skipio's mobile phone and sent the text to the police station.

"Help! Help me... Please!!!!"

She waited for confirmation that the message had been sent and they left.

The motorbike raced off into the night and disappeared into the darkness while above them a huge wave of thumping acoustic shockwaves resounded in the air sounding like a massed army firing machine guns and mortars at the same time.

Zita knew the Dutch have a unique way of celebrating New Year, preferring to stay at home to celebrate quietly with their family until the stroke of midnight, when they would dash out onto the streets and indulge in a freestyle orgy of pyrotechnics. Holland is probably the only country where so many fireworks are let off in such a short space of time in the streets and public areas, creating mayhem reminiscent of a war zone.

She and Liam had made the decision to act during their trip to Zandvoort, on Boxing Day, and spent the next few days setting up clues to implicate De Groot and his men. She knew De Groot would be on his own at Kasteel Meerwijk on New Year's Eve and Luuk, Jaap, Vim, Jan, Piet, Erag and Skipio would be left to their own devices. She collected hairs from their hair brushes and combs and carefully threaded them into the linings of worn and creased overalls. She took fingerprints from cups and glasses with lifting tape and then imprinted them onto the syringes and scalpel. She hid some of them, along with a few identical fireworks, lighter and small vials of the lethal concoctions she had used to inject into Skipio, in the drawers and wardrobes belonging to Luuk and Jaap at De Groot's house.

The motorbike slowed down near the bridge on the corner of Berenstraat before arriving at Zita's houseboat. Once inside the houseboat, they stood in silence looking at each other, until simultaneously; they let out a huge sigh of relief before releasing their feelings, with ear shattering celebratory screams of satisfaction. Their euphoria was short-lived when Zita looked towards the clock. Realising they needed to rush, Liam quickly changed into the clothes he had worn earlier while Zita cut the studs and zips from the overalls, opened the stove and one at a time pushed them into it. While they burned, she went up on deck and threw the studs and zips high in the air where they scattered as they fell back into the canal.

CHAPTER FIVE

My Secret Place

De Groot had already drunk several glasses of cognac when at midnight his mobile pinged incessantly with New Year wishes. As he walked to his private suite with Lutya and Bobbie, he scrolled through his texts. Once inside, the girls poured three glasses of champagne, removed their dresses and gyrated in their alluring underwear to *"The Launch"*, a track produced by DJ Jean and Klubbheads.

De Groot had little or no interest in sex and was preoccupied as he continued to flick through all the texts on his expensive mobile phone.

One text was very different and it grabbed his full attention.

"Everyone is gone. The police are coming for you."

He read and reread it several times.

The alcohol fuelled colour drained from his cheeks and he began to sweat profusely. While the volume of the music intensified, the girls lay provocatively on the huge bed, each of them vying for his attention.

Tonight, his mind was elsewhere.

Lutya stood up and slunk towards him and attempted to remove his shirt. He growled at her and pushed her away. He grabbed his jacket, raced out of his suite and, deep in thought, staggered to the walled car park. He started his Mercedes and accelerated hard, his tyres pitching the gravel onto nearby vehicles as he speeded between the open electronic gates before closing them behind him.

Although he had been drinking heavily, he knew he had to get away and, if he was stopped, he would have to deal with it.

He gunned the accelerator and made his way towards Amsterdam.

Turning onto the deserted N326 he drove a hundred and thirteen kilometres until he reached the A10, on the outskirts of Amsterdam. He left the A10 at Ringweg Zuid, then to Beethovenstraat, a side road which ran beneath the A10 and the main railway line to Schiphol airport. He drove across Water Street, an area of private land owned by a mysterious consortium of developers, until he reached the insignificant and dilapidated rows of arches beneath the main railway lines and the A10. He took a remote-control unit from his inside jacket pocket, clicked it and waited. An electronically operated door in the railway arch opened in exactly one and a half seconds and he drove into his most secret place - De Groot's "bunker" - a converted double railway arch. He turned off his lights and sat in the darkness waiting for the external door to close. As soon as it was closed he flashed his headlights four times and the inner doors opened to reveal a brightly lit area with white tiled floor and walls. He had it built in the early eighties, using tradesmen from Germany, Belgium, Poland, Serbia and France for each part of the works to ensure that only he knew that it existed The untraceable bodies of the key workers were found randomly on various building sites outside of the city over a long period and were not considered to have had any connection with each other. He had used his bunker once before for an extended period, when the police carried out a purge around Amsterdam and he needed to disappear for a while. He had maintained this hideaway for almost twenty years and at that time wondered if he would ever need it again but something told him that his luck would not last forever and he had to have a guaranteed exit route.

Once inside his secret stronghold De Groot parked the Mercedes beside a BMW and telephoned the plasterer, a man who De Groot had always retained on standby for this inevitable eventuality.

The plasterer immediately made his way to Centraal Station, opened the delegated locker and removed the fake passport with his photograph and credit card in the name of Meener De Groot. He left for Schiphol airport and took the first one-way flight to Madeira and an unexpected holiday at the five-star Reid's Hotel overlooking Funchal. He would fly back to Amsterdam a week later using his own passport and paying for his flight with his own credit card.

De Groot took a key from behind a wall tile and unlocked the metal clad door at the far end of the room, entered the self-contained flat and undressed. He carefully folded and hung his clothes neatly on hangers in the air-conditioned room. He rubbed the shaving foam into his face and began to shave taking care to leave a thin line of blonde bristle above his top lip. He showered and cleaned his teeth before unlocking a second area and carefully choosing his change of clothes. He turned on the television and briefly watched the Millennium firework celebrations. He shook his head when he realised, he was wasting valuable time and turned it off preferring to listen to a CD by *Klaus Mertens*. He pulled on a pair of neatly ironed chinos, pale olive polo shirt, light socks, brown shoes and a beige jacket. He took a small case from the top shelf, unlocked it and carefully fitted soft blue contact lenses before finishing off his look with a pair of silver framed glasses. He smiled briefly at himself in the mirror, closed both cupboards, and then locked the metal door before returning the key behind the wall tile. He walked across to the dark blue 1995 BMW and flicked up the boot. He slid his hand deep inside and opened a secret compartment beneath the rear seats and removed a metal case. His fingers carefully skimmed through the contents and removed a German passport. He flicked it open and compared the picture to his *new* look and once more smiled at himself in the mirror.

While he was in Untersuchungshaftanstalt prison in Holstenglacis 3, St Pauli, Hamburg, De Groot spent much of his time learning to speak German. He shared a cell with Hans Feldman, a notorious drug dealer from the city. Hans taught him German with the distinct Hamburg dialect and twang. He told him stories of the violent and heady sixties when Hamburg was home to dozens of English groups and the Beatles when they played at the Indra and Star Club in Große Freiheit and the Top Ten on the Reeperbahn.

When De Groot was released from prison in 1978, he decided to stay in the Hansa city of Hamburg and, using the contacts given to him by Hans, worked as a barman in various clubs and bars in St Pauli, on the Reeperbahn, the notorious Red-Light District. As his mentor suggested, De Groot changed his name; he chose Dieter Stange - the name of a boy, who had died at the age of five. At the same time he changed his appearance - but only slightly, with blue contact lenses, a carefully sculpted pencil moustache and silver framed glasses with clear glass. It was all he needed, very simple and easy to change his persona when required.

Dieter Stange gradually built up a new life for himself. He spoke with the instantly recognisable Hamburg tone and, within a few months, opened two bank accounts, passed his driving test in the city and secured a German driving license.

41

He bought the second-hand BMW the following day and a few weeks later, with the help of Hans, he took over ownership of a bar in 10 -12 Talstraße, which was once used by musicians in the sixties when it was known as the Mambo-Schänke. It was perfect, with two flats immediately above the bar, which he rented out, and a bedsit on the top floor where he lived. It had a fire escape which gave him access to the roof and, if needed, an exit route to adjacent buildings. He obtained a national insurance number, regularly made his annual tax returns and obtained a German passport, along with several credit and debit cards. He learnt a lot about the underworld in Hamburg and, when he felt he was ready, he returned to Amsterdam and put much of it into practise.

He continued to return to Hamburg, in the HH registered BMW, on a regular basis and built up a business that was the envy of many people in St Pauli. Amsterdam was his first love and he was proud of his reputation and the power he had gained and regularly returned to the city. He would park his BMW in his secret underground garage before emerging as Bram De Groot, driving the Amsterdam registered Mercedes.

His Dutch mobile bleeped with a message.

'We resign... Happy New Year'

He read and reread it and smiled to himself. 'We'll see,' he said, with a strong German accent. He stood erect before talking to himself. 'I remember you from *Malaga...*' He stabbed his index finger into the air and laughed loudly. 'Even if you don't remember me - Meener Liam... fucking, Reilly!'

His whole body stiffened as he took himself back to the previous year at the funeral of Laurie Feldmann, an elderly English criminal and one of the many who had decided to hide in Spain on the Costa del Sol. De Groot had reluctantly used him, along with many others, to help him launder his takings from the illegal activities of his vast empire in Amsterdam.

De Groot, Liam, Freddie and a handful of close criminal associates attended Laurie's funeral. Liam had paid very little attention to those who attended the funeral in the tiny church in Mijas Pueblo, thirty kilometres from Malaga. But on the other hand, De Groot took his time to identify and memorise in great detail everyone in attendance. He never knew when he may need the services of any of them in the future.

De Groot looked around before tightening his fists, raising them high in the air and in a fit of rage screamed out. Suddenly, he seemed revitalised and ready to complete his transformation. He turned off the Dutch mobile, removed the German mobile from the box and clipped in the battery before turning it on. He then removed the battery from his other phone placing it in the boot. He played the message on his German phone. 'Hello this is, Dieter Stange... I'm unable to take your call at the moment, please leave a message.' He smiled to himself and repeated the message to himself several times. It was his way of becoming Dieter Stange.

He slipped the mobile into his jacket pocket, opened a separate compartment in the metal case and removed small quantities of German deutsche marks, Dutch guilders and euros. He didn't need to carry much cash but felt that he had to have some money on him. He flicked through each currency and removed any notes that looked new and returned them to the case. He checked the dates on the German credit and debit cards and placed them, along with the notes, in a worn wallet. He completed the contents with two business cards from his Hamburg bar, a card identifying his blood group, some recent receipts and a receipt for the second mobile phone paid for on his German credit card. The few odd coins he placed in his trouser pockets. He pulled a dark brown, well worn, knee length leather coat and holdall from the secret compartment and removed the contents placing them neatly inside the boot. He eyed everything in turn and concentrated on what he may need and what would be practical items for his trip before he repacked the holdall. He opened the leather wash bag and took everything out. He carefully checked the part-used items. The toothpaste, toothbrush, shampoo, shaving foam, razor blade, aftershave and hair brush, all bought recently in Hamburg. He meticulously replaced it all every time he went there to ensure that it had recent dates and price labels on it. He could leave nothing to chance. He opened the German passport and held it close to the mirror, and as his forefinger traced the moustache, he compared himself with the photo. A wide grin spread across his face. *Without any doubt it was the same person.* He checked himself in the mirror for the third time before he locked both cars, turned off the light and walked out into the explosive New Year's night.

He crossed the deserted street and walked towards Centraal railway station, stopping at the first phone box. He made three calls before making his way up onto the platform of Amsterdam Zuid WTC and bought a single ticket to Schiphol airport from the machine.

He had always expected to make this journey but not this soon, for this reason, or in this way.

The plasterer walked into the departure lounge and after giving De Groot a cursory nod walked to his gate and flight for a week of winter sun in Madeira.

Liam and Zita arrived at the Love Shack on the motorbike a few minutes after midnight and she threw Skipio's phone into the canal. The lights were on but they had been deliberately kept low. Liam had made the decision to close for the evening and didn't want any unwanted drunks or customers descending on them.

Inside the bar Peggy, Helga and Saskia were entertaining their richest clients, who had paid a premium for the extended privilege. Matthijs Kikkert, the contractor who had renovated the Red Cat many months earlier, held his young wife, Fenna, close to him as they slow danced to the music.

Detective Andrea Ribeker, leaned on the piano and gazed lovingly at Bernie, her female partner, as she played a never-ending selection of traditional Dutch, English and German tunes. Vil, the youngest of the girls, who had decided she didn't want any clients with her, served drinks from behind the bar.

Even Liam whistled tunelessly to himself as he stored his motorbike in the basement.

Zita had bought three bags of olliebollen, in various flavours, from a street stall on their way back to the Love Shack. She arranged them neatly on plates along the bar and while Bernie continued to play, everyone else rushed excitedly to grab their share.

Zita put two of them on a separate plate and took them over to Detective Andrea Ribeker and Bernie, placing them carefully on top of the piano.

Liam returned from the cellar and smiled to himself when he saw how much everyone was enjoying themselves. He stood behind the coffee machine and waited for the hot water to filter through the freshly ground coffee. He made himself an espresso and sat down at the table, decorated earlier by the girls. On cue young Rafi and his mother Asmara carried in her speciality rijstaffel, placed the colourful assorted dishes on the candle lit tables and joined them in the celebrations.

Liam lifted his cup high in the air and exhaled with a sense of deep satisfaction and relief, before finally speaking. 'Happy New Year to all of you,' he said, as he took a sip of his espresso. They all smiled back at him and chattered excitedly as they deliberated over their choice from Asmara's fantastic New Year banquet.

CHAPTER SIX

Live and Let Die

Acting on an anonymous phone call, the police raced to De Groot's unnamed house, in P.C. Hooftstraat, situated in the exclusive suburbs of Amsterdam. They surrounded the house and after a lengthy stand-off they arrested Jaap, Luuk, Vim and Jan but Erag Gasha managed to escape.

Erag Gasha, the young Albanian was different from De Groot's other henchmen. He had lived alone on a small farm along a gravel lane, off of the road leading to Dragot, several kilometres from the town of Belsh, in the county of Elbasan, in central Albania which had a population of less than fifteen thousand. The hills and mountains with its natural lakes covered much of the dirt-poor country crisscrossed with clusters of tiny villages where the farmers concentrated on agriculture, growing wheat and root vegetables. Erag was an experienced hunter of wolves and bears and spent much of the year outdoors which had resulted in him having a heavily veined and weather-beaten face. He was followed at all times by his two devoted dogs - Albanian Shara mountain dogs, large and strongly built with dense dark coats and wolf like heads.

He had a reputation of being a butcher with many of the nearby villagers and when he was drunk, he could frequently be heard bragging of executing any animal with his bare hands.

When the communist regime collapsed in 1990, and following the elections in March 1992 amid the economic failure, the Albanian lek was close to worthless. With the social unrest that followed many of its inhabitants left for European countries and America.

In 1997, Erag also made the decision to leave his farm and follow in their footsteps into Europe. Before he could leave, he had no option but to kill his trusty dogs - cutting their throats and burying them in his yard. For the first time in his life he experienced feelings and felt heartbroken. Undeterred, he stole a flatbed lorry loaded with vegetables and made his way to Germany where he sold them. Now with money that was worth something he made his way into Holland and within days found himself in Amsterdam. He was soon recruited by Meco, a fellow Albanian, who had high aspirations of taking over De Groot's thriving criminal empire.

In the spring of 1999 Meco made his move to seize the Love Shack a few weeks before it was due to open. He totally misjudged it. De Groot was already aware of his attempt so when Meco, along with his henchmen, made his move and challenged Liam, he was met by Zita, Skipio, Jaap and Luuk who thwarted his attempt. De Groot used the attempted coup to set an example to future aggressors by murdering the attackers and leaving Meco to endure a slow and painful death in the Amsterdam Torture Museum.

Erag attempted to get away in Meco's Mercedes but crashed in front of Centraal Station. Luuk caught up with him, threw him in the boot and took him to one of the De Groot's many warehouses on the edge of the city. Skipio tortured him for several hours but, when De Groot realised that he couldn't be broken, he was impressed and much to everyone's surprise decided to let him live. He held the Albanian under guard in his safe house in Huidenstraat, off Keizersgracht, for several weeks while he carried out a detailed background check on him. He was fascinated at what he heard and Erag was immediately recruited to collect protection money from those that were frequently reluctant to pay. Within a few short weeks he was known by everyone for his aggression and De Groot's takings flourished.

CHAPTER SEVEN

Escape

While the police dealt with Luuk, Jaap, Vim and Jan at the Amsterdam Police Headquarters in Elandsgracht, detectives were investigating the explosion and the remains of the motor boat and body parts scattered in the Singel. The following day forensics found hairs, fibres and fingerprints that matched the DNA of De Groot and all of his men in the overalls left by Zita and Liam in the rubbish bins at the Waalseilandsgracht Brug.

All of those captured would soon be charged with Skipio's murder, extortion and other unsolved crimes and a warrant was issued by Europol for the apprehension and arrest of Bram De Groot.

As Dieter Stange's plane took off from Schiphol airport it flew high above the city and he could see for himself the flames of the burning Love Shack. He ordered a drink and pushed himself deep into his seat and reread the previous day's newspaper.

When his plane arrived at Hamburg airport, he immediately made his way to the check-in desk. Without saying a word, he was given an automatic upgrade to First Class. He walked into the departure lounge, bought a copy of the Hamburger Abendblatt, a magazine, a bottle of Asbach, a bottle of Kirsch and a Mozartkugeln - a ball shaped,

50

chocolate-coated cake, with a pistachio and almond marzipan centre and an outer layer of nougat coated with bittersweet chocolate.

He sat in the executive departure lounge and repeatedly checked his watch while he crunched his way through the Mozartkugeln.

Four hours later, on the morning of 1st January 2000, the plane touched down at Arrecife airport, Lanzarote, carrying De Groot's alter ego, Dieter Stange.

He passed effortlessly through customs and sat at the café, in arrivals, drinking a large coffee. He alternated his attention between checking his watch and glancing up at the huge television screen at the rolling news, which included the massive firework displays across Amsterdam.

A Breaking News update flashed up on the screen. He sat forward and watched intently; captivated as he watched the events unfold at the burning inferno that was once the Love Shack. This was a bittersweet moment for De Groot. He gazed intently at the screen as he watched the fire brigade try in vain to control the fire that had engulfed part of his empire that was once the Love Shack.

He shook his head and almost immediately self-congratulated himself with a shrug of his shoulders followed by a wide grin of satisfaction that spread slowly across his face. It quickly turned to anger as he watched his building burning to the ground in front of him.

A hand gently touched his shoulder and he turned his attention away from the television and, without looking around, closed his eyes and smiled to himself. 'Hello, Keeva,' he said, softly. He turned to face the young Irish waitress who once worked at the Red Cat and left a few weeks after Liam arrived in Amsterdam and transformed it into what was to be known as the Love Shack.

He continued. 'I'm so glad you're here.'

'Me too,' replied Keeva, with a mischievous giggle.

He stood up from the table and they held hands as they left the airport building and walked to his car.

'I didn't expect to be here until the spring. Did you?' he asked.

She put her arm around his waist and purred in his left ear with her soft southern Irish accent. 'Why not?' said Keeva, his secret, long distance lover. She rubbed his shoulder lovingly and giggled. 'The sooner the better, eh?'

He pulled her slowly towards him and kissed her passionately.

Reluctantly their lips separated and they walked arm in arm until they reached his rare silver 1993 Mercedes - 500 SL 6.0, Brabus Edition, convertible. He threw his bag into the space behind the front seats before removing his jacket and flinging it there too. Once in the car he fired up the powerful engine, flicked the CD player and turned up the music. He pushed himself deep into his seat, exhaled and smiled to himself as the two of them drove leisurely down to Playa Blanca to wait for the ferry.

De Groot had little to do with the girls that earned him so much of his wealth but Keeva was special and when she arrived, he set about grooming her for his future life away from the city.

Keeva handed him his Panama hat. 'You must take care... You know you burn when you are just looking at the sun.'

As he placed it on his head he smiled. 'I know. But that's a small price to pay for being here without the shit back in Mokum. I'm sure I can manage that...'

'Course you can,' purred Keeva.

They drove onto the early morning ferry to the nearby island of Fuerteventura.

The ferry took a little over thirty minutes to reach Corralejo and as soon as they landed, he parked at a bar overlooking the beach where they had a very enjoyable champagne breakfast.

De Groot looked out across the Atlantic. 'I don't intend spending all my time here, you know.' He topped up their champagne and continued. 'We can travel.' He turned to her and smiled. 'We can go anywhere - absolutely anywhere.' He stroked her right hand. 'Is there anywhere you have always wanted to visit?'

'Well, Bram, I would like to take you to Ireland and you can see where I lived... and perhaps meet my family.'

He pulled his hand sharply away from her. 'I don't think that is a very good idea. Do you?'

Now it was her turn to look out at the sparkling sea. 'Well... maybe not.'

He pushed his chair back and stood up from the table. 'Come on let's go home.' He grinned broadly and hugged her. '*Our* home,' he said softly.

He tilted his head to one side and his demeanour suddenly changed. 'Listen, Keeva. From now on I *am* Dieter Stange. Remember that.' He hugged her tight and squeezed her tiny body. 'I am no longer, Bram De Groot.' He grinned. 'He has gone...' He paused, lowered his head and continued. 'Forever,' he said, emphasising every syllable.

He grinned and looked directly at her and winked. 'Erm... But... Maybe... Erm, Bram De Groot... *to you...*' He lifted his left shoulder expressively. 'Sometimes, when we are alone, eh?'

CHAPTER EIGHT

We Didn't Start the Fire

The embers of the burnt-out Love Shack continued to smoulder well into the next day and heavy smoke from the fire and fireworks still hung over much of the city partially obscuring the weak winter sun. The television crews were still reporting from the scene on the opposite side of the Oudezijds Voorburgwal canal.

Near Oudezijds Kolk, the end of the canal on the Armbrug - Arm Bridge, two black leather clad bikers leaned brazenly on their handlebars and watched intently as the chaos continued to unfold. One of them slowly raised his visor and thrust his fists high into the air and let out a euphoric scream before throttling away.

The reporter spoke to camera. 'This is a massive fire and we have no idea how it started.' He turned towards the burnt-out Love Shack and the camera tracked the firemen as they carried out the first fatalities in body bags.

He turned away and pushed at his earpiece and nodded. Unable to hide his shock he continued to speak at speed. 'We are hearing that there are no survivors.' He stopped to catch his breath and cough the smoke from his lungs. He looked across at Detective Piet Ackerman who was talking to a group of policemen.

The interviewer walked across and interrupted him. 'I'm joined by Detective Piet Ackerman. Good morning detective. Is it true that there are no survivors?'

The Detective replied in a sombre tone. 'Yes. We are fearful that there are no survivors.' He coughed nervously and forced a smile. 'But... we can never give up hope...' His tone changed to a sombre deep respect. 'Only time will tell.'

One of the firemen reached across and handed the detective a badly damaged framed photograph of all the residents taken at the Love Shack at a party on Christmas Eve. The glass was still warm and as he nervously tried to brush off the smoke stains he cut himself on the broken glass. Ignoring the blood, he faced it towards the camera and as he traced their obscured faces including his colleague, Detective Ackerman deliberately failed to identify and name any of them. 'These are the people we fear may have *died* here last night'. He took a huge breath and coughed hard. 'In this sad... and... and... a horrific fire.'

CHAPTER NINE

It's Only Just Begun

Ten hours earlier

As the first Molotov cocktail smashed through the window of the Love Shack, they all turned towards it. The flaming bottle was followed in quick succession by three more.

At first, they all froze and looked on in disbelief at what was happening.

In a split second, the flames ignited the flammable curtains and blinds and another flash of petrol shot across the bar setting fire to Fenna's silk shawl. She screamed out as the flames licked around her face. Matthijs grabbed and flayed his arms around her as he tried to extinguish the fireball. His desperation was in vain and he too was soon engulfed in flames.

The light bulbs were the next to be affected as they let out frightening gunshot sounding explosions leaving the fierce and threatening flames as they spread through the bar.

There was chaos and sheer panic.

Flames licked around the bar and soon found their way along the counter and the open bottles of spirits left for the guests to help themselves. The food on the table ignited and the partially drunk glasses of alcohol pinged and exploded shooting fragments of glass into anyone close by.

The businessmen grabbed their female escorts, cast them aside and pushed past the screaming Fenna and Matthijs whose clothes were now burning out of control. They crashed into the flaming rijstaffel sending the food everywhere and making the floor slippery as they made a futile attempt to reach the flaming front door. They turned back and, after flinging the burning chairs and tables aside, they tripped over each other as they made for the stairs.

Toxic and hot black smoke filled the bar, searing everyone's nostrils before it spread throughout the ground floor. It was propelled by the flames up the stairs into the rooms and eventually reaching Liam's flat on the top floor.

It was mayhem as everyone screamed and trampled over each other in a desperate attempt to escape the inferno.

The terrible triplets: fear, panic and chaos suddenly loomed as the occupants tried to escape the inferno.

Zita had already decided on an exit route from the Love Shack. Ever fearful of an attack from De Groot or one of his enemies she made it her business to always seek out an exit route; something that had been repeatedly hammered into her by her mentors in the Mossad.

So, when the fire started she was immediately ready to move. But this time, rather than securing the safety of herself and her customary, *client, target, double agent or spy,* she had to consider the many other people, her friends in the Love Shack, who she desperately needed to save.

With her hand over her mouth, she screamed through her closed fingers. 'Keep as near to the floor as you can!' She removed her hand and attempted to take a breath of any clean air before continuing. She coughed violently before swallowing and taking another breath of the foul air. 'If your clothes burn, drop onto the floor and roll. OK?'

Helga, Saskia, Peggy and Vil uttered their terrified distorted replies.

Liam had made a vain attempt to help Matthijs and Fenna but it was already too late. Their burning clothes and blackened contorted bodies now lay entwined in front of the bar.

Zita continued with a high-pitched scream. 'If we get out... we will meet at my houseboat!' After inhaling the smoke, she coughed heavily again and as the excruciating pain swept throughout her already damaged throat, she screeched one last instruction. 'At the end of Berenstraat... on Prinsengracht!' She took one last huge breath and screamed as loud as she could. 'Look for the name - Madonna! The lights are on!'

In a split second the whole building was filled with acrid smoke and fumes and heat from the raging fire. Red hot roof tiles and burning timber crashed down onto the lower floors igniting everything in its wake and as the carcass of the piano burned through, the red-hot metal strings dinged randomly, creating a cacophony of sound.

Peggy, Helga and Saskia's paying clients were not so lucky. Having been drinking heavily throughout the evening they were incapable of comprehending the instructions Zita had shouted to them.

Andrea Ribeker made her way blindly through the smoke as she attempted to find Bernie, her young female lover. She pushed past the three businessmen who were now slumped on the narrow burning stairs and writhing in agony as they struggled with the impossibility of finding clean air. Instead they took fatal gulps of the poisonous air.

Unable to move them, Ribeker climbed awkwardly over their overweight bodies, squeezing out any air left in their already failing lungs. She continued up the burning staircase as each tread collapsed behind her. She had no option but to take huge gasps of the foul and polluted air as she attempted, in vain, to yell out her lover's name. When she finally reached

Bernie's empty room, she was exhausted and overcome by the heat and smoke.

Unbeknown to Ribeker, Bernie was already safe in the rear yard and racing to safety in Warmoesstraat. Now it was her turn to worry. She tried to return to the flaming building but was held back by Peggy and Helga, who in desperation grabbed her arms in a vicelike grip and dragged her away screaming.

As the last survivors escaped thorough the rear kitchen window the fire now took hold igniting the cooking oil, flour, sugar and rice causing random explosions behind them and heightening the already impossible catastrophe.

The fire engines turntables already positioned in Warmoesstraat were aiming their hoses across the roofs and onto the rear of the Love Shack. The water was a welcome relief to the acrid smoke and fumes as it fell onto the survivors as they ran through the yard and to safety. They crossed the Singel and Herengracht canal and made their way to the houseboat beneath a sky on fire with the madness of the night and the unrelenting fireworks and deafening explosions above them.

CHAPTER TEN

Never Say You Can't Survive

Bernie, Helga, Saskia, Peggy and Vil made their way to the houseboat, lit on the outside by coloured lights which festooned the deck garden. They were soon joined by Asmara, Rafi and Liam who was having real issues with his already damaged throat and struggled to breathe.

The girls still wore the expensive clothes chosen for what was to have been a very special night of celebration but now within a few short hours the transformation and deterioration was unimaginable. Peggy's matching red suede jacket, silk blouse and clinging mini skirt were in tatters. Without raising her burned hands, she scratched her chin with the corner of the front collar of her once brightly coloured jacket, now blackened with ash.

Helga, still wearing the face mask that matched her once elegant, shimmering silver dress, was splattered with ash and blood. What remained of it was lacklustre and ripped to shreds.

Saskia's colourful silk suit was torn, burnt and unrecognisable.

For New Year's Eve Bernie had chosen to wear the black dinner suit that she so proudly wore for the first time when she made her appearance with the Dutch National Student Orchestra two years earlier at the Royal Concertgebouw. Whilst it wasn't burned it was stained with smoke, ash and

Peggy's blood. She knew she would not be able to wear it again. She no longer cared and dug her blackened nails deep into the cuffs, tearing the shiny satin on the cuffs where it joined the black material. *All she wanted was her Andrea.*

Vil's clothes were the least damaged. Although she didn't have a client with her she wore her thin olive green figure hugging designer leather jacket and trouser suit, bought for her by one of her clients from an exclusive boutique in Amsterdam's 9 Straatjes. It was stained with the blood from the cuts on her face, neck and hands and as she checked her bright red nail varnish she screamed out.

The shrieks heightened everyone's distress and they all turned and peered at her apprehensively.

She held out her fingers and waved them in front of her. 'Look! My varnish is damaged!'

Their resonating obscenities resulted in her immediate embarrassment and silence.

Peggy, echoing what everyone was thinking and wanted to say, was the only one to speak up. 'What the *hell* are you thinking? Do you think your fucking nails are more important than all of us… injured, and those that have died?'

Vil blushed, shrank back into her seat and covered her face.

No one escaped.

Everyone had singed hair matted with splinters of burnt timber, soot, and ash, asbestos and plastic which now fell onto their shoulders as they repeatedly screwed up their pained and blackened faces and coughed violently in an attempt to clear the poisonous air from their lungs. Peggy and Saskia fiddled nervously with their various nose and lip rings, studs, and earrings while they watched and waited.

Still in shock and dazed by the night's events they all huddled together and, relieved to have survived the terrifying ordeal, they chattered nervously and systematically broke into a series of random and nervy smiles.

The roof light blinds and window curtains were ineffective and couldn't hide the bright light from the fireworks that continued relentlessly to illuminate the night sky.

They heard the sound of footsteps above them.

They all froze, held their breath and waited.

Liam raced into the kitchen, grabbed a large carving knife from the nearest drawer, stood at the door and held it menacingly in front of him.

This further raised the level of fear.

The hatch slid open and the uninvited guest stepped slowly down the wooden stairs.

An exhausted Zita helped the injured Ribeker down the stairs. They were the last two people to escape alive from the Love Shack.

The badly burned Detective Ribeker took her time to look around fearfully at each of the survivors. Bernie was sat in the corner, squeezed tightly between Helga and Peggy and was barely distinguishable in the poor light. Andrea Ribeker strained her eyes as she gazed from one survivor to the next. When she finally saw her she screamed out. 'Bernadette! Thank, God you're safe!'

Bernie struggled to stand and fell back into the seat. She looked up unable to speak and gazed lovingly at Ribeker. She made a massive effort and finally pushed herself up and staggered towards her girlfriend. 'Wow,' she screamed. She took a huge gulp of the clean air and smiled broadly at the female detective. 'That's the first time you called me by my full name!'

Ribeker grabbed Bernie and almost squeezed the life out of her before realising how badly she was burned and pulled back as she winced in pain.

Bernie forced a smile. 'I was worried if we would all get out in time...' She looked directly into Andrea Ribeker's eyes and attempted to rub the soot and dust from her cheeks. Ribeker winced as Bernie's fingers brushed against the tiny fragments of glass buried in her face. She stopped abruptly and pulled her head back. 'But...' She looked confused. 'How did you get out?'

Ribeker cautiously wiped at her blistered mouth and smiled as she looked around the room silently counting everyone. She sighed heavily and took her time to catch her breath. 'But I left it too late and as I climbed the stairs...' She sniffed and wiped at her bleeding nose. 'I forgot that the spirits...'

Bernie gasped. 'Spirits?'

Ribeker forced a painful laugh. 'The spirits... the bottles of alcohol behind the bar... They were so dangerous.' She winced again in pain. 'They exploded and the glass flew everywhere and into my body.' She shuddered as she reflected. 'I was unconscious... trapped in *your* room... But something...' She shook her head. 'I don't know what... what made me wake up and I managed to get up to the attic.' She looked around again at everyone. 'How was it we all managed to escape from that hell?' she said, with a long wheezy release of her smoky breath.'

'Not everyone did,' said Zita. 'Only *we* made it,' she said, looking around at each of the bloodied survivors in turn. 'Some have died,' she said, with an honest sadness in her voice.

Ribeker winced, closed her eyes and nodded.

Zita continued. 'I guided everyone to the kitchen window before the explosion and the inferno.'

Liam took a huge gulp of air and answered for them. 'Yeah. We were lucky all right. It was mad, crazy. Did you see the streets packed with drunks and fucking tourists, rubber necking?' He attempted to take a huge breath but instead choked on the toxic phlegm that filled his pained throat.

Zita helped him to release some of the poison from his already damaged lungs and weakened throat. She handed him a cloth and he groaned in pain as he wiped the vile filth away from his mouth and chin.

He took a shallow breath and continued in a strained and painful voice. 'No one was looking for us... or...' He gulped. '*Interested*... in any of us.' He grinned for the first time and exhaled. 'No... Fuck 'em... We're all safe,' he said, defiantly. 'Who cares?'

He let out a huge sigh which signalled to everyone else to exhale deeply.

Zita left the room and reappeared seconds later clasping a hand gun with a silencer. She looked around at everyone for any comments before sliding it into her rear jean pocket.

There was collective silence.

Perhaps having seen the gun, at last, they had a strange feeling of security.

Liam continued to struggle for breath and grabbed huge gulps of air before coughing another deep painful cough.

Liam spoke to Andrea Ribeker. 'So, how *did* you get out?'

She replied proudly as she wiped at her eyes. 'He... A fireman rescued me.' She looked around at the each of the girls in turn before returning to refix her gaze on Zita.

'A fireman?' said Zita.

'Yes, in Amsterdam the fire service is always prepared on this crazy night.' She shrugged. 'They arrived in time...' She smiled, 'And, yes, he carried me through the burning roof and onto the ladder.'

They all gasped and mouthed their shock. 'The roof?'

Zita smiled. 'Yes, she was lucky to make it from the roof.' Bernie grinned and clapped her appreciation. Zita continued. 'I could not leave until I knew that you were all safe.'

Someone knocked on the open hatch and stepped nervously inside.

Zita pulled the gun and pointed it towards the stairs.

The occupants could only see the heavy boots and held their breath in anticipation of the impending threat. They all shrank back into the darkness and their uncomfortable, makeshift seats as the paramedic lowered his head and smiled before he stepped nervously down the steps and into the dimly lit, shadowy room.

He shot them another reassuring smile and raised his hand before speaking. 'It's alright. You must not worry. I came on my bike,' he said, with a comforting voice. 'It's parked on the other side of the canal in Elandsstraat,' he said, reassuringly. 'I guessed there may be a problem for you all.'

Everyone let out welcome sighs of relief, unnoticed, Zita slid the gun into her pocket and pulled her jacket over it.

The paramedic looked furtively around at everyone before deciding who needed his help the most. He checked out Rafi before turning his attention to Andrea Ribeker who was clearly in agony.

While he worked on Ribeker's hands Zita scrutinised the rest of the survivors who were still in shock and in need of treatment. She signalled to the paramedic. 'Andrea was the last one to come out,' she said.

The paramedic shot her an astonished looked and mouthed his reaction. 'Wow.'

Zita nodded to him. 'Yeah, we are the only survivors.' She sniffed and wiped at her eyes. 'Do you realise that everyone else has died.' She broke down and sobbed for the first time in the life she had been trained for. 'I'm so sorry. I wanted to save them all but–'

'You did your best. It's not your fault. Whoever started the fire is to blame,' said Ribeker, her voice faltering. Her face suddenly turned blue as she desperately tried to suck air through her burnt lips. She slumped to the floor and her whole body began to convulse.

The paramedic reacted immediately. He reached across to the detective, pushed her tongue aside, checked her airways and began CPR, pressing rhythmically on her chest.

Bernie was frantic. 'Help her. You have to help her!' She broke down, frantically banging her damaged hands on the floor.

Zita pulled Bernie away. 'You need to give him space to work. OK?'

Ribeker suddenly spluttered and coughed and the paramedic placed her in the recovery position before reaching for his radio. He continued to give her his full attention while he waited for backup.

Seconds later two more paramedics arrived and, after getting their whispered instructions from the first paramedic, they carefully lifted the detective into a vac chair and up into the ambulance before it screamed away with its blue light flashing and siren blaring.

The first paramedic now turned his attention to Liam who was finding it much harder to breathe. He propped his head, removed an oxygen mask from his bag and used it to cover Liam's nose and mouth.

He then turned to Peggy and while he proceeded to clean her cuts and treat her burns, he looked across at Saskia and the bubbling burns on her arms and legs. 'They will come back to help you all. Don't worry. Please try to relax,' he said.

Liam briefly removed the oxygen mask and waved his hand at Zita signalling for her to come to him. 'Listen,' he said weakly. She moved closer to him and waited intently as he emphasised every word. 'That fire.' He swallowed hard and wiped at his watery eyes as he remembered that *his* Love Shack was totally destroyed. He continued. 'Who the fuck set that up?'

He made a half-hearted attempt to punch the air and replaced the mask over his mouth and nose.

Zita nodded in agreement and muttered, 'De Groot?'

Liam slowly nodded. 'Yeah... Course it was.'

CHAPTER ELEVEN

Stand by Me

Detective Piet Ackerman's stood on the canal opposite the burning building. His radio crackled, he pulled it close to his mouth clicked the switch, and answered it. He struggled to hear the caller through the continuing explosive mayhem. When he finally got to hear the message, he raced to his car and, with his blue light flashing and siren droning and the fireworks continuing to explode overhead, he picked his way through the drunken and euphoric revellers celebrating the New Year.

When he reached the houseboat, he slid the hatch open and eight pairs of terrified eyes looked towards it.

Detective Piet Ackerman, with his gun primed, waited guardedly on the top step, shone his torch into the greyness, and took his time to move it slowly from person to person until he recognised everyone. 'How the fuck did you all get out of that?' he screamed.

No one had the energy to answer him.

He made his way apprehensively down the remainder of the stairs and into a room where the air was thick with the stench of burnt clothes, singed hair, soot and smoke ash.

He took his time to stare at each person in turn, counting them in his head. For some reason he flipped and waved his gun in the air and they all shrank back. 'So, where the hell is Andrea?' he boomed.

Bernie looked up at him and replied in a quivering voice. 'She's on her way to hospital–'

'What?' he screamed.

Zita walked across and put her arms around him. 'She'll be fine,' she said. She looked across at Bernie. 'She's in the best place,' she said, reassuringly.

She could see that Bernie didn't believe her.

'Really... she is,' she said, softly.

Ackerman reached for his radio and glared menacingly at the paramedic. 'Which one?'

Bernie replied succinctly. 'UMC.'

Ackerman screamed instructions into his radio. 'Get onto the ambulance heading from Berenstraat to UMC and reroute them to the hospital in Haarlem.'

Zita looked at him open mouthed until she realised what he was doing and raised her index finger. She waved it slowly towards him and grinned. 'Yeah, good call,' she mouthed.

The Detective continued. 'If De Groot doesn't believe the news and wants to be sure... or...' He paused and tilted his head backwards before he continued. 'Or... wants to find any of you.' He took his time to stare hard at everyone in turn. 'Where is the first place he will have them look?'

Zita nodded back at him. 'OK.'

'Haarlem is far enough away to be safe.' Ackerman nodded. 'Yeah. We need to keep the news that you've all survived...' He leaned forward. 'A secret. Let's feed them the false news. When the time's right... perhaps...' He grinned. 'We can tell them you all survived. OK?'

Zita stood up and shuffled across to him, raised her right arm and slowly drew it past everyone. 'Do you realise, if the girls...' She paused and looked across at Liam and offered a smile. 'And Liam...'

He grunted back to her through the mask.

She continued. 'If the girls were in their rooms and not in the bar having a special dinner then...' She pointed at the girls before she continued. 'None of them would have got out of there.'

Liam reached up and lifted the oxygen mask. 'How the hell did we all get out of there anyhow?' he screeched. 'I can't believe we did.'

'Do you know what?' said Zita, 'When you have the fear of death you suddenly feel more alive.'

A beat.

She looked at Ackerman and continued. 'Before the Love Shack opened, I had already worked out *my* exit.' She grinned, sniffed and wiped at her blackened face. 'Remember it was my job to do those things.' She coughed and continued. 'I knew there was no way out of the front door and...' She attempted to bite her bottom lip but realising it was burned she licked it and continued. 'If there ever was a fire...' She paused and closed her eyes and as she remembered the earlier events, she shuddered. 'There must always be an escape route - a plan B,' she said, emphatically.

They all murmured and nodded.

Zita continued. 'But... we should all thank Rafi.' She laughed. 'He had already found his Plan B *too*. Escape through the window, eh?' She grinned at him. 'That's been his way in and out of the Love Shack for a very long time.'

Rafi shuffled in his seat and grinned brazenly at the detective.

His mother, Asmara, smiled proudly and pulled him closer towards her.

Those that didn't have painfully burnt hands clapped their appreciation.

Rafi blushed through his smoke covered face and wiped his hand across his blackened and bleeding pink lips.

Zita kissed his smoke blackened cheek.

She continued. 'Plan B was to go through the window and... and out into the Koopermoolen yard and then... Warmoesstraat.'

While they all descended into nonsensical conversation Zita walked into the kitchen, boiled water in a large saucepan, removed the limited cups and mugs from the cupboard and lined them up on the worktop. She opened another cupboard and removed a sealed pack of Dutch Bros coffee and a jar of Manuka honey, kept solely for Liam. When the water boiled, she turned off the hob, filled the coffee pot and poured it into the mugs.

She walked in with a tray and after checking she had enough mugs, poured their coffee.

She passed the first mug to Detective Ackerman and worked her way through the group handing out mugs of coffee with an option to add a spoon of honey.

The detective sipped at his coffee, licked his lips and commented. 'Nice.' He took a second sip before speaking. 'We've rounded up most of De Groot's men... but...' He took another sip of his coffee. 'Do any of you think *he* could still be hiding in the city?'

Zita wiped the back of her blistered hand across her forehead. 'He is too proud to do that. He wouldn't want any of his *clients* to find out he arranged the fire. His credibility would suffer.'

'Really?' questioned Ackerman.

'Yes.' She shook her head. 'He threatens a lot of people but to kill so many - all of us - in that way and at the same time would be a disaster for him.'

'So where could he go?'

Zita offered her thoughts. 'Another country?'

'We've checked Schiphol... nothing...' He shook his head. 'Nothing.'

'Really?' questioned Zita.

Detective Ackerman could see the girls' taut faces displaying their discomfort, anguish and pain. 'You all need to go to hospital and get treated.'

Zita whispered in his ear and he reached for his radio. 'But not yet.' He spent the next few minutes talking to his office and then the hospital. When he'd finished, he flipped it into his jacket pocket and turned to them. 'All arranged. OK. Give them a few minutes and we'll get you away.'

'Listen to me. As you know people have died. And I feel very sad for their families but to the outside world you *all* need to have died too.'

They gasped.

'Whoever did this is still out there and if they know you are alive, they will try again.' He took a deep breath and exhaled noisily. 'So, Zita's idea was good. We will issue a statement saying that there are *no* survivors. Once you are better, we can decide what to do then. We won't issue any names to the press so you will be safe and your families won't worry.'

There was a gasp of relief.

'I need to ask if anyone knows you worked and lived at the Love Shack.'

They all shook their heads.

The paramedics returned and although Liam tried to remove the mask one of the paramedics held it in place. As they lifted him into the vac chair and moved towards the stairs, he raised his hand to answer Ackerman's question but no one noticed.

Zita spoke directly to the girls. 'Once you are treated, you must all stay here for a few days and then you can move into one of De Groot's secret houses.'

They all looked at her and mouthed the same word - *secret*.

She nodded. 'Yes, secret.'

'Surely, De Groot knows you live on this houseboat?' asked Peggy.

They all looked around at each other and gasped. 'Yeah.'

Zita shook her head. 'No one knows where I live.' She paused. 'Well. Liam and...' She smiled. 'And... now you all do.'

The sense of relief was immediate.

Zita forced a tired smile. 'Whenever I was working, I always went to either De Groot's house or his office.' She smiled proudly. 'I even had them drop me in Elandsstraat and then I would walk or jog back here.' She shook her head. 'Sometimes I took a taxi to Rozenstraat and then doubled back. 'Easy, eh?'

When the last ambulance left, Zita treated her own wounds and then returned to De Groot's office where she removed everything of value and transferred all the money in his bank accounts to her anonymous backup accounts in Switzerland.

CHAPTER TWELVE

Don't Give Up

Detective Ackerman decided to continue to hide the fact that there were no survivors from the media following the Love Shack fire and he confirmed it during several press conferences and television interviews covered by the media across Europe.

On the second of January 2000, De Groot read it in the report in the Het Parool, a Dutch newspaper printed in the Canary Islands. He pulled Keeva towards him and gloated by tapping hard at the page reporting the news.

Everyone spent several weeks in the Haarlem hospital under tight police guard. The damage to Liam's throat was serious and it continued to bleed heavily. After a thorough examination the specialist explained that, due to Liam's previous throat injuries the caustic fumes and smoke had caused much more damage. The ear, nose and throat specialist stood at the end of Liam's bed and explained the problem. 'It will take some time before we can repair the damage to your throat.'

Liam looked back at him and rolled his eyes.

The specialist couldn't hide his disapproval. 'I am telling you that once you leave here, you will need to take care of yourself.' He looked directly at Liam and emphasised his concern with firm words. 'Or you *will* lose the voice.' He paused. 'And there will be nothing I can do to help you.' His demeanour changed. 'Do you smoke?'

Liam nodded nervously.

The consultant stood up and fired a look of disgust at his patient. 'That is crazy. Don't! You can't do that anymore. OK?'

Zita was already planning her next move, and spent much of her time visiting everyone in hospital. She sat on Liam's bed looked down at him and grabbed his hand. 'We'll go away when you're better. OK?'

He forced a smile from beneath his mask.

The consultant coughed to gain their attention and continued. 'You will need many more visits to me for minor surgery but we can do that without you needing to stay in here. We will arrange that and perhaps you can attend with Ms Ribeker?'

As well as the inhalation of smoke Detective Andrea Ribeker had major burns to her hands which needed skin grafts but the doctors would not consider them until the tiniest fragments of glass were removed. She had shards of glass all over her body and it took the surgeons several hours to remove them all. They told her it would leave some scars but they assured her that in time most of them would be unnoticeable.

The funerals for the wealthy punters who died in the Love Shack fire were held in private, a decision made by their respective families, who were all aware of the truth and where they died and wanted to keep it as low key as possible. However, the funerals of Matthijs and Fenna Kikkert were public and the service was held in the Oude Kerk, Amsterdam's oldest building constructed in the thirteenth century, and just a few hundred metres for the burnt-out shell of the Love Shack. Their grieving teenage children, respective grandparents, close relatives and all of their employees, many of their customers attended. The plasterer was incredibly upset and chewed nervously at his finger nails knowing he was in some way responsible He chose to stand at the side of the distraught congregation and feigning sickness, he left before the end of the service.

Detective Ackerman wanted to continue with the fake news and insisted that no one from the Love Shack should attend any of the funerals. Everyone sat in the hospital and in silence watched the funerals on television. As the service progressed, they started to fidget and fret as their anger grew.

Peggy spoke out. 'De Groot is such a worthless piece of shit… what right did he have to decide who lives and who dies?'

It was the twenty eighth of January and their first day together on the houseboat. Everyone was still showing signs of shock, exhaustion and tiredness. Ribeker's hands were still heavily bandaged and Liam had a portable oxygen tank and mask. Saskia, Helga Vil and Bernie still had plasters and temporary dressings on their arms and legs while Peggy, as well as her arms and legs, had a dressing across one eye and large plaster on her forehead.

Asmara and Rafi were almost back to normal and very bored.

Boredom had begun to set in everywhere.

Detective Piet Ackerman sat in the only armchair and finished his cigarette.

Zita's face took on a concerned stare. 'Well, have you caught them all?'

Ackerman nodded animatedly and then stopped suddenly. 'All except...' He paused and lowered his voice, closed his eyes, coughed and continued nervously. 'The Albanian–'

'Erag!' screamed Zita.

'Yeah,' said Ackerman, nodding in agreement. He continued guardedly. 'Erm, the Albanian... He *is* still around. My men have seen him.' He reached into his pocket for a cigarette and lit it. 'You just need to be careful.' He paused to take a long thoughtful drag on his cigarette. 'But every time he gives them the slip. He's a crazy bastard, that one.'

'Bastard? He's a fucking animal,' screamed Zita.

The detective turned and spoke directly to her and Liam. 'I'm sure he is. We've checked up on him with Europol and you are correct.'

Zita looked at him. 'Surely, it's Interpol?'

Ackerman shook his head. 'It all changed a couple of years back.' He grinned and inhaled deeply. 'We use Europol now. It's much the same set up but with a different name.'

Zita scoffed.

The detective continued. 'His full name is Erag Gasha. His record is too long to even mention... robbery, murder...' He turned and looked towards the girls. 'And *rape*.' He closed his tired eyes and wiped his hand across his face. 'In fact, he has done and... and been in involved in anything you can imagine.'

Zita feigned shock. 'Really?'

'So how the hell did he get into the country?' asked Liam.

Ackerman lowered his eyes and looked directly back at him. 'May I ask how you entered our country?'

'Touché,' mumbled Liam.

Detective Ackerman cleared his throat before he continued. 'There is another problem...' Their mouths dropped open while they waited for him to continue. 'We still can't find De Groot–'

'Maybe he left the country?' gushed Liam.

The Detective licked his lips. 'We checked flights out of Schiphol. There were only three that left early on New Year's Day, to London, Hamburg and Madeira.'

'Madeira?' asked Zita.

He took his time and talked into his radio before he continued. 'Yep. Just the three...' He paused and looked directly at Zita. 'Yes, including Madeira.'

Zita sat back and picked nervously at her finger nails. 'It is important...' She looked across at Liam. 'Yes?'

He nodded his response.

'I'll let you know when I hear anything. OK?' said Ackerman.

Liam grunted his indifference.

Zita walked into the kitchen, refilled the large saucepan and boiled it before making another round of drinks.

Ribeker took her time to look at everyone before returning to Asmara and Rafi. She smiled as she peered through the bandages. 'I know someone who would love to have you living and working with them.'

They both tilted their heads and looked back at her quizzically.

The female detective continued. 'Don't worry, you will love it and they will arrange for Rafi to go to school.' She turned and looked at the girls from the Love Shack. 'Everyone else...' She paused and thought carefully about what she was about to say. 'The rest of you *do* need to go home...' She paused and sighed. 'Leave Amsterdam.'

They all exhaled noisily before they reluctantly acknowledged what she was saying with mumbles of agreement.

She continued. 'Detective Ackerman will continue to tell the media that everyone died in the fire.'

Detective Ackerman turned his attention to Zita and Liam. 'Can I suggest you also leave Amsterdam for a while until things die down?' They both screwed up their faces. He continued. 'We'll keep in touch and when I feel it's safe you can come back.'

'But Andrea still needs treatment at the hospital,' muttered Bernie.

Liam looked towards the female detective and continued. 'So, we can't leave yet.'

Ackerman nodded. 'Sure, I understand,' he said, reluctantly.

Zita nodded her agreement.

Peggy made to stand but thought better of it and slumped onto the chair. 'Why can't we stay here too? I can't go back to Nijmegen...' she spluttered. 'What would I do?' She sighed and reluctantly she slowly nodded agreement. 'OK. You are right.'

Ackerman partially closed his eyes before he replied. 'Perhaps we can arrange for you all to go to a women's refuge?'

All of the girls shrieked simultaneously. 'No way!'

Ackerman continued. 'We need to agree on something. You will all need clothes and money?'

They all nodded and replied in unison. 'Yes, we will.'

Zita brought her hand down hard on the table with a single slap and they looked towards her and awaited her revelation. 'Maybe there is an alternative...'

They all fired her a mutual grin and waited.

She continued with her guarded suggestion. 'Maybe for a week or so?'

They all nodded excitedly.

'I'll check out one of De Groot's special houses and perhaps we can all stay there until it's safe and then you can you decide… what you want to do… and… where you want to go.' She looked around at each of them in turn. 'Alright?'

They all shrieked at the same time. 'Great!'

A few days later, after relieving himself of his need of the oxygen tank, Liam left the houseboat, pulled up his hoodie and walked out into the freezing night for the first time on his own since the fire.

The whole of De Wallen was unusually quiet with only a handful of drunken tourists ambling from bar to bar. He stood on the other side of the Oudezijds Voorburgwal canal, leaned on the railings and foolishly lit a cigarette. He had been warned that to continue smoking could totally destroy his voice but for this emotive moment he knew he needed it. He covered his mouth, leaving enough room for the cigarette, and gazed blindly at what was once the Love Shack. Now a burnt-out shell with the adjoining buildings supported by a metal framework of scaffold and a large timber hoarding covered what was the ground floor. He cursed to himself as he read the large signs advertising the planned opening of a massage parlour.

He crossed Armbrug and walked down Warmoesstraat. When he reached the Koopermoolen Hotel he slipped into the rear courtyard that backed onto the Love Shack.

He stopped briefly as he recalled the weeks he had spent at the hotel and Anje, the receptionist, who had helped him to find the girls, while the Love Shack was being renovated.

He had a lot to thank her for and still wondered what had happened to her and where she was now.

He ripped off the timber cladding that now covered the burnt-out window that had been their escape route weeks earlier and climbed into the fire ravaged building. He pulled a torch from his jacket pocket, flicked it and aimed it at what was once the bar and his retro coffee machine.

Having not seen the television reports it was much worse than he had expected.

Everything was destroyed.

His newly discovered life was once again in tatters.

Was it his fault - again?

He believed it was and suddenly sunk into deep depression.

His pride and joy was unrecognisable. The stairs no longer existed and the floors and rooms above him were gone. He leaned back and looked up through the blackened void at the clear moonlit sky above him. He stood in the centre of the eerie burnt out devastation and shook uncontrollably. He tightened his fists in rage and then exhaled shakily before cursing De Groot for his greed and total lack of empathy and the loss of life and the wanton destruction he had instigated. He seethed with anger. 'You bastard!' he growled. 'Why? And for what?' He kicked out and grabbed at his pained throat. 'Greed?'

Liam had so many contradicting thoughts racing through his head: *He wasn't too worried about the rich punters who had died. What prompted them to choose to leave their families, instead of preferring to spend New Year's Eve with their paid for "lovers" - prostitutes? But he did have genuine remorse for the death of Matthijs Kikkert and Fenna, his young wife - nicer and more deserving people. Why had he survived? Was he meant to be alive? What did the future hold for him now? Did he even have a future?*

He finally pulled himself together and wiped at his tearful eyes with his blackened hands. He kicked his way through the twisted debris, grabbed a piece of metal and smashed through what was left of the basement door and shone his torch into the darkness.

As he slowly took in the catastrophic destruction again, he cursed De Groot. His classic motorbike was a perverse relic, destroyed by the intense heat, and tables and chairs no more than grotesque twisted pieces of metal. He fought his way further into the basement between the debris and removed a blackened brick in the wall farthest from the door. He smiled as he took out the money he had saved.

He forced a pained smile.

He had always insisted that he held onto the passports and papers of all of the residents of the Love Shack as well as their hefty deposits. He withdrew what would be their lifelines and to some a modicum of a future, carefully stuffed everything into his deep jacket pockets and zipped them up.

Liam left the empty shell and walked slowly along Warmoesstraat. A car drove past and braked to a halt a few feet ahead of him. Liam instinctively clenched his fists and waited. The window wound down and Detective Piet Ackerman poked his head out. 'Hello, Liam. Good to see you up and about.'

Liam grunted his response, relaxed his hands and pushed them deeper into his trouser pockets.

Ackerman noticed that Liam was clutching something. He tried to lighten the conversation and said a strange thing. 'I suppose that classic bike of yours is gone?'

Liam glared at him. 'People have died and you talk about a fucking bike! Fuck you!'

Ackerman lowered his head in disgust at what he'd just said. 'Sorry, Liam,' he said, sympathetically.

Liam's head shook violently. He inhaled, sucked at this bottom lip, forced his dirty index finger into his already twisted mouth and chewed at it. 'Nothing left now,' he murmured, reflecting on the past few weeks. He sniffed and looked into space. 'Fuck all!'

'Sorry. I just know how proud you were of–'

'Of?' rebuked replied Liam, tersely. He turned and looked around blindly. 'Everything is fucked up...' He strained to continue and as he struggled to breathe he expelled a painful cough. 'Now,' he drawled.

'Do you want a lift?'

'No thanks. I'm fine.'

The detective spoke as he wound up his window. 'Take care, Liam.'

Liam leaned against the shop window and watched the detective drive down the street and when he was out of sight, he rubbed his thumb blindly at the twisted badge he had removed from the petrol tank of his burnt-out motorbike and grinned.

Liam thought to himself. *What the fuck is wrong with me? Why am I being so friendly with the law? I hate them - I always have. He was so angry with himself and for the first time in his pathetic life questioned his long held resentment of the police.*

CHAPTER THIRTEEN

Rescue Me

The survivors from the Love Shack sat drinking coffee in the houseboat lounge. Zita coughed nervously taking care not to pick out anyone in particular before she spoke. 'Asmara and Rafi have already got somewhere else to live and work in Leidseplein.' She grinned. 'It was easy... she was in great demand. You all know she makes the best Rijstaffel in Mokum.'

They nodded their agreement.

Zita continued. 'So, we now need to decide what we should all do.'

Silence.

'Do you feel safe enough to go home *now*?'

Zita's words were acknowledged with more muted silence and they all shared the look of sheer terror before lowering their heads in disbelief.

Ackerman looked across at Zita and spoke for the first time. 'How long do you think you'll survive De Groot's bully boy, Erag, the Albanian...' He coughed into his closed hand. 'When he finds out you're still alive?'

Zita looked at him. 'Yeah, I know.'

Peggy looked at her, open mouthed. 'So wha..?

Andrea Ribeker grinned and looked across at Peggy and then each of them in turn before speaking. 'With respect...'

Her tone changed and she continued in a confident voice. 'You *can* look after yourselves.'

Ackerman continued to show his concern and rolled his eyes at Ribeker. 'They do need to be careful. Erag has the heart of a monster... He's a murderer.' He paused and exhaled. 'And a cold-blooded butcher.' He focused his attention on Ribeker. 'You know what we've seen of his handiwork?'

Ribeker nodded.

Liam placed his mug on the coffee table and took a deep breath. He spoke softly. 'Well then... *what* is the alternative?'

They looked at him open mouthed.

Zita interrupted and tapped Liam's arm. 'I agree that at some point you will all need to go home.' She paused. 'But... not yet.' She looked at each of them in turn. 'I have an idea.' She saw the immediate relief with confused smiles of appreciation. 'I told you I would look at some of De Groot's safe houses and we can all move into one of those for a few weeks and... you will have time to think. OK?'

They all gasped. 'Really?'

'Yes, you'll be safe. He used it for holding his trafficked girls until he placed them in his clubs. It's really close to here. And...' She looked at Liam for his agreement.

Although he had no idea what she was talking about, he nodded.

Zita continued. 'We'll keep you safe until you decide what you want to do next. OK?'

The following evening Zita took them in pairs to the five-storey property at 25 Huidenstraat above The Lost Tulip Café. It was huge, five bedrooms with more than enough beds for everyone, a huge sitting room, a large kitchen-diner, three showers with a toilet and bath. She had already stocked the fridge and freezer with everything they were likely to need.

There was no television, radio or phone. Something that De Groot deliberately omitted in an effort to make sure that his "guests" had no contact with what was going on in the outside world.

Ribeker and Bernie chose the bedroom on the top floor and after exploring all the rooms the remaining girls decided to pair up in their chosen rooms on the third floor.

The house had a door entry system and the code agreed between Ackerman, Ribeker, Zita and Liam was three short buzzes and one long. They told everyone in the house that the door was only to be released if that signal was heard.

To give the girls' reassurance and security Zita and Liam took it in turns to sleep in the lounge and as they were all still taking time to recover from their injuries, not all visible, it was agreed that everyone would go to their rooms at ten o'clock at night.

Liam and Ribeker still needed to visit the hospital in Haarlem every other day for treatment and Zita arranged for one of her contacts to take them. On the days they didn't attend hospital Zita left the house, checked on the houseboat and made her plans.

Ribeker and Liam were up early and, after making sure no one saw them, they walked to the street corner and jumped into the waiting car before being driven away. They arrived back at Huidenstraat tired and exhausted to see the last of the sunset fading behind the canal. After thanking the driver, they cautiously made their way to the door of the safe house.

Liam pressed the intercom. Three short bursts and one long.

'Coming,' said the weak and trembling voice.

He looked at Ribeker. 'What the fuck?'

She looked around cautiously and then spoke. 'Liam, something is wrong - very wrong.'

86

Liam stroked the stubble on his face. 'Um. Yeah, it is.' While he thought, he slid his forefinger back and forth across his teeth. 'I'm going in–'

'How?'

The café was still open and he pointed at the open door. 'Through there.'

'Why don't you wait until I've called Ackerman?'

Liam ignored her and stomped into the crowded Lost Tulip Café.

He forced his way between the cramped occupied tables forcing the customers to lean uncomfortably into them. One of the young waitresses tugged Liam's shirt. He grunted, grabbed her arm and shunted her violently, sending her careering into the nearest table where the food, plates and cutlery crashed onto the tiled floor. He raced into the kitchen, pushed his way past the young chef and ran outside, slamming the door firmly behind him. He stood in the tiny rear yard and took a minute to decide on his next move. Most of the properties in old Amsterdam were interlinked and often shared rear fire escapes. He pushed himself up onto the roof of the cold store and took a painful breath. He swallowed a handful of painkillers, shook his head and made his way across the roof and onto the fire escape that had never been used. He stopped and took several more painful breaths before inching his way up the ladder.

Peggy had been passing water to the heavily bound Helga, Saskia, Bernie and Vil and helping them to drink. When she heard the door buzzer, she dropped the bottle and raced across the room, grabbed the handset and spoke. She knew it could only be Liam and Ribeker and hoped and prayed they would realise something was wrong.

Liam reached the first-floor window and peered inside. The light was on and he could see the horror and torturous mayhem that had gone on while he was at the hospital.

He exhaled with shock.

All the girls were naked, badly beaten up and bleeding.

Helga was tied to Bernie and Saskia to Vil, all with filthy rope and duct tape. They all had cigarette burns on different parts of their bodies and Saskia and Helga's beautiful body artwork was now a bloody mess where Erag had drunkenly traced their tattoos with a blade. Zita was tied to a chair, her bruised and bloodied face a mess and her bowed head resting awkwardly on her chest. The blood from one of her earlier attacks had dried and darkened on her perfect rounded breasts, stomach and legs. Liam could only look on in silence and listen to Peggy's blood curdling screams as Erag chased after her. He grabbed her arm and then tugged at her bloodied shoulder length hair before dragging her across the room and relentlessly beating her. She fell to the floor and lay motionless beneath the window.

Liam felt helpless but all he could do was wait for his opportunity.

Erag finally left the room and walked into the kitchen to grab yet another bottle of Jenever, his favourite Dutch liquor.

Liam tapped gently on the window. Zita was the first to hear him and she lifted her head and turned her sad and battered face towards him. *For the first time Liam realised that she wasn't infallible. But then he knew no one was. There was always someone better and he had always hoped that he would never meet them.*

Peggy stirred and slid nearer to the window and struggled to lift her tiny body high enough to unbolt it.

A beat.

Liam slid it open and climbed in. He closed it quietly and stood behind the kitchen door and struggled painfully to hold his breath. As Erag swaggered back into the lounge swigging the potent alcohol Liam smashed him on the side of the head with a clenched fist and then elbowed him in the chest. Erag was briefly stunned and Liam seized what he knew would be his only chance. He grunted then head butted the Albanian, kicked him in the groin, picked up a heavy hardwood chair and smashed it over his head. Erag moaned and groaned but he was strong and the alcohol in his system ensured that the attack had little or no effect. After shaking away the unexpected assault he straightened his muscular frame and faced Liam square on. A vein visibly throbbed on the right side of his forehead as he glared threateningly at him. He opened and then clenched his massive hands and scoffed in his own unintelligible language. He looked slowly around the room and drew Liam's attention to the brutality he had already meted out on each girl in turn finishing with a shrug and stabbing finger towards Zita. He now turned his attention back to Liam and took his time to size up his attacker as he readied himself to make his move. A move that Liam knew he didn't have the energy to counter.

Liam stood and grabbed deep painful breaths as he tried to gather any remaining energy.

A long beat.

Erag stopped and wobbled and his eyes gazed sightlessly ahead.

The diminutive Peggy stood behind her attacker and, having severed his spinal cord, twisted and jerked her hands, before yanking the scissors out of the Albanian's back. After a frenzied howl of satisfaction, she let out a series of repetitive ear shattering, high pitched screams each time she indiscriminately stabbed his arms, neck and legs.

Erag slumped awkwardly onto the floor and let out a series of shuddering breaths as he attempted to get up.

Liam wasted no time; he kicked out at him until there was little or no movement before turning his attention to Zita and cutting through her bound hands, feet and chest. 'Are you alright?' he gasped.

She pushed him away and rose demonically from the chair, her perfect naked body slashed and covered in bruises and caked in dried blood. She shook her head wildly to release her pain and crept slowly across the bloody timber floor as though she was stalking a wild animal. She seized Erag's filthy hair with her left hand lifted him partially off the floor before ripping out his throat with the other hand and letting out a sustained savage scream of victory.

Helga, Bernie, Saskia and Vil gasped with mixed emotions. *Pleased their torturer was dead, something he deserved, but shocked at the barbaric way in which he had been killed.*

Liam stood and watched the blood dripping from Zita's bruised fingers and as he exhaled he shouted out one word. 'FUCK!' He shook his head and took a deep breath and exhaled with an anxious shudder. 'So, how the hell did he get in here?'

'I heard him this afternoon... when I was laying on my bed,' spluttered Bernie.

Zita struggled to speak. 'I went to see what it was and he pushed me off the ladder.'

'The bastard,' yelled Liam. Something he immediately regretted, as despite the painkillers, pain ripped through his body

Zita made an attempt to control herself by taking deep breaths. 'He was here all the time - hiding in the attic,' she shrieked. 'It's been our worst nightmare–'

'So that's how you ended up like this?' Liam grinned at her. 'I must say I never expected to see you at the wrong end of a fight.'

Zita huffed and shot him the vilest of looks. 'Fuck you!'

He lowered his head submissively and mouthed his apology to her. 'Sorry.'

Zita tried to clear the dried blood from her flared nostrils with her freshly bloodied hand smearing it across her face. She immediately realised what she had done, looked down at her hand, and continued. 'When he discovered Bernie, Helga, Saskia, Peggy and Vil, he was shocked. He said he thought we were are all dead. He was so angry. "How does that happen?" he said.' She swallowed hard and lowered her voice. 'Then it began.'

Poking at her nostril had made her nose bleed again and she swallowed the warm blood with a gulp. 'He was an animal. He said, '"I want both of you..."' She shook her head. 'I didn't understand what he was wanting. He laughed into my face. "The Englishman... I want him." He screamed at me. "I will kill him and all of you... and rip out your hearts... then I can leave this shitty city."' Zita pulled back and wiped at her bleeding nose with the cleaner hand. 'Do you know he was so mad that you weren't here with us? He said. "You are such stupid - people." He grinned at us. "I am going to cause all of you a lot of pain," he said.'

Liam had seen the results of Erag's actions first hand and he winced.

'He told us take off our clothes.' She shrugged. 'We *didn't.*' She forced a pained grin and looked around at each of the girls in turn.

They forced a collective grin.

'He grabbed Saskia by the throat and pushed a knife into it. Yes... It did bleed.'

Saskia partially lifted her hand away from her throat and blood began to seep between her fingers.

'OK,' said Liam, squeamishly. He raised his hands. 'I don't want to see it.'

91

Zita blushed. 'Do you imagine what he said?'

Liam shook his head.

'He said! "Come on girls... he snarled at us, "You take your clothes off when you're paid. Do it for me for free! NOW!"'

She turned to Liam. 'I know you have seen it. We did it, of course,' she said, trying to hide their eventual submission. She sniffed and looked towards the hook in the ceiling and the rope still hanging in the corner of the room.

Liam saw it for the first time. 'Fuck.'

'He dragged Helga across the room with her hair.'

Helga could still feel the pain and shuddered.

Zita continued. 'And he put the rope around her neck.' She showed that she was angry with herself by kicking out into space with her bare feet. 'It is my job and...' She breathed raggedly. 'Do you know the hook was already there? And... and... and I didn't see it before that time?' She turned back to the girls. 'And you didn't see it also? Did you?'

They all shook their heads.

'After that... it was hell.'

Saskia spoke for the first time. 'Then... the animal... he... he...' She finished with a fiendish shriek. 'He sucked the blood from my neck!'

Liam was stunned at Erag's aggression and shook his head in disbelief.

Zita reached across and tried to console Saskia before she continued. 'He burnt us with cigarettes, lashed out at all of us, tied up the girls and then tied me to the chair... And...' She couldn't bear to tell Liam what he had done to her and instead she kicked out at her chair with the duct tape still attached to it. It flew towards Saskia and Vil. They drew up their legs before it crashed into the bloody settee where they were sitting.

Ribeker had followed Liam into the café and pushed the waitress into the same table. She grabbed the phone from the wall in the café and called Ackerman who immediately arranged for an armed unit to join him.

Minutes later the sound of sirens were heard in Huidenstraat followed by a line of cars and vans that filled the street. A dozen heavily armed policemen smashed down the door and raced up the stairs followed by Ackerman and finally by an apprehensive Ribeker who, fearing the worst, held back.

While the armed police checked every room, Ackerman looked on in disbelief at the naked girls as they slowly cut through each other's ropes and duct tape before taking time to look down at the bloody Albanian. 'I thought he was long gone,' said Ackerman. 'We've not seen anything of him for days.'

Liam struggled to breathe.

Zita spat thick clots onto the already bloody floor and grinned at the detective. 'You have now,' she said, sadistically as the blood dripped from her split mouth.

Liam left the room and walked through the bedrooms grabbing handfuls of clothes while Ackerman used the time to furtively ogle each of the naked girls while faking an empathetic nod. When he noticed the piercings in places that he had only seen on dead bodies he was suddenly aroused. In an attempt to divert his urging, he turned away from them, pulled on a pair of latex gloves and picked up the scissors and blade that Erag had used to carve up the girls and slipping them into separate plastic bags.

Ribeker spent much of her time sitting with Bernie and whispering words of reassurance in her ear.

Liam returned to the lounge and threw the clothes randomly at the naked girls who grabbed at them and dressed frantically to cover their ravaged and bloody bodies.

Zita pulled on an ill-fitting dress and, as she pawed at the dried blood on her face, she whispered to Liam. 'Thanks.'

He gave her a hug and a soft kiss on the forehead.

She winced in pain before turning to Ribeker and then Liam. 'So how are you two?'

'We're fine,' they said in unison.

They both lied. *In their own way they were still trying to take in the events that had unfolded while they were away and in a selfish way were pleased, they hadn't been there. While at the same time realising, with some relief, that if they had been in the house then things could have turned out very differently.*

The paramedics arrived and began to check over the girls and patching up the worst of their injuries. But it was clear they all needed a lot of specialist treatment and operations from the various surgeons who had the unenviable job of trying to hide or disguise their injuries and burns and tidy up the scars with plastic surgery.

Ackerman made a call and after clicking off his radio told them that they could all be treated at a private clinic on the outskirts of the city. Their evacuation was kept low key and didn't happen until the café below them was cleared of all the customers and staff.

Unmarked police cars took them to the clinic.

Liam shared a room with Zita and Ackerman shared with Bernie, while Helga, Saskia and Vil all chose to have their own room.

Liam continued the regular treatment at Haarlem for his damaged throat and Ribeker for her burns and counselling, which only Ackerman knew about, for her mental health issues.

Detective Ackerman still didn't want to reveal to anyone outside of his close circle that any of the residents of the Love Shack had survived so while they were having treatment he used the time to make sure that the death of an anonymous attacker was widely broadcast across every television station, radio and newspaper across Holland. He then followed that up with a dedicated and thorough search of the city for any of De Groot's remaining henchmen.

There were none. In fact, some of the city's long-term criminals had also left.

He now felt confident that finally everyone was safe.

CHAPTER FOURTEEN

Yesterday's Gone

It was almost six weeks before they were able to leave the clinic and they were driven to Zita's houseboat in two taxis, fifteen minutes apart. The plant pots on the open deck were now a mass of brightly coloured tulips, daffodils and the smaller pots with wallflowers and pansies. Zita had healed well and although she still had occasional nosebleeds, she had been able to return to her houseboat and her fitness regime a few days before the other girls were released.

While she waited on the deck for the rest of the girls, she took her time to admire the colourful flowers and plants and recalled how much had happened, all of it totally unexpected, since she had planted them back in the autumn.

Liam, Ackerman and Ribeker were already waiting in the lounge and as each of the girls arrived they were greeted with a series of firm hugs before sitting down. While Zita made the coffee, she gave them time to relax, the noisy chatter was incessant as they compared their injuries and tried to identify their now healing scars.

Liam helped Zita to serve the coffee and when everyone was settled, she coughed loudly for their attention. 'Today is my birthday,' she said, with a wide smile.

While everyone cheered, Liam looked on in disgust.

She mouthed to him. 'It's OK... Later.'

He couldn't hide the disappointment of her not telling him earlier and he sipped at his coffee, deep in thought.

She grinned broadly as she reached into her brown leather bag and handed Helga, Bernie, Saskia, Peggy and Vil bulging envelopes. 'A gift from De Groot,' she said, glibly. 'It's good for me to give you all something on *my* birthday. And... be sure to pay it into your bank accounts when you can.'

Zita looked at Ackerman and waited for his response but he flicked his hand indifferently. He had no interest at all in De Groot's money all he wanted was to find him and put him behind bars forever.

She grinned at him and mouthed her words. 'Thank you.'

He lowered his eyes and nodded.

The girls were still in shock not only from the fire but the torture meted out to them by Erag. They didn't hide their suspicion and sat gripping the envelopes tightly in their hands until Saskia succumbed and opened hers. When she saw the contents she gasped before fanning the money and revealing it to everyone. Saskia Peggy and Vil soon shared her surprise and tore open their envelopes each taking their time to count their unexpected gift of the equivalent of three thousand pounds in Dutch, German and Belgian notes.

Bernie passed her envelope to Ribeker who shook her head in disbelief as she counted the notes.

Zita reached into her bag and passed the last envelope containing pound notes to Liam. He looked at her in shock. 'For me?' he mouthed.

'Yes. For you,' she said, with a wide grin.

Zita had deposited most of the money stolen from De Groot into several new bank accounts but kept some of the money collected over the Christmas and New Year holiday for the girls and placed it in the envelopes when she knew they were about to be released from the clinic.

Now it was Liam who surprised them. He sat forward and proudly handed each of them their passports and deposits he had removed from the cellar safe at the Love Shack when he made his final heart-breaking visit after the fire. 'You can all go home now?' They gawped at him. 'Assuming that's what you want, uh?'

Bernie chose to stay in Amsterdam and move in with Detective Andrea Ribeker and return to her music while Helga, Saskia and Vil chose to go home. Peggy had other ideas and carefully chose her words. 'I am going to do something I want to do for myself,' she said, with an impish giggle.

They all looked at her and waited for her to tell them what it was.

She clicked her tongue. 'I will become a sports instructor,' she said. 'Think of all those beautiful bodies... of the men,' she said, drooling. 'And... this time *I* can decide which of them I want to fuck.'

They all clapped, shrieked and cheered.

After everyone had gone Liam sat back in his favourite chair and looked up at the sun streaming through the roof light.

Zita walked in with two glasses of freshly squeezed orange juice and passed one to him.

'Thanks,' he said, offering his appreciation with a nod.

She waited until he took the first sip and as a smile of pleasure crossed his face she lifted her glass and smiled back at him. 'Liam, you never had a birthday since you arrived here.'

He shrugged.

'When is that?'

'Pff.' He shook his head as he spoke. 'It's the twenty second of September,' he said, brusquely.

She briefly closed her eyes. 'But that was *last* year,' she said, with a look of confusion. 'Why didn't you tell me dat–?'

'You know when that was... don't you?'

'No! How could I?' she shrieked.

He shuddered and nodded erratically. 'When I tell you... *you will* know.' He paused. 'How could I ever forget it?'

'How come?'

He stood up and tilted his glass accidentally spilling juice on the colourful Moroccan mat. 'It was...' He squeezed his chin. 'It was when....' He coughed repeatedly as he tried to clear his clogged and enraged throat. 'When that Greek bastard...' He exhaled sharply. 'Attacked me! 'He clutched at his throat. 'Surely *you* remember that?'

She closed her eyes and remembered the horrific scene she discovered in his flat in the Love Shack so many months earlier. When she finally opened them, she spoke in a soft sympathetic voice. 'Yes, Liam.' She stood and hugged him tight. 'I can never forget that most terrible day...'

CHAPTER FIFTEEN

Get Away

Now that Liam had any direct threat from De Groot removed, he shared the houseboat with Zita and he loved it. It was a new and different world and he couldn't resist spending hours sitting on the deck and looking out onto the canal and waving majestically at the passing tourist boats. He frequently pinched himself and smiled knowing that he now lived in his new home in this wonderful city.

Following a delicious takeaway dinner delivered from the restaurant where Asmara now worked Zita and Liam sat listening to her belated birthday present from him. *The Man Who* CD from Travis was released a few weeks after the fire at the Love Shack. She reached across and turned the music down and exhibiting a thoughtful expression she looked into Liam's eyes. 'I love this music, Liam. Thank you.'

He blushed as he smiled at her genuine appreciation - something he had seldom met.

She continued. 'Liam... I will be sure to remember you next birthday,' she said.

He shrugged. 'Does it matter?'

She fired him a huge grin. 'Of course, it does... It is important to everyone.'

He knew she had already made a mental note of the date before she spoke. 'Um. I think we need to get away for a while. Have you got any ideas?'

Liam tried to smile.

He failed.

'I lost everything in the fire.' He closed his eyes and thought. 'In fact, I have nothing now... except...' He reached into his trouser pocket and pulled out some crumpled ten-pound notes and Dutch guilders.

Zita smiled and reached into her jacket pocket and pulled out a passport. 'There you are,' she said. It was the fake passport that De Groot had arranged for him when he first travelled to Fuerteventura with the laundered money; bundles of Dutch guilders and Deutsch marks.

He flicked it open. 'So, I'm back to being Robert Webster... Am I?'

'Well... until you want to go home and start again. And... if you want a true passport... with your own name... You can get it then.'

Liam sighed and shook his head. 'Who cares?'

Zita shot him a smug look. 'And, I've got money.' She left the room to return with a worn leather travel bag. She dropped it on the floor, opened it and grabbed handfuls of notes in different currencies and waved them at him excitedly.

Liam looked on speechless. *Dishonest money - earned without a fight, for the first time in his life.*

Zita continued. 'This is some of the money from Christmas and the New Year. Collected from all of De Groot's bars, brothels and clubs... Everywhere.' She giggled. 'Of course, I used some of his money for the girls... but only the small money - the petty cash.'

Liam shrugged.

'This is *our* money now. Payment for the hell... And my time working for that bastard!' She sat back, and as she relaxed, she exhaled. 'So, what do we do now?'

Liam stifled a yawn and shrugged. 'Dunno, what do you want to do?'

She smiled. 'We can travel... to Berlin... then Hamburg?'

Liam nodded. 'Yeah, why not.' He grinned wryly and spoke out loud. 'I've not been any fucking where really.'

'It will do you good to get away and will help to widen your view of the world.'

He replied glibly. 'If you say so.'

He suddenly fell silent.

'What is the matter, Liam?'

He lowered his head before blurting out his words. 'Teach me.'

'Me? Teach you?' She frowned. 'Teach you what?'

'You know. What you do...' He paused. 'Or did.'

She lowered her voice. 'Liam, I can only teach you about death...'

He stood and without saying a word walked up the stairs and onto the deck.

Zita waited for few minutes and followed him.

'Is that what you want me to teach you, Liam?' she said softly.

He kicked out. 'I don't know.' He shook his head in frustration. 'You know so fucking much and... and I know...' He scoffed. 'Fuck all.'

'Why do you curse so much, Liam? Is it anger? Maybe you are cursing against yourself.' She reached out and placed her arm across his shoulder. 'Liam.' She pulled him towards her. 'Of course, I will teach you everything... and we can see places together... places I know you will love.'

He wiped the tears from his eyes and forced a smile. 'Thank you.'

Liam had not had his hair cut since a week before the fire in December, more than four months earlier, and it was now touching his shoulders which he sometimes tied into a pitiful excuse for a pony tail. Zita treated him to a haircut at The Old Fire House, he had only been there once before, when Keeva took him before the opening of the Love Shack, and although it brought back mixed memories he decided it would be a new start for his new life as a traveller to places he had never imagined.

CHAPTER SIXTEEN

Born to Run

Tsotne Tabagari was born in Tbilisi the capital city of Georgia in 1971.The city lay on the banks of the Mtkavi or Kura River surrounded by hills and mountains. The City's back streets were a mishmash of rundown buildings.

Georgia is located on the crossroads of Western Asia and Eastern Europe and for much of his childhood he, like all Georgians, were part of the Soviet Union, but in 1991 it changed. Everyone believed that things would immediately get better but the opposite happened and for much of the following decade there were civil conflicts which resulted in an economic crisis.

Back in 1958 a twenty-metre high aluminium statue of Kartvlis Deda, designed by the prominent Georgian sculpture Elquja Amashukeki, was erected on Sololaki Hill when Tbilisi celebrated its 1500th anniversary. Kartvlis Deda was considered to be the "Mother of Georgia" and the statue depicts her holding a cup of wine in one hand, which stands for hospitality, and a sword in the other, which represents the Georgian's love of freedom and fierceness to fight for their liberty. Tsotne fell in love with that statue and the Georgian motto - "Friends will be welcomed with wine, enemies with a sword!"

Tsotne was sickly and small for his age and often bullied by other kids. They would kidnap him and drop him in the deep open drains and he couldn't get out. On one occasion he nearly drowned when they had unexpected torrential rain and the culverts filled. He survived and it increased his resolve and determination to prove his bullies wrong and one day to be a household name in Georgia.

Years later when he was training for his early fights, he would run up the hill and spend a few moments staring at the statue to build up his confidence.

At the age of eighteen and at a little over five foot tall he knew what he wanted to do but wasn't ready. He was conscripted into the army and he used that time as a way of achieving his dream. Although conscription was only for twelve months he stayed on and the following year he began training in martial arts. He thrived and was soon fighting fellow soldiers and winning.

He always won.

While on leave he started taking small fights in the clubs around the Vaziani Military Base twenty kilometres outside Tbilisi. But the rewards were meagre, a few lari for a win. He continued to win every fight and his reputation grew outside of his home city. He started full-on training at the Ringside Muay Thai Gym in ZP Palace Hotel in Tbilisi which in time resulted in major fights at the Tbilisi Sport Palace.

With the continuous wins his life changed and so did his physique and then his name. He had ambitions to fight outside of Georgia and wanted a name that anyone could pronounce. After lengthy deliberation he changed his name to Toto. From then on, and although he was still only a few inches over five foot, he was infallible. He learnt English and he had a dream and a plan to leave his country and make money. It was his way of proving his bullies wrong. He left the army in the summer of 1997 and from then on whenever he had a fight, and with his fighting nickname of *Poster Boy,* he always entered the cage wearing a Derby County football shirt - POOM 1.

Mart Poom, the Estonian goalkeeper was signed by Derby County in March 1997 and he played against Manchester United at Old Trafford the following month.

After the match, Toto read in the newspaper that Poom didn't have a team shirt so their kit manager bought a Manchester United shirt from their shop and covered Russell Hoult's name with black tape putting POOM 1 on top of it. From that day Mart Poom became his hero.

Toto travelled to Germany and arrived in Hamburg in 1998 and within a few months had fights in the lower end of the fight card in the Hansa city. He continued to take fights in Hamburg and, after betting on him and winning big, Dieter Stange arranged bouts for him against all-comers across the country. As a result, Toto and *Poster Boy's* name was soon synonymous with the sport throughout Germany.

Toto and Dieter built up an enviable partnership and Toto was soon seen as the one to beat. But Toto had a nagging uneasiness and became suspicious of his mentor, Dieter Stange, because for much of every month he seemed to disappear from Hamburg. This came to a head when Dieter failed to turn up for several meetings at the bar beneath his flat in Talstraße and was uncontactable for days on end. Toto challenged Dieter but he waved it off with spurious excuses.

It spurred Toto on and he made the reluctant decision to trail Dieter. He borrowed a car from one of his keenest fans, filled it with diesel and parked twenty metres from Dieter Stange's flat. He followed him every day until one late afternoon he drove out of Hamburg. He followed him driving on the autobahn non-stop for four hundred and seventy kilometres and almost five hours before arriving in Amsterdam. He watched him pull up and stop in a rundown area before driving into a railway arch beneath the main line. He was confused so he waited for several hours until, to his amazement, Dieter Stange didn't reappear. Instead De Groot emerged in his Amsterdam registered car. He followed him and when he saw him park his car and walk away confidently and into his office, he knew that Stange and De Groot were without doubt the same person.

He was the first and only person to know about the secret of De Groot's double life. He knew he couldn't get into his hideaway but vowed one day to return and use it to his advantage.

Toto's initial plan had been to set up in Amsterdam in competition with De Groot but following his disappearance in January 2000, several months later, he opened his massage parlour in what was once the derelict Love Shack and used Hamburg as his "training" ground. He moved into Dieter Stange's flat in Talstraße and waited until May when he returned to Georgia. He recruited the most suitable criminals recently released from Gldani #8 prison in Tbilisi and moved them into his flat in Talstraße.

CHAPTER SEVENTEEN

Come What May

While Zita bought drinks at the Centraal Station buffet Liam walked to a telephone and called his father.

Tommy, his younger brother answered. 'Hello. Who is it?'

Liam struggled to speak.

'Is that you, Li?' asked Tommy, excitedly.

Liam coughed and mumbled his reply. 'Yeah, I need to speak to Dad...'

Tommy fired a series of questions but Liam ignored all of them.

He coughed and continued. 'Can *you* let me speak to Dad?' He swallowed hard and screamed out. 'NOW!'

Tommy dropped the phone and raced into the lounge. He grabbed his father's arm dragged him out of his favourite armchair and into the hall. As he handed the phone to his father he spoke. 'It's Li...' He sighed and continued. 'He sounds rough... really rough...'

His father cleared his throat before speaking. 'Hello... is that you, Liam?'

'Hello, Dad.'

There was only silence at the other end.

'Yeah, it's me, Dad.'

His father partially closed his eyes and screwed up his face. 'Liam, is that really you?'

'Yeah. It is.'

His father took a huge breath. 'We thought you'd fuckin' copped it...' He snorted and forced a half laugh. 'We all saw it. It was all over the TV...' He sniffed hard before he continued. 'And... Do you know what?' His father paused a minute before he continued with an almighty roar. 'No fucker *cared* or... dropped a tear.'

Silence.

Liam swallowed hard. 'We were fucked... firebombed'

His father smiled to himself and grunted.

Liam continued. 'But...' He grinned. 'Some of us got out.'

'So why the fuck did they say you all died–'

'Dad...' He held his throat and struggled to breath before continuing in a subdued voice. 'It's a long story...' He gulped for air. 'But we will find the bastards who did it–'

He flicked his head mockingly. 'Course you will, son.' He showed his disinterest by immediately changing the subject. 'Have you phoned, Kath and the kids?'

Liam sighed. 'I can't. Not yet... but I will when the time is right.'

'So... when will the *"time be right,"* Liam?'

Liam coughed a deep and painful cough and tried to swallow but the pain was too great. He only managed a gasp.

'What's happened to your voice?'

'*That* is a very long story,' he said, faking a laugh.

'Remember... You make sure you find 'em and do what you do so well, eh?'

Liam coughed again and tasted the blood, from his damaged throat.

'Listen, son. Kath and the kids are beginning to forget you ever existed. I thought you would have only gone for a couple of months but it's almost two years now–'

'Fifteen months, that's all.'

His father grunted. 'So, when are *you* coming back?'

'Not yet. I'm not ready to face them all. I'll let you know when I am.'

'OK, but make sure you give Kath a call–'

'I'd rather you do that, Dad... I said I'm not ready yet.'

There was a lengthy pause.

'There won't be any money for a little while. I've lost everything this time,' said Liam. 'But I am arranging a way to do it.' He breathed heavily.

His father raised his voice. 'Come on, Liam.'

Liam imagined him smiling proudly. 'You left here with nothing didn't ya? So, you will find a way. You'll survive... bastards like you always do...'

Liam could hear his father lighting a cigarette. 'Why are you still smoking, you know it's going to kill yer?'

His father coughed painfully and then spoke. 'Maybe it will.' He took a drag and continued. 'You know Kath still hasn't forgiven you. Time won't heal things this time, son.'

The phone clicked and disconnected.

Tommy had been listening in the hall and as soon as his father put down the receiver, he moved towards him. 'Li's not coming back is he?'

His father shook his head. 'Sorry, Tommy, I don't believe he'll be back for quite a while.'

Tommy lashed out and broke down, punched the front door and ran off into the night.

Zita rushed across to the box and grabbed Liam. 'Come on our train is ready to leave.'

They raced for the train and took their seats.

Liam was still in shock at the way his father had spoken to him but he gradually realised that he was right after all. He felt guilty at having spoken to Tommy the way he had but he only had limited time before the train was due to leave.

Rather than book a flight, taking into account check-in, passport control and waiting times, it would take the same time on the train so she chose the latter. There were no passenger inspections except for checking their tickets so Zita decided on the air-conditioned train which took a little over six hours to arrive at the Hauptbahnhof, in the centre of Berlin. They took the U Bahn to Weinmeister Straße and Gip Straße which was followed by a three-minute walk to Adina Apartment Hotel at Hackescher Markt in what was previously East Berlin.

They checked in and Zita paid for a six week stay at the second-floor apartment overlooking the street below.

As they walked towards the lift, Liam looked at her. 'Are we staying here for six weeks?' he asked, apprehensively.

Zita grinned. 'We are… and…' She grinned. 'We aren't,' she said.

'I don't understand.'

' You will see why I did this… later.'

Liam shrugged and followed her into the empty lift.

Zita explained why she had done it. 'We will be travelling to Hamburg and then we will take a holiday and we will come back after that.'

He was stunned at her answer and followed her out of the lift in silence. *He had so many questions and he needed answers but he was prepared to wait for them.*

They threw their worn travel holdalls onto the huge bed and, after a taking a shower, they walked out into the warm evening and dinner in the bar next door. The atmosphere in Berlin was so different to Amsterdam. There were few tourists and the locals were clearly relishing their freedom gained from the Communist Party a mere nine years earlier.

The next morning Zita was up early and keen to explore. After breakfast they took the U Bahn to Bülow Straße. They walked

111

up the stairs and out onto the busy street. Liam sensed Zita's mind was elsewhere and they walked in silence until they reached a row of shops and offices dominated by the overhead viaduct which carried part of the train line above the city.

Liam sighed and finally spoke. 'What is it? What's wrong?'

She snapped at him. '*Nothing.*'

'I know you.' He sighed again. 'I know there is.'

Zita broke down and wrung her hands as she looked around her. She sat down on a bench outside of what was once the Liverpool Hoop - the Tanzsalon der Jugend in 6 Bülow Straße. Liam sat beside her and turned his head as he tried to make sense of the names above the entrances behind them. He was fortunate the signs had images; one was a cookery school and the other a gym.

Zita looked at him. 'This is not like it was in 1967, my mother loved music and coming to this club, especially the Manchester Playboys from England. She came to see them every week for the month they played here.'

Liam tried to imagine what it was like so long ago, when he was still just a kid.

He failed.

Zita swallowed hard and pointed towards the steel stanchions supporting the overhead rail line. 'This is where my mother was...' She sighed heavily and wiped at her eyes. 'RAPED!'

Liam pulled her towards him. '1967 was a long time ago wasn't it?' He paused and forced a smile. 'And...*you* wouldn't exist if that hadn't happened to her... would you?'

'Is that such a good reason?' said Zita, as she shuddered and sucked in air.

Liam stroked his neck and looked around for the words before answering her. 'Well, isn't it?'

Zita reflected. 'Do you know my mother died waiting for *him* to come back for her?'

'Why would she want to see him again after that?'

'I don't know, Liam.'

'Did she honestly believe that he would come and find her?'

'She was so sure he would.'

'And?'

She sniffed, wiped at her tears and looked hard at Liam. 'Do you know what it's like to have a secret that you can't tell to anyone?'

He nodded thoughtfully. 'Yeah. Course, I know that.'

'You can never put what's happened back in the box when it's been opened,' said Zita.

A train rumbled noisily overhead and they looked at each other as they had their own thoughts.

Zita wiped her tears, took a deep breath and spoke. 'I was removed from Mossad.'

Liam stroked her shoulder. 'Is that why you ended up in Amsterdam?'

She sniffed her tears away. 'Remember what De Groot said?'

Liam nodded and tilted his head forward.

'You *don't*, do you?'

Liam shook his head. 'No. I have no idea what the hell you're talking about.'

'OK. De Groot said that most of the people that end up in that city are there for a reason - they had nowhere else to go.' She stared hard at Liam. 'Can you remember?' She paused and then continued in a softer voice. 'Why *you* came here?'

Liam swallowed hard and took an incredibly deep breath. 'Course I do...' He choked with embarrassment. 'I was drunk and set fire to... to... to me own fucking house.' He sighed heavily and reflected. 'I nearly lost my wife and kids.'

113

She was visibly shocked.

'I didn't care if I woke up the morning after.' He ignored her expression and continued at speed. 'I saved them all.' He grinned. 'Even got a mention in the paper for doing it - said I was a hero.' He let out a loud comedic laugh. 'Me. A fucking hero! Can you believe that?'

'Why? How can that be?' she gushed.

'It was all a lie. The newspapers always make shit up.' He cursed. 'Only my father knew what happened.' He pushed out his chest. 'But guess what?'

She shook her wildly and mouthed her question. 'What?'

'He told me to fuck off! Can you believe that? Your own father telling you to fuck off!'

Her expression didn't change.

Liam shrugged his shoulders. 'Tommy, my young brother, nicked a car...' He laughed loudly. 'Not just any car, a fucking BMW and... And... And drove me to Dover in style.' He reflected and then continued. 'I bought a ticket and took the first boat out of the country,' he said, flippantly. 'So that's how I ended up in that crazy place. And then... within a couple of hours arrested for fucking murder! Can you believe that?'

'Didn't De Groot get you out of the police cells after you were arrested?'

'Yes, the bastard did... but at a price' He clicked his teeth. 'And it was at *his* price - and no negotiation,' he screamed, venting his anger.

'That's right... but you ended up with the Love Shack–'

'I did, but I had to bust my balls to make it work.' He looked into space and then slowly turned to grin at her. 'And *it did*.' He sneered. 'And now it's gone.' He looked directly at her. 'Well... isn't it?'

She breathed in noisily through her nostrils and wiped at it with her sleeve, she forced a smile. 'Yes, I suppose it is,' she said, her voice fading with emotion.

'So... after today *you* can start again.' He paused. 'You can put your demons to rest too.'

'How do I do that, Liam?'

'It was more than thirty years ago and... and... now everything has changed.' He looked around at the shops, cafés and offices that had replaced the club and businesses that had long closed down.

'The club's gone and...' She paused and sniffed and rubbed her eyes. 'And with it... the memories, eh?'

Another train raced overhead and Zita looked around and then tilted her head to look up at the metal framework above them. She closed her eyes, exhaled and shook her head. 'Um... maybe not all.'

Liam followed her eyes and gazed up to the dark metal girders which was the viaduct carrying the U Bahn high above them. 'Well, I doubt if *that's* changed much in thirty years,' he said.

As they stepped into the road a gleaming 1959, red and white fin-tailed Cadillac with Berlin plates, shipped over many years earlier the by the American servicemen, appeared from nowhere and blasted its horn as it drove at them.

Zita's mind was elsewhere.

Liam grabbed her arm and dragged her back.

They both looked at the driver and glared before collectively raising their fists. 'What the fuck?' he screamed.

Zita shook her head. 'That is a crazy German man... A dummkopf!'

'What?' Liam sniggered blindly. 'I would agree with that.'

She spoke as they walked. 'In 1991 after the wall came down many of the GI's started to go home so they sold their cars to German men - it was too expensive to send them back.' She clicked her tongue. 'Do you know that more than fifteen thousand ex-American military still live in Berlin?'

'Wow,' he said. He bit at his inner lip and felt that he was ready to finally ask Zita a question he had wanted to ask for a very long time. He forced a cough before speaking. 'So, tell me why you ended up with me and the other wasters in Amsterdam?'

'It is a long story, Liam. A very long story.'

'So, tell me then.'

'Well, Berlin is where I started the search for my father.' She tugged at his arm. 'Come on I'll show you.'

They took the U-Bahn from Nollendorf platz to Thielplatz, in the Dahlem district, and walked out onto the platform that was once Berlin's former American Sector. They took the escalator and when they reached the street Liam was gobsmacked at the difference in the Schöneberg area compared to what they had left just eight stations earlier. They walked slowly through the area of Steglitz-Zehlendorf, once the home of yet another "Little America," and like Ramstein, the huge air force base in Germany, and the other bases around the world where troops were still stationed. Berlin's McNair Barracks with its stores, cinemas, bowling alleys, American diners and sports centres which were once home to more than 30,000 troops were now either put to another use or remained closed and dilapidated.

They returned to the subway and walked until Zita motioned to Liam to stop. She opened the door and they walked into the American barbeque diner.

Had they just walked into America?

Zita explained. 'This was opened for the Americans soon after the war but when they went home the American owner stayed behind. It is a very famous place and is just like the diners across America.'

They sat in a booth and Zita ordered two coffees and four doughnuts from the pseudo American sounding waitress.

CHAPTER EIGHTEEN

Too Late Now

While American fifties music filled every corner of the diner, they sat in the booth and took their time to look around at the walls completely covered with the black and white framed photographs of singers, comedians, actors and musicians who had visited this part of the city to entertain the troops after the war. While they waited for their order, they attempted to recognise the once "famous" faces.

They soon gave up.

Liam tapped Zita's arm. 'You never finished telling me about your father.'

She was very surprised at his question. She swallowed hard and straightened up.

'Did you find him here?' said Liam.

'He had left a long time ago.'

'So?'

Zita was reluctant to continue but Liam pressed her.

Her pretty face became almost unrecognisable as it was slowly transformed into what appeared to be a spine-chilling, macabre mask. 'OK.' She sneered, showing her clenched teeth. 'So, I used my contacts - called in a few favours... And... yes, I found him–'

'You found him?'

'Yes, I did,' she said, as her head shook uncontrollably. 'He was living in Atlanta, Georgia.'

'And?' Liam bit enthusiastically into his second donut. 'Did you want to see him - to meet him?'

She nodded. 'Of course, I did,' she replied tersely. 'I wanted to see what he was really like... Even after all dese years.'

'So?' said Liam. He emptied his mug, tilted his head and waited.

She bit into her bottom lip. 'I flew to Columbus Metropolitan Airport which was almost a hundred and fifty kilometres from where he lived. Then I hired a car, drove to Atlanta and took a taxi and parked at a bar two kilometres from Piedmont Heights.'

Liam looked confused.

'He lived in a bar?'

'No. But nearby.' She smiled. 'I jogged the rest of the way until I reached the end of his tree-lined street. I caught my breath and walked until I saw the number 4128 on the letter box.' She feigned shock. 'There was an old and fat, grey haired, black man on the drive washing his car.' She remembered. 'An old red Mustang–'

'Nice car.'

She passed his ridiculous comment away with a lazy wave.

'Was it him?'

She frowned. 'Wait a moment... and I will tell you.'

She ordered more drinks from the waitress and continued. 'I walked up to him and he lowered the hosepipe, reached for the tap and left it to run slowly.' She briefly closed her eyes and exhaled deeply. She scoffed at Liam. 'And... yes, I told him it *was* a nice car.'

Liam blushed awkwardly.

'He just grinned proudly and said "thanks". Then he said, "Do you live around here?" I told him I didn't... and he ignored me and returned to washing his car. I can remember walking closer to him and I asked if he was one time in Berlin and if he knew Benjamin Reynolds. He stopped and glared at me and then laughed so loud that his wide open mouth showed his dirty, filthy teeth.'

She looked at Liam and grinned. 'He didn't have many.'

Liam shrugged.

Zita wrung her hands. 'He asked me why I wanted to know. I remember stuttering as I tried to come up with an excuse - the excuse I had rehearsed so many times during the journey.'

She paused while the waitress put the drinks on the table and took the empty plates and mugs away.

'So what did you say?'

She scowled. '*Wait* Liam. This is very difficult!'

'Sorry.' He forced a cough, raised his hands and stretched his fingers in submission. 'Take your time. OK?'

She stirred her coffee erratically until Liam reached out and took the spoon away from her and placed it on the table. She smiled at him, cleared her throat and continued. 'I asked if he was in the army... in Berlin in '67 and... He looked at me confused... But then he looked nervous...' She exhaled and took a deep breath. 'Then he nodded,' she said, as she exhaled.

'Wow.'

'Then... he stared at me... As if I was *mad*.'

Liam lifted his head. 'Um.'

Zita continued. 'He asked who I was.'

Liam fiddled with his mug. 'Right?'

'I screamed at him. YOU RAPED MY MOTHER!' She took a huge breath and continued. 'In BERLIN!'

Liam shushed her to be quiet. He looked around but the few customers in the diner were half listening to the music and hadn't heard, or taken any notice.

Zita looked furtively around and lowered her voice. 'Then he changed. He *became* a madman. He was crazy. He picked up the hosepipe and turned it at me and told me to fuck off!'

'The next thing I said was... was... I am *your* daughter–'

'Fuck,' muttered Liam. 'You said it just like that - straight out?' He began to laugh.

'Yes.' She said proudly. 'Just like that... those are my real words.'

Liam still had the remains of the smile on his face.

'Do you know *he* laughed at me - just like you did?' she shrugged. 'What a bastard. He *said*, "I ain't got *no* kids."'

'Fuck.'

'I couldn't believe he said dose things.' She breathed erratically. 'I didn't know what to do. I looked around. There were no people. So, I rushed at him. I took the hosepipe and pulled it around his neck.'

'Fuck.'

She swallowed hard. 'Then...'

Liam slid the mugs to one side, reached across the table, lowered her trembling hands and gently stroked them.

She stiffened. 'I pushed him into the car and...' She sniffed. 'He was *my father* but... he said he didn't do it to my mother... and every time he said that...' She sobbed. 'I stabbed him... And then...' She exhaled. 'I pushed the pipe into his mouth and... and down his throat.' She reflected. 'He may explode...' She raised her shoulders. 'I don't know... then maybe *die* for sure.' She slowly lowered her shoulders and looked at Liam through her rueful eyes. 'Can you believe that... that my own father would not accept me?'

Liam lied. 'No, I can't.' *He knew that his father had come close to disowning him but instead he'd forced him to leave everything behind and take that ferry.*

'I broke the Mossad ethics - "By way of deception thou shalt make war." She paused. '"But our goal is *not* to take vengeance on its enemies." I was confused by it. He w*as* my father but maybe *not* my enemy? So... it *was* war and I *could* kill him... Yeas?'

She saw Liam's response by the uncomfortable look on his face. 'You must remember, Liam we have lived in separate worlds - many miles apart.' She paused. 'And, sometimes I was lost in my cover and I wondered if *anything* was real.'

Liam shuffled uncomfortably in the booth.

'I left people broken or dead. It was my work.' She wiped her eyes. 'But now I know *some* difference.'

Liam couldn't react. Instead he gazed at her with a look of utter astonishment and confused at what she had just said. *How could Zita, his only friend and lover, be so different, one minute thoughtful and caring and then seconds later morph into a violent murderer? He thought hard and then realised that he was the same, albeit light on caring.*

She finished drying her eyes with her serviette and continued. 'So now you see why I was forced to leave... Mossad and... and... the work... I loved.'

He lied again. 'Yeah, I understand.'

She pushed herself back hard into the booth and smiled at him. 'And that is why I... like so many other people...' She tilted her head and forced a sorrowful look. 'And... like you,' she sighed, 'I also arrived in Amsterdam.'

They left the diner and walked in silence for almost an hour until they reached Kurfürsdendamm and the Artisan deco Café where they continued their silence while they drank tea and thought their own thoughts and looked blindly out of the window and the strangers walking past.

121

Zita placed her cup on the saucer and finally spoke. 'What about your demons, Liam?'

He rubbed at his stubbly cheek and thought hard. Still thinking, he picked up his mug, closed his eyes and finished the cold coffee before speaking. 'De Groot is still my demon.' He slid the cup and saucer across the table. 'I lost the first thing I ever cared about.' He fiddled with the spoon. 'Something I'd done without thieving and... for once... on me own.'

Zita inhaled loudly and smiled at him. 'We can fix that–'

'How?'

'First let me take you to Hamburg and show you where I lived and maybe after that we can fix it,' she said, emphasising the words - fix it.

CHAPTER NINETEEN

Times like These

Trains ran almost every hour from Berlin to Hamburg and in a little over two hours they arrived at the Hamburg Hauptbahnhof. They took a bus to the Hotel Pacific at 30-31 Neuer Pferdemarkt which was a short walk from Zita's home where she had lived with her mother and coincidently it was very close to 10-12 Talstraße where Dieter Stange had lived above his bar.

Zita checked them in at the hotel and while she was waiting for the key she turned to Liam and smiled. 'This is the place where all the bands that played at the Star Club stayed in the sixties.'

Liam looked at her quizzically.

'You know... The *Beatles*?'

The desk clerk looked up, grinned proudly and spoke to them in English. 'Ja, dey all stayed with us in here.' He pointed at the framed black and white photographs that covered one wall. 'It was a very long time ago - Ja?'

'Um,' muttered Liam, highlighting his lack of interest. He straightened up and continued with a shrug. 'I preferred the Stones, anyway.'

Zita looked at the desk clerk and together they shook their heads in disagreement. She turned to Liam. 'My mother told me that music in the city changed when the Star Club closed at the end of December 1969.'

Liam clearly still had no interest.

'I will show you tomorrow. OK?'

The following morning, she gave him a guided tour of St Pauli. 'This is a very famous area, Liam.' She took him to Große Freiheit and stood outside the Indra Club looking at the plaque on the wall while she explained when the Beatles first played there.

He wasn't impressed. 'I still prefer The Stones,' he said, with a grunt.

As they walked down the cobbled street she continued. 'Do you know the Star Club was once a cinema but as there were very few new German films many of the cinemas either closed or were changed into music clubs and the Star Club was one of the first to do that.' They walked past a catholic church and stopped. 'The Star Club was next door to this church. It opened in 1962 and the Beatles played there for many weeks until December the thirty first when they had their first hit record. It closed in 1969 and after there was a fire and nothing is left except this,' she said, pointing at the plaque where the Star Club once stood.

They walked past the Greta and Alfonse bar and out onto the Reeperbahn. She pointed up at the dilapidated sign above the innocuous looking entrance where the now closed Top Ten Club once pounded with the music of English bands.

Liam took his time to look around and finally feigned interest. 'This is not much different than London. Why the big deal?'

'This is where the Beatles also played.' Her face turned into a wide grin.

'And do you know what?'

'What?'

'Well... after Berlin the Manchester Playboys were playing at both clubs and my mother saw them here too.' She shrieked. 'When she was pregnant! Can you believe that?'

Liam was bored and showed it by shaking his head.

Zita ignored him and grabbed his hand. 'We will come back tonight and you will see...'

They took a taxi to the impressive Four Seasons Hotel which overlooked the Alster River, a tributary of the Elbe, and had a very expensive late lunch.

Zita scoffed and then laughed loudly. 'When the US President wanted to stay here his security people wanted to drain it.' She laughed. 'Crazy isn't it?'

Liam shrugged his disinterest.

As they left they looked out across the calm water at the swans swimming majestically across it. 'Do you know that in the winter the swans are taken away for safety?'

He shook his head. 'What the?'

'Come on. I will show you much more.'

They strolled past the Hamburg football stadium and onto the massive static fairground that was open for much of the year.

Liam had never seen anything like it. It dwarfed what he'd visited in Battersea Park and even the Kursaal in Southend.

They crossed the busy road and onto the Reeperbahn which was now an avenue of music from the bars and clubs and all trying to compete for customers, flashing lights and the wide pavement crowded with local people, rowdy tourists, seaman and drunks.

Zita stopped and looked at him. 'Do you agree with me now?'

Liam nodded. 'Yeah... it is different.'

She glared at him.

He chuckled. 'Yeah, alright - very different.'

'Can you imagine what it was like when I was growing up here?'

'Yeah - madness.' He thought and was about to say. *No wonder you're so fucked up. But changed his mind and remained silent.*

She tugged his arm. 'I will show you where I lived with my mother.'

They turned right into Talstraße and then into Hein Hoyer Straße and walked almost to the end of the street. She stopped on the left-hand side outside number sixty-five. She put a foot on the first step and pointed at the number at the side of the entrance. 'This is where I was born.' She tugged at Liam and they crossed the cobbled street and she looked up. 'On the second floor where we lived for many years...' She paused. 'Before I travelled to Israel. Can you believe I lived amongst this people?'

Liam shrugged.

'The strippers and prostitutes...'

He shook his head in disbelief. 'No, I can't.'

'My mother had three jobs to support us, washing clothes in the laundry, cooking in the bars at night and then in very early morning... Cleaning...' Her mood changed. 'It was very hard for her but she did it - *every* day.'

Liam pulled her close to him.

She continued. 'When I left, she returned to Berlin and waited for her G.I.' She reflected. 'Her American.'

'The rapist?'

She nodded.

'Fuck.'

'And do *you* know... he never came back.'

She paused and wiped at her eyes. 'I never saw my mother again. She died while I was away... of a broken heart.'

They walked back onto the Reeperbahn in silence and took the U Bahn for one stop to Landungsbrücken. They left the train and stepped out onto the open elevated station with a phenomenal view of the huge harbour with its ships, barges, ferries, tourists and imposing tower of the fischmarkt.

They walked down to the landing stage and sat watching the feverish activity of the tourists and young local people until it was almost midnight.

Zita stood. 'Come on let's go back to the hotel now. I have many things to do in the morning.' She giggled. 'You can have a breakfast in bed... and a lay in, yeas?'

Zita was up early the following day and after Liam's breakfast arrived, she buttered his toast and poured his tea. While he was eating, she changed, checked her wallet and pulled on her jacket. 'I'm going shopping,' she said.

'What for?'

'Wait and see.'

As she closed the door Liam lay back on the bed switched on the television and, realising all stations were in German, fell asleep.

She walked down to reception and asked the hotel porter if he would sell her two suitcases from left luggage. He walked her down to the basement which was stacked with everything from dust covered guitars, some in cases, drums, speakers and amplifiers and even an electric organ all left behind by homesick musicians in the sixties. After leaving their bands and unable to carry their equipment, they returned to England on the train. The rest of the items were a treasure trove including expensive golf clubs, umbrellas, prams and push chairs, overcoats, shoes and even two wigs hanging from the ceiling. She had a massive choice of cases and decided on two that were very different and easily recognisable. A 1980's hard-shelled dark blue Samsonite and a dark brown battered

Constellation suitcase. After paying him four hundred Deutsche marks he said he would have them cleaned and taken up to their room.

Zita took the tube a few stops up to Altona and Schanzenviertels the newly opened Flohschanze flea market in the decommissioned animal abattoir in Neuer Kamp1 Straße. She took her time and picked her way between the mass of stalls and filled several large plastic bags with clothes for Liam. A casual suit, several pairs of casual trousers, designer shirts, tee shirts and shoes, and for herself, two dresses, blouses and skirts and three backpacks, one much smaller than the other two. Once back in the room she flattened and packed the second-hand clothes into them.

Liam looked up at her.

'So, when will you tell me what the fuck is going on?'

She huffed. 'I said we were taking a holiday so we need these things… so please wait a little longer, Liam.'

He shrugged, closed his eyes and pretended to sleep.

After lunch in the bar next to the hotel they took the U Bahn from the St Pauli station and five stops later arrived at Mönckebergstraße and the large department stores. They bought toiletries, an electric razor, aftershave and perfume, something she seldom wore, sun cream, two electric tooth brushes and toothpaste and a selection of travel tablets. Zita let Liam choose his underwear and socks but when it came to buying her undies Liam found it too embarrassing to stay with her and waited in a nearby café.

Zita woke early on Sunday morning and was already dressed before she nudged Liam into life. 'Come on get up. I have a surprise for you.'

He checked the wall clock. 'Now? Five o'clock in the bloody morning?'

'Yes. I want to you show you something.'

'Something else?' How much more?'

She grinned. 'Liam you will love it.'

They walked down a deserted Große Freiheit and across the Reeperbahn and side streets joining the growing crowds until they finally reached the famous fischmarkt.

It was packed.

The bars were overflowing with people singing and dancing to the live music that varied from folk, jazz, rock and traditional German music and even an oompah band in the large corner bar.

Zita steered him away from the bars and bought two frigadellen in thick cut bread each on a cardboard tray. She covered the bread with mayonnaise, ketchup and mustard before handing it to him. She watched and waited as he reluctantly bit into it.

His reaction was sheer pleasure.

He loved it.

She bought him another one and he ate that just as quickly.

They spent the next two hours pushing their way through the crowds and walking between the stalls and vans selling everything from live fish and so many different fish on ice, crabs, shrimps and prawns, rabbits, chicken, ducks, paintings, Tee-shirts, jeans, CD's and stall after stall of hot food and drink. Zita guided him inside the huge cavernous fischmarkt and the largest frying pan he'd ever seen filled with paella.

'So... what do you think of the fischmarkt now?'

He closed his eyes and took his time to inhale the wonderful smells. He finally opened them, shook his head and spoke. 'You know...' He grinned. 'I *love* it.'

'So, it was worth getting up so early?'

He licked his lips and tasted the frigadellen, ketchup, mustard and mayonnaise. 'Yeah.' He looked around. 'This is more like it for me.'

'My mother told me that the musicians always came here on Sunday mornings after finishing their last set at the Star Club at six in the morning. And do you know?'

'What?'

'They didn't go to bed.' She giggled. 'Instead they played and then went to bed on *Monday* morning.'

Once back in their room at the Pacific hotel they both slept until early afternoon. Zita woke first and went down to reception and rebooked their room for one night the following week. She handed the hotel porter the largest of the suitcases and asked if he could have the clothes washed and ironed and the suit and dresses dry cleaned and store the other case securely for her.

She passed him five hundred Dutch guilders and arranged to collect the cases when they came back the following week.

CHAPTER TWENTY

Travelling Light

They took the train to Amsterdam and as soon as they arrived back on the houseboat, Zita went below and opened the roof lights and windows while Liam sat down on the deck and returned to the week-old English newspaper he'd picked up on the train.

Fifteen minutes later Detective Ackerman drove down Berenstraat and when he saw Liam on the deck he parked his unmarked police car and joined him. 'Hello,' he said.

Liam reluctantly lowered the newspaper and forced a smile 'Hi.'

'You've been away quite a while,' said Ackerman, with a grin. 'Good time?'

Liam nodded. 'All right.'

Zita heard Ackerman on deck and to complete their subterfuge she placed a handful of clean clothes in the washing machine after making sure that there was nothing left that could give any clues to where they had stayed. *She had been taught to destroy anything that could incriminate her or give clues to her actions or previous whereabouts well before returning from an assignment.*

There was nothing.

She walked up onto the deck carrying a tray with three mugs. She placed the tray on the table and, after brushing Liam's knee. 'Yeah we did,' she said, confirming what he had

131

just said. She passed him his tea and continued with a forced weariness. 'I need to sort out a few things on here,' she said, shaking her head. 'I've neglected it for so long.'

Ackerman cast a fleeting eye of disinterest around the tidy deck and shrugged. 'OK,' he said.

Zita lifted the second mug and smiled at him.

His wide grin and enthusiastic nod confirmed his acceptance.

She passed it to him and continued. 'We're only back for a few days.'

The detective sipped at his coffee, tightened his lips and sucked on them. 'Um... OK.'

She smiled. 'And then... we're going *back* to Berlin.

'Yeah - why not.' He forced a grin. 'You've both had a hard time. You deserve it.'

Liam nodded his agreement as he folded his newspaper and eyed Zita, surprised at her decision, before dropping it on the deck beside his chair.

Ackerman took a cigarette from his pocket, Liam watched enviously and waited while he took his time to light it.

Liam coughed and rubbed at his painful throat.

Ackerman took an extended drag before speaking. 'So, Liam, how is it?'

Liam tilted his head to one side and shot him a confused look.

Ackerman coughed and stroked his throat with his thumb. 'Your throat?'

Liam replied with a slow shrug. 'It's getting better,' he said, with a sigh. 'But I still get spasms of pain if I get stressed... or...' He looked at Ackerman's cigarette. 'From smoke.'

Ackerman ignored him and took another drag before he studied the glowing end of his cigarette and returning to Liam. 'Right.'

Liam noticed the dark sooty brown birds as they swooped down and skimmed the surface of the canal picking up insects before zooming high into the air.

Ackerman joined him and tracked one of them as he spoke. 'Aren't they beautiful?'

Liam nodded. 'Yeah... Fantastic.'

'They are swifts.'

Liam shook his head.

The Detective continued. 'Do you know they come to Amsterdam for only three months each year to breed? You only see them here in... May, June and July...'

'Wow.'

'And then they fly back to Africa.'

Zita coughed to gain their attention and changed the subject. 'Any news on De Groot?' She looked directly at Ackerman. 'It's been a while now.'

'Yeah, it has. Apart from arriving in Madeira last January he seems to have vanished into thin air,' he said.

'How can you be sure about that?' asked Liam. 'Surely he can be tracked?'

'Not always. He's a devious bastard - been around a very long time.' The Detective looked at Zita and continued. 'I'm sure he always had his way out - *his* escape route.'

Zita grinned back at him and nodded. 'Yeah... For sure.'

A huge smile crossed the detective's face as he exhaled a cloud of smoke. 'His enemies are already fighting each other to carve up his operation.' He rocked in the chair. 'He's lost his grip this time. We now have all of his people, well... those still alive.' He grinned. 'Do you know I still wonder how that *huge* Greek bastard ended up in Waalseilandsgracht?' He turned to each of them in turn hoping for a reaction.

There was none.

He continued. 'Well, what was left of him?' He grinned. 'That must have taken some planning. Don't you think?'

Liam looked at Zita and they both shrugged their shoulders.

Liam took a deep breath while he thought of a reply. 'There were enough of them to do something like that.'

Ackerman grinned. 'Um... Sure,' he said, as he exhaled yet another thick cloud of smoke.

Liam coughed hard and spluttered.

Zita shot the detective a disparaging glare.

He looked at Liam and reluctantly stubbed it out in the unused ashtray.

'Sorry, Liam,' he said, shamelessly. He took a huge breath and smiled before he continued. 'Do you know what? While you've been away there's a new kid on the block *and*... he's out to take over De Groot's empire. He's already opened a massage parlour in...' He paused, and looked apprehensively towards Liam.

Liam knew what was coming.

Ackerman continued. 'In what was the Love Shack–'

'Bastard,' seethed Liam.

Zita reached across and tried to console him with a gentle squeeze of his shoulder. She looked across at Ackerman. 'Who is he?'

'He calls himself Toto and he's a cage fighter from Georgia.'

Liam's ears pricked up. 'A cage fighter. Really?'

'Yeah. We've already checked him out. He's a clever bastard too. He's well ahead of his time and he's already worked out which are De Groot's most profitable clubs, hotels and brothels and is targeting them.' The detective cleared his throat. 'He's massed a load of heavies... Georgians... up in Hamburg. He's just waiting for the right time to strike.'

Zita was initially lost for words and she stood. 'So much has happened while we've been away. Shall we have another coffee?'

Ackerman took a cigarette from the packet. 'Good idea, eh, Liam?'

Liam grunted. 'Tea for me...'

Zita shook her head and feigned surprise. 'Course.'

While they waited on deck Ackerman moved as far away from Liam as he could and lit another cigarette. 'You know, Liam, nothing ever stands still.'

'I know that.'

'Toto's not his real name... It's Tsotne Tabagari. According to Europol he's a weird bastard and tiny. His nickname back home was the *dwarf*. He's just over five-foot-tall but built... like... what you would say, "built like a brick shithouse."'

Liam grinned. 'Yeah, it's a name we use in England.' His grin broadened. 'For *big* bastards.'

Zita heard what he'd said as she walked across the deck. She looked confused. 'That is not sense.'

Liam laughed.

She turned to Ackerman. 'But you said he was small.'

Ackerman replied. 'He is small... but all muscle and... full of anger.'

Zita tilted her head towards Liam. 'Sometimes like you, eh, Liam?'

He snorted.

While enjoying their drinks they took in the warm sunshine and waved to the passing tourist boats. They indulged in small talk until the name of Liam's nemesis was mentioned.

Ackerman flicked his cigarette butt into the canal and spoke. 'Well. If De Groot is still around maybe he will show his hand now, eh?' he said.

Zita shook her head. 'Maybe, but we don't believe he's still in the Netherlands. Do we Liam?'

Liam shook his head. 'No, I'm sure he's long gone.'

Ackerman stood and walked off the boat and onto the cobbled road. After looking for any cyclists heading in his direction, he turned back. 'Enjoy Berlin.'

They both raised their hands and while Zita busied herself checking her potted plants Liam sat gently rubbing his throat.

CHAPTER TWENTY-ONE

It's All Gone

Since arriving on Fuerteventura Dieter Stange and Keeva had wined and dined anyone that mattered at the top restaurants and hotels on the island or occasionally across in Lanzarote.

Dieter Stange was rich.

But when they were together, rather than see him as his alter ego, Keeva couldn't help but see him as Bram De Groot, the Dutchman.

She suggested they took time out for themselves and this evening spent time together chilling out on the roof garden amongst the luxuriant shrubs, plants and flowers. De Groot was cooking their dinner on his pride and joy, a huge state of the art gas barbeque.

The relaxing sound of the fountain filled the warm evening air as the water cascaded and trickled over the colourful pebbles. He briefly stopped cooking and they slow danced to the George Michael *Older* CD.

It was perfect.

Paradise.

Keeva closed her eyes and faced the last of the evening sun. 'I love this place... Do you?'

He grunted. 'Yeah. Course.'

He seemed reluctant to continue.

Keeva sensed his angst and pulled back. 'But?'

'I don't know how long I can stay *here*.' He shook his head and a tear appeared in his eye. He wiped at it. 'I miss Mokum–'

'You know… you can *never* go back.'

He pushed himself away from her and wiped his eyes before closing them. 'Maybe Hamburg?'

Keeva snapped at him. 'You can't! Europol will be looking for you... *Both* of you.' She licked the red lipstick on her top lip and gave him a mischievous grin. 'What difference does it make whether you're Bram De Groot or Dieter Stange, now?'

He was about to reply but he heard the telephone ring down in his office. He looked apprehensively towards the steps.

Dieter Stange seldom had calls so, eager to answer the caller, he flung the grease stained towel over his shoulder and hurried down to his office leaving the barbeque unattended.

As the German caller continued to speak Dieter became more and more angry, his face turning crimson. At the end of the call he smashed the receiver down onto the phone and still wringing his hands, made his way up towards the roof.

While he walked, he wiped at his anger with the greasy towel.

It didn't work.

When he reached the top of the steps, he could see that the barbeque was well alight with flames stretching high into the evening sky.

He screamed at Keeva, 'Get some fucking water... NOW!'

She shot him a blank look.

He screamed back at her. 'Why the fuck didn't you do something about that?'

She turned and as she took her time to walk towards the gardener's cabin, hidden behind some of the largest shrubs, she looked back at the Dutchman, fired him an indignant look and unusually for her she answered back cockily. 'You told me never to touch it.' She smirked at him. 'So, I didn't!'

'Just get something you... you... you stupid bitch!'

She returned with a fire extinguisher and handed it to De Groot. He pulled the tag, aimed the dry powder at the flames and the barbeque fizzled to destruction. He grunted to himself as he watched the dying moments of his pride and joy and the huge palls of dense smoke that briefly obliterated the last minutes of the setting sun.

Keeva passed him his beer and they sat down.

He took a few sips before speaking. 'That bastard... The fucking dwarf... has moved into my flat in Hamburg!' He threw his bottle towards the fountain.

He missed.

Instead it smashed, scattering shards of glass across the roof.

He shook as he tugged at his hair and raged. 'He is fucking... everywhere. He's... he's... he's in *my* city. He's rebuilt the Love Shack... and... and turned it into a fucking massage parlour!'

She sucked at her bottom lip. 'Is it really that bad?' She took her time to look at him. She didn't like what she saw and turned away before continuing. 'I mean... did you really care that much about the rundown shit house?'

'That's not the fucking point. He's got my girls from the Casteel working for him and the bastard and his imported cronies are collecting protection money from *my* people!'

He stood up and with his feet crunching the glass, he stomped across the roof kicking out blindly at the flower beds and trimmed shrubs.

'How did you find out about that?'

'I just got that call... from Hamburg,' he said, his crimson face contorted in anger. 'Didn't I?'

139

He grabbed a bottle of Jägermeister from the drinks trolley, unscrewed the top, threw it away and took a huge swig.

He followed it up with a second even bigger swig. His body stiffened and he jerked uncontrollably. 'I'm going back to sort out this shit!'

Keeva spoke softly as she tried hard to appease him. 'You can't ever go back, Bram—'

'Wait and see,' he said, 'I can do what the fuck I want!'

'Yes, but you have lost all your power as well as... new money.' She struggled to continue. 'Forget the past.' She lowered her voice in an attempt to console him. 'You have a new life now - a wonderful life.'

De Groot threw the bottle into the air before it crashed down and smashed on the terrazzo. He reached out, grabbed her tousled hair and struck out with his clenched fist.

Keeva's blood spewed into the air as her face exploded into a bloody mess.

She fell to the ground and with open fingers tried in vain to squeeze the ripped skin and deep lacerations in her lips, eye brows and forehead together.

De Groot turned away and stomped across the roof until he reached the gently gurgling fountain. He stopped and lowered his head but as he felt the warmth on the back of his neck, he raised it and looked out across at the last of the evening sun on the Atlantic. Realising what he had done, he shuffled on the spot rubbing his deck shoes back and forth on the pieces of glass and sticky terrazzo paving before letting out a howl reminiscent of a wounded animal.

He shook his head, turned and walked slowly back to a shocked Keeva who trembled and sniffed as she made a futile attempt to wipe at her beat-up and bloody face with her sleeve and the greasy towel from the barbeque.

De Groot couldn't look directly at her brutally ravaged face and instead made an attempt to whisper in her ear from behind her.

She pulled away. 'Fuck you,' she said, through her chattering teeth.

De Groot said something he vowed years earlier, never to say. He swallowed hard and spoke with a stutter. 'I... I... I'm sorry, Keeva.'

The gushing blood had affected her ability to see clearly but, after shaking her head and releasing some of the clots and peering through her partial enforced blindness, she made a determined attempt to see him before she spoke. With a derogatory show of bravado, she fired her confused emotions at her attacker. Her voice crackled with each heartfelt word. 'You're such a cruel bastard?' She shook uncontrollably as she attempted to wipe the now sticky darkening blood from around her eyes and face. She sighed raggedly. 'Why? Why did you do that?' She took a deep shuddering breath before she continued in a raised voice. 'I'm the only one in the world that cares about you!' Her bloody eyes burned her anger into him. 'Do you know that?'

He closed his eyes and, as the tears ran down his cheeks, he once again repeated the words he vowed never to say. 'I'm so very... very sorry,' he said. Hesitantly he slowly raised his arms and reached out to her.

She shook her head and refused to look at him.

He turned her towards him. 'Look at me. Will you just look at me?'

She sobbed and rubbed at the dry blood that now covered much of her face.

He pleaded. 'You *know* you mean the world to me, Keeva.' He sucked air. 'You are my world... you always will be.'

She slid nervously away from him.

He reached out for her and as she jabbed her elbows into his flabby stomach he let out a pained grunt of discomfort.

She tried to smirk but only succeeded with limited painful satisfaction. She turned to face him and when he finally hugged her, she could feel the sense of regret in his trembling body. 'You can't do this to me *ever* again,' she said, firmly. She sobbed quietly in his arms. 'You *do* know that *don't* you?'

He squeezed her tiny frame even tighter into his, nodded his reply and spoke. 'You need to go to hospital. Come on.'

He released her but stopped abruptly. He looked into her bloody face and quivering hands and issued his orders. 'Remember... you *fell*.'

He waited for some semblance of agreement from her.

There wasn't any.

De Groot continued. 'Right?'

She shook her head propelling new innocent blood into the air as she screamed at him. 'You really are a BASTARD!'

'I know,' he said ruefully. 'But you know I can never change completely.'

She whispered to save her breath. 'Thank God for that.'

He forced a smile.

She grinned at him mischievously and briefly ignoring her injuries she spoke excitedly. 'I'm pregnant!'

'What?'

CHAPTER TWENTY-TWO

Sailing

Zita carried a tray up onto the deck of the houseboat and after pouring them drinks she sat close to Liam and spoke in an unusually timid voice. 'Well, Liam I am sorry for not telling you what we are doing...' She paused effectively. 'But you will see why I needed to keep it to myself until this time.'

He looked at her and snorted.

'It's what I have been trained to do...' She offered an apology by pushing her bottom lip up over her top lip.

He grunted.

'But I had to be sure everything was ready.'

Silence.

She grinned broadly. 'We are going...' Her face exploded in the widest of grins. 'We're going...' She took a hug breath and yelped. 'We are going on a *cruise–*'

'Fuck. A cruise! Why? What the hell for?'

'We need a holiday and to finish some things...'

'What?'

'It's a surprise–'

'Is that why we bought all that second - hand crap from the market stalls?'

'Yes, it is.' She passed Liam her passport and waited apprehensively while he flicked through the pages.

He suddenly stopped. And as he raised his head his eyes opened extraordinarily wide. 'What the–?'

'Yes, Liam. I am *your wife*... I'm Julie Webster.' She laughed. 'We are married!' She giggled childishly. 'It will be much easier for us on the cruise.'

Liam was speechless.

'Can you believe it?' She giggled. 'We are... Mr and Mrs *Webster*.'

Liam showed no emotion and she continued. 'Only for this time.' She pointed at him and slowly shook her head. 'Don't worry.'

His face changed to the broadest of grins. 'I'm not,' he said with a chuckle. 'Why now?'

'You'll see. We really do need a holiday. It will do us both good.'

Liam gave a low sigh and sipped at his tea.

They took the train back to Hamburg and the Pacific Hotel. They stayed for one night and Zita collected their second-hand suitcases, already packed with freshly washed and ironed clothes, from reception and the following morning they took a taxi. It drove between the major demolition and construction works for what was to be the new cruise terminal in Altona, approved a few months earlier in February. It pulled up outside of the existing dilapidated building. Their luggage was taken from them and placed on huge trolleys and whisked away. Liam felt intimidated as they entered the archaic bustling warehouse, passing armed policemen, officious looking men and women, customs and finally some of the crew. Zita showed their tickets and travel insurance to a young woman and after having their credit cards and passports scanned, they were each handed a boarding card.

Zita grabbed Liam's hand and followed other passengers along the meandering timber decked corridors until they reached an extended deck where two Asian photographers were lying in wait. They welcomed everyone with broad smiles and directed Zita and Liam to stand behind an old oak ship's wheel in front of a huge photograph of a sunny beach. Zita immediately raised her hand and walked towards them. She whispered to each of them in turn and slid a handful of Deutsch marks into their eager hands. They lowered their cameras and stepped back, bowed, raised their heads and displayed thankful grins before motioning to the next passengers to move along and stand behind the wheel and smile.

Zita and Liam finally walked out into daylight and onto the huge quayside. Two distinctly different ships faced them; a huge modern cruise ship which could only be referred to as a floating hotel with deck after deck towering above them and beside it a vessel dwarfed with just eight passenger decks. It was much smaller and older than the other and Liam stood nervously, shook his head and held his breath before Zita guided him towards it.

He sighed with relief. 'Thank God for that,' he said.

'I would never want to travel on something like that,' she said. 'Do you know it has more than three thousand passengers?'

He shook his head with surprise. 'Three thou–'

She grabbed his shoulder and turned him and pointed at the smaller ship. 'This one has seven hundred passengers and three hundred crew. It is a wonderful old ship. It has so much character. You will soon see.'

They walked up the gangway and onto the ship and after showing their boarding cards they were led by a steward, wearing white gloves, to their outside cabin on the sixth deck.

He unlocked the door, opened it and let them walk in. 'Your luggage will be with you very soon,' he said, 'My name is Pito.' He smiled at them and continued. 'And I will be your cabin steward for this cruise.'

They both nodded.

'If you need anything... and I mean *anything* during the cruise...' He took his time to smile again. 'Please let me know.'

They thanked him and as he handed them their keys he smiled once more and closed the door.

While Zita opened the wardrobe and locked their passports, money and documentation in the wall safe, Liam stood and took in what would be their home for the next twelve days. Behind each of the twin beds was a porthole, on one side were wardrobes and drawers and a dressing table, with a hair drier and telephone while on the other side was the compact bathroom with a shower, wash hand basin and toilet.

Zita looked at him with puppy eyes. 'I'm sorry. I know we have twin beds but I'm sure we can share one of them...' She paused. 'If you want to?'

He replied immediately and grinned. 'Course I do.'

Zita handed the second key to Liam. 'Keep this with you always and your boarding card.' She slipped hers into her pocket. 'I must do the same.'

After the obligatory lifeboat drill, Zita took Liam's arm. 'Shall we explore now and... maybe have some lunch?'

'Yeah. Let's do it.'

When they returned to their cabin their cases were outside the door. Liam picked them up and placed one on each bed. Zita took the second case containing their backpacks and pushed it under her bed.

Liam had paid little or no attention to the itinerary and Zita felt the time was right to tell him where they were going.

'Liam, we're going on a cruise to the Canary Islands.'

Liam looked up at her. 'Where? Why now?'

She nodded.

'Isn't that where–'

She raised her index finger and held it to her lips. 'Shush.'

He gave his usual response with a grunt.

She grinned back at him. 'You will see why we do this.'

CHAPTER TWENTY-THREE

Light Up the Skies above Me

Liam was incredibly embarrassed when they went for dinner in the restaurant. He couldn't read the German menu and even when Zita explained what it was, he still didn't understand.

On the second evening he looked at her with sad confused eyes. 'Are you ashamed of me?' he said, softly.

'Liam, do you know what you're saying?

He sighed heavily and closed his eyes. 'Yes, I do,' he muttered.

It was a signal for her to make a decision. Whereas she was in total control of her own feelings for much of the time she knew that Liam was like a coiled spring. She noticed it as he fought to hide his obvious embarrassment from the waiters and the frustration that could soon be released with an outburst of anger and possible violence. So, she took the decision to limit them having dinner in the restaurant and generally they ate in the bistro, a buffet style restaurant, where they sat together at a table well away from the other passengers.

However at lunchtimes Liam felt more relaxed and although they had to share a table with other travellers in the restaurant it was a combination of self-service buffet or ordering from the menu. Zita would order from the menu and Liam was more than happy to choose his food from the buffet.

Passengers were seated in order of arrival and would often share with six or more fellow passengers. One lunchtime when they were joined at a table by other passengers he watched mystified as one man took a silver chain from his jacket pocket, hung it around his neck and let his wife clip his serviette at each end, to protect his shirt from getting stained with his food.

The seating was completed with the magician who was one of the guest performers on the ship and two other passengers who sat at the round eight-seater table leaving one empty chair.

Liam waited for the magician to finish his dessert and then turned to him. 'We saw you last night. We loved the show.'

He nodded his appreciation.

'Do you mind if I ask you a couple of questions?'

The magician smiled and nodded. 'No problem.' He paused. 'But you do know I can't tell you how I do them–'

'I understand that.'

Zita watched Liam's unexpected interest.

Liam grinned and coughed. 'So, how do you practise your tricks?'

The magician moved his plate away and replied animatedly, moving his hands in front of him as though he was performing a trick. 'I used to practice for hours in front of a mirror...' He looked across at Zita.

She offered a smile.

He continued. 'It was too much.' He laughed. 'I was looking at myself and...' He laughed raucously. 'And I knew what I was doing.'

Liam tilted his head questioning what he'd said.

The magician grinned. 'These days it is better to film it on video camera and I watch it back many times. When I have perfected the trick I do it with very slow movement - and not too fast...' He grinned. 'If it is too fast... it looks *fake*,' he said, laughing loudly.

Liam was about to reply. *But it is fake.* But didn't.

It took a few seconds for him to understand what the magician meant and he grinned back at him. 'Got it,' he said pointing his index finger into the air.

The three of them watched a passenger on the opposite side of their table as he expertly skinned an apple and sliced it with perfect precision, as though he was performing a surgery. He placed the crafted pieces on a side plate arranged them neatly and passed them to his elderly wife. When he finished, he set the core neatly on his plate and wiped his pocket knife before slipping it into his trouser pocket.

The following evening, rather than eat in the restaurant, Zita and Liam decided not to get changed and instead had dinner in the bistro.

She grabbed his arm and guided him between the numerous food counters. 'It's the same food here as in the restaurant but we must serve ourselves.' She smiled. 'And, yes, you can see the food and you can choose what you want to eat.'

Unable to make up his mind Liam walked from counter to counter of the hot and cold food eyeing up the impressive choice of food until he finally chose several slices of roast beef, mashed potato and gravy.

He joined Zita who was already enjoying a plate of fish and salad at a table far away from anyone else. 'I prefer this to sitting in the restaurant with the posers,' said Liam, as he emptied his plate and walked off to choose a dessert.

Once finished they walked through the automatic doors arm in arm and wandered slowly across the deserted deck. It was a cool evening and Zita briefly shivered when she stopped to look up at the thousands of stars in the sky above them. 'Aren't they fantastic?'

'I didn't realise there were so many,' said Liam.

'There are millions of dem,' she said.

She spun Liam around and pointed directly above them. 'Look. That is the Plough. Isn't it great?'

'Fuck. How do you know all this stuff?'

'To survive... We must always know where we were or... we would go in the wrong direction. Maybe into trouble...'

Liam pulled away from her and shook his head wildly. 'Are you kiddin' me? Was it really that...?' He stammered as he tried to find the right word. Instead after a few seconds deliberating, he continued. 'Dangerous - always fucking life or death?'

Zita laughed. 'Oh, yes, Liam. It was.' She paused and bit her bottom lip as she relived her past. 'But I loved it.' Her whole body stiffened and she turned to Liam. 'You did bad stuff, yeas? So, did you *get off on it*?'

He nodded. 'Course I did.' He pulled her close to him. 'We are very much the same.' He squeezed her tight. 'Aren't we?'

She pulled away and ran across the deck. 'Come on let's go and face the breeze,' she said, playfully.

The security man smiled at them as they ran past him.

Liam followed her up the stairs and they stopped to look down, fascinated by the unbroken trail left by the bubbling swell illuminated by the full moon.

Although he had seen her mutilate any threat or kill at a stroke, he tried to comprehend that she was capable of such horror when she also had childlike traits.

Liam was in a deep sleep when Zita reached down and gently shook him. 'Quick, quick, Liam. Get up!' she screamed.

He jumped out of bed and tripped on the suitcase that had slid out from under the bed during the night. 'What the fuck is going on?'

Zita thrust the white towelling dressing gown into his hands and dropped his disposable slippers onto his bed. 'Put dese on... Now!'

He struggled to get dressed and still half asleep. He stopped at the cabin door, swung on the frame, and called out to her. 'Don't we need our life jackets?'

'Come, Liam. There is no time for that now...'

He shook his head wildly, felt in the pocket for his key card and, closing their cabin door behind him, followed her.

She hurried along the corridor and up several flights of stairs until she reached the open top deck. He found it hard to keep up with her in the ill-fitting slippers but eventually joined her on the deserted deck.

'Look,' she shrieked, pointing towards the distant horizon. She pushed him into the hardwood rail damp with dew and put her arms around him. 'Isn't it fantastic?'

At that moment the horizon began to turn a pale blue and then pink. In seconds it reddened followed minutes later by the first glimpse of the rising sun.

Liam exhaled as he spoke. 'That is fantastic... Fucking great.'

Zita shrieked with delight. 'I'm so pleased you like it. I wanted you to see at least one sunrise on our trip.' She kissed him on the forehead. 'Do you forgive me for frightening you?'

He turned and squeezed her tight. 'Course I do.'

She pulled away and still holding his hand walked towards the stairs. 'Come on, let's go for breakfast.'

For the first time he appreciated choosing what he really wanted to eat. He loved a fried breakfast, something he had most mornings when he was home and today he ate more than he'd ever eaten before at that time of the day.

After breakfast they walked out on deck, sat at a table and watched as a handful of the regular fitness freaky passengers struggled to aimlessly walk around and around the deck above them.

Two of the passengers swept past Liam and Zita on collapsible bikes. He reached out and grabbed at Zita's arm. 'How the hell did they get to bring those on to the ship?'

Zita shrugged. 'Who cares...' she said, as she made her way across the deck to one of the engineers who was checking the lifeboats. She spoke to him in his own language.

Liam listened but all he understood were the words, "fifty dollars."

The second engineer silently quizzed Zita but she waved it off.

After lunch in the bistro Liam sat in the shade in the nominated smoking area on deck eight. He lit his daily cigarette while he waited for Zita and watched as two overweight Filipino crew members in dark blue overalls, woolly beanie hats and sunglasses, using paint brushes fixed to sticks with silver gaffa tape, cleaned the aluminium frames with detergent.

Zita left the gym with a towel around her neck and still wearing her loose-fitting track suit, not the best to show off her perfect body, took her time to walk down the stairs and join him. She was still sweating and looked the perfect athlete. She displayed an extended expulsion of contentment. 'Why don't you try it? You'll love it...'

'Nah... Never been in one - it's for poofs and...'

Zita glared at him.

He stopped abruptly and blushed as he faked a cough. 'No... Not me.' He stuttered. 'You... you... carry on...'

Zita thought for a beat.

She checked the two glasses of water on the table, picked up the sparkling water and sipped at it. 'Look, you know *you've* achieved so much,' she said.

Liam looked at her blankly.

She rubbed at her wet hair with the towel and continued with a smile. 'It's been almost eleven months since you… drank anything bad…'

She waited for a response. There wasn't one so she continued. 'Good news, eh?'

Liam blushed as he remembered his outrageously drunken night in Lanzarote before he was due to deliver the cash to De Groot on Fuerteventura and how Zita had to help him sober up and get his hotel room cleaned of vomit. He didn't reply, instead he raised his shoulders and neck briefly until he relaxed. His eyes tracked the waitress carrying a tray of brightly coloured cocktails and beer as she walked across the deck to a table of already noisy and drunken German passengers. Zita noticed his interest, pulled him towards her and looked him in the eye. 'See how foolish they are?' She smiled. 'You should be so proud–'

'What me?'

She smiled and directed Liam towards the waitress as she placed the drinks in front of the waiting drunks. 'Yes. Especially with those temptations all around you…'

The passengers cheered as the waitress placed the glasses on their table before breaking into a raucous discordant German song.

Their singing was interrupted by the crackling tannoy around the whole ship.

The waitress turned towards the nearest speaker and tilted her head.

'CODE Alpha - members to Reception.'

The barman hurriedly left his station and raced off.

Zita looked at Liam and whispered. 'Someone has died–'

'What?'

'That's the code some cruise ships use.'

'Really? Are they that organised?'

'They have to be. If you think that there are more seven hundred passengers and crew on the ship... Those things do happen...' She smiled at him. 'Only sometimes... Don't worry.'

Liam looked around the deck picking out the elderly passengers and reflected before he spoke. 'Often...' He took a deep breath and continued. 'I reckon.'

The nominated crew members made their way to reception and attended to the elderly man who had collapsed. The medico was already in attendance and after attempting CPR, pronounced the passenger dead. The man's wife screamed out until she was helped to her cabin by two of the trained receptionists.

Within a few minutes it was as though nothing had happened and the German guests ordered another round of drinks.

Liam and Zita frequently remarked to each other at an exceptionally overweight passenger who always wore the same clothes and carried a yellow pencil with a rubber on one end. He lay on a sun lounger on deck for hours and had a severely sunburnt face. One evening when they shared the lift, Zita asked him why he carried his pencil everywhere. He grinned and said that the buttons had millions of germs on them and demonstrated by using the rubber to press the floor numbers.

CHAPTER TWENTY-FOUR

Riders on the Storm

At six thirty on the fifth evening of the cruise the tannoy crackled before sounding a triple bleep which was heard throughout the ship. The first show in the huge theatre paused while the captain conveyed his message to a capacity audience through the P.A. system.

'This is your captain… Captain Aegeus speaking,' he said in German.

The passengers stopped and looked towards the nearest speakers and waited.

He gave the current position of the ship using latitude and longitude measurements, which meant nothing to any of them, before he continued. 'We are now crossing the North Sea and have received a storm warning from the meteorological office. Please be warned that we will be experiencing a storm with a minimum of force ten winds and we are expecting a swell of eleven to twelve metres.' His Greek accent became more evident as he continued to deliver his warning. 'We would ask all guests to take very special care when moving around the ship. Please use the handrails and do not walk onto any of the open decks. When opening your cabin door… take special care.' The tannoy crackled and he could be heard to take a huge breath before he continued. 'Please ensure that the bathroom doors are firmly closed. We will now be undertaking the relevant safety precautions around the ship which we expect to remain in place until midday tomorrow. We apologise for any inconvenience.' His microphone crackled before he continued. 'Thank you.' The tannoy crackled again and a triple bleep signalled the end of the captain's message.

As soon as he finished, the hubbub resumed.

Zita took her time and translated what the captain had just said.

Liam's response was a shrug of the shoulders.

Passengers had initially listened with interest but before he had finished, they returned to eating their early dinner and chatter while others ordered more drinks in the numerous themed bars.

In less than hour, heavy pre-formed metal plates, each numbered with the corresponding cabins on the fourth and fifth decks, lined every corridor. Over the next two hours engineers swarmed along the lower decks, entered every cabin and screwed the heavy plates to the windows. Sick bags appeared along every corridor placed just a few feet apart and pushed into the handrails while others were strategically placed on the stair cases and in the lifts.

Liam and Zita struggled to make their way across the deserted windswept deck eight and sat briefly at a bolted down table protected by the wind and rain and watched with trepidation. The water in the on-deck swimming pool water crashed from side to side and broke over the seating area and onto the deck. They peered over the side at the huge waves and the white flashes of sheer power illuminated by the ship's lights as they broke against the ship's hull and the lower decks.

Chairs and sun loungers were tied down on the lower open decks and all doors leading out onto them were cordoned off with tape and signs were hastily tied to all external doors informing passengers not to open them.

For the time being - it was business as usual.

The full power of the storm arrived much earlier than anticipated and as the swell rose to more than eleven metres high the ship rocked and rolled, buffeted by the huge waves which swamped most of the open decks. As a result, anything not fixed down began to slide back and forth and the crew raced around the closed decks securing it. Walking normally for any passenger was no longer possible and those that chose to move around the ship staggered from handrail to handrail or table to table grabbing anything that was secured. The crew had been unable to empty the on-deck swimming pool and now with every unpredictable pitch of the ship the water splashed from side to side before breaking into huge waves that inundated the deck.

Immediately after finishing their dinner in the buffet Zita and Liam made their way to their cabin on deck six, taking twice as long as normal to make the journey from the lift to their cabin. Like so many experienced passengers, Zita, would be taking precautions to minimise any damage to anything in the cabin so she and Liam staggered back

She took her time and secured everything. This time she wasn't quick enough and, despite her best endeavours, the two litre bottles of water and the glasses fell and crashed onto the carpeted floor before rolling around the cabin. The wardrobe doors flew open and their suitcases, stowed beneath their beds, slid across the cabin. Despite closing their cabin and bathroom doors as the storm reached its peak they crashed open as the ship was buffeted violently by the powerful winds. They could feel the alternate thuds as the waves crashed into the stern and broke, sending huge waves up and over the lower decks. She tried in vain to make things secure but it was futile and as the ship bucked and swayed beneath her feet, after falling several times, she returned to relative safety by joining Liam in his bed.

A much-relieved Liam stirred and taking care not to wake Zita, he sat up. He looked around the cabin and was relieved to see that nothing was damaged and most things were where they should be except for a litre plastic bottle of water that had found its way into one of his slippers. Dawn was about to break and Liam pulled back the curtain above his bed and looked out of the porthole at the now calm sea that showed no sign of the previous night's storm. He watched blindly as the pink fingers of light broke on the distant horizon. He had become fascinated by sunrise after his first time up on deck with Zita when they had watched the sun come up together.

There was a light tap on the door.

Zita stirred awkwardly and dug her elbow into Liam's ribs. 'Your turn today,' she said, groggily.

Liam pulled on his dressing gown and took his time to walk towards the door and, after checking the viewer, he opened it to reveal a smiling female steward carrying a tray. 'Breakfast,' she said, with yet another smile. He wondered how she could make one-word sound so meaningful and cheery so early in the day.

He opened the door fully, let her walk into their cabin and watched as she took care to place the tray in the space already prepared on the dressing table. She straightened the knife and spoon and smiled yet again.

Liam nodded with relief. 'Thank you,' he said, forcing a tired smile.

He poured Zita's coffee and his tea, buttered the toast and joined her back in bed. 'Pito must have overslept,' he said, with a dry laugh.

She checked the time, flicked off the light, pulled back the curtain on the porthole above her bed and waited. Within a few minutes the sun began to stream through the porthole and filled their cabin. They lay back and watched the strange ever-changing shapes on the ceiling cabin caused by the early morning sun reflecting on the sea.

Liam knelt up and looked out of the porthole. 'Hey, Zita, come and look at the sea shine,' he said, excitedly.

Zita was already sitting up in bed and brushing her hair. She stopped and turned to him. 'How did you remember that?'

Liam grinned. 'It was the first thing I heard you say when we arrived in Lanzarote last year,' he said

Up on the forward deck twelve a military helicopter from the British base in Gibraltar hovered above the ship waiting to take off the passenger who had broken their hip in a fall during the storm. While passengers, some of them sporting cannulas, bandages and plasters, highlighting their injuries sustained during the storm, lined the lower decks filming and watching with trepidation, thinking their own very different thoughts. They watched the crew in spacemen-like Marine firefighting gear, which incorporated a yellow outer layer signifying an emergency, take up their well-rehearsed positions on the top deck while other similarly dressed crew held fire extinguishers at the ready as a precaution.

The injured elderly man, stretchered by four trained members of the crew, was brought up from the medical centre on deck three in the ship's cargo lift and onto deck twelve. The winchman was lowered from the helicopter onto the deck with a Stokes basket and the injured man was carefully strapped in before being winched up. He was followed by his wife who was quickly winched up lifted inside the helicopter before it raced noisily away. Many of the passengers remained on deck watching until the helicopter disappeared into the distance and the hospital awaiting them in Gibraltar.

That afternoon Zita met the engineer on deck four as arranged and he handed her a small bag. She paid him, took the bag to the cabin and locked it in the safe.

CHAPTER TWENTY-FIVE

Rollercoaster

On the day after the fire Toto set about planning what was to be his first venture to have the Love Shack rebuilt and run it as a high-class massage parlour and brothel. The forensics department took a few days to complete their investigations before the police released the property. It was agreed that there was no doubt it had been arson but they had been unable to identify who was responsible. Like so many incidents in De Wallen it was put down as infighting or gang warfare.

Despite using labour from Georgia, the reconstruction was much more expensive than Toto had ever imagined and he used most of the winnings he had set aside from his fights, knowing that it was only a matter of time until those costs would be replenished many times over.

Two weeks after the fire at the Love Shack, he had moved into Dieter Stange's top floor flat in 10-12 Talstraße. He had heard from Erag the day after the fire that De Groot had left mainland Europe to live on an island but he had no idea where. He didn't care and he immediately began to put his long-held plan into effect. All the costs for the Hamburg flat were paid by standing order or direct debit from Dieter Stange's bank account so, apart from his food, Toto was able to live there for free and unhindered. He continued his harsh training regime and took fights wherever he could get them.

As his reputation continued to grow, he was able to command much higher fees.

As well as cage fighting, he also had a plan to take over De Groot's territory in Amsterdam and it was too good an opportunity to waste.

In late March he had brought in like-minded, violent fellow Georgians to join him and he began to put his plan into action. He needed to maintain his distance from them and once he felt confident that there was no bother from the Hamburg underworld, he moved them into the flat and went back to his original flat in Altona. He then proceeded to follow De Groot's policy and along with his hand-picked ignorant and naive muscle made frequent trips to Amsterdam.

When the Love Shack reopened in early April, he used the top floor flat as his base when he and his men were in the city. By mid-April, he controlled a third of the Dutchman's empire of clubs, strip joints and bars.

His energy was boundless and as well as controlling his team and collecting fees even higher than De Groot he took bigger and bigger fights in Amsterdam which soon resulted in lucrative offers to fight in the velodromes of Rotterdam, Groningen and Apeldoorn as well as the ice rinks and sports halls across Germany. He would often take two fights in a week and by the end of May he was acknowledged as one of the best cage fighters in Holland and Germany, and the one to beat.

He never lost.

De Groot was following Toto's fighting success from afar with his daily fix from the national German and Dutch newspapers as well as the local daily papers: The Hamburger Abendblatt and Amsterdam's De Volkskrant. The unexpected reports of Toto taking over his beloved Mokum business, coupled with his success as a cage fighter, incensed De Groot so much that he quickly began to reach heights of anger verging on madness.

Keeva did her best to console him but he was becoming impossible to satisfy with his frequent fits of rage and verbal abuse and threats that he would return to Amsterdam, and retake what was rightfully his. She knew was no longer possible, and would be his undoing if he dared.

She liked her life on the island and the luxury he afforded her.

It was Keeva who suggested the alternative.

As the ship cruised out of the North Sea, Zita and Liam took advantage of the warm weather. They changed and went up on deck. He sat near to the pool and took off his shirt and gazed at Zita who looked stunning in her bikini. She slid into the pool and joined the much older overweight and regular cruise fattened women and took part in the aerobics class. Liam looked from one to the other, comparing them, and then turned to their husbands who had propped themselves up on the sun loungers and ogled Zita while they pretended to offer occasionally fake smiles to their wives.

For the first time since meeting Zita, Liam felt jealous.

Very jealous.

Liam wished he could have joined her but he couldn't swim, he'd never had lessons.

To one end of the pool a petite woman, who had undergone a mastectomy, sat on the edge and dipped her feet in the water. She looked down, at her slipped colourful bikini and then furtively around before choosing a time to quickly adjust it.

Zita leapt out of the pool while the women waited in line for their turn to climb the ladder. Still dripping, she sat on the sun lounger next to Liam. 'You ought to try and sunbathe for a while. But you know you will burn without it. Remember Papagayo beach.' She paused and licked her lips. 'When we were naked...' He remembered and after wishing they were there now, obviously embarrassed, he blushed before grinning suggestively back at her.

She slid across to his sun lounger and took her time to cover his exposed pale freckly upper body with factor fifty sunscreen. 'Now you can relax...' She paused. 'But you must remember... to roll over sometimes.'

He grunted his reply.

As the sun began to set and the warm wind gently wafted across the deck it was quickly transformed. While the band set up their equipment on a small raised stage close to the bar the waiters walked around the deck offering a colourful selection of cocktails with exotic names. Every available waiter from the three on-board restaurants appeared with folded tables and carefully positioned them on all sides of the pool. The head chef gave his instructions to countless sous chefs as they ceremoniously carried out two small pigs on rotisseries to huge applause instigated by the waiters. They placed them in opposite corners of the pool area and within fifteen minutes every available space on the tables was filled with a luxurious hot and cold buffet including mouth-watering gateaux and figures of dolphins and angels that had been skilfully carved from huge blocks of ice.

On cue the band played and, as reggae music boomed across the deck, the party started. The ship's dancers, singers and entertainers raced around the deck placing paper garlands around the passengers' necks and encouraging them to join them and dance in front of the band.

It was magic.

Zita hesitated before ordering brightly coloured mocktails and they sat back and watched in disbelief as those not drinking or dancing gorged themselves on the incredible feast.

Liam looked at her and laughed. 'Is this really happening?'

Zita nodded. 'Yes, Liam.' She reached across and pinched him.

He sipped at his mocktail and licked his lips. 'I love it,' he said.

'So do I,' she said, giggling at him.

'But it's not a world I could get used to,' he said, in a raised voice as he struggled to be heard above the music.

She grinned back at him and spoke into his ear. 'Nor me,' she lied, looking enviously across at the dancers. 'But it's still great isn't it?'

Zita cuddled into Liam and she grinned to herself as the warm wind picked up and blew across the deck brushing her face.

Life was good.

Idyllic.

It was well into the night when the music stopped. The waiters and crew almost invisibly cleared the deck around the pool and the musicians stripped down their equipment and moved it to the late-night bars ready to set it up again and play into the night for those passengers not wanting to go to bed.

Zita and Liam walked up to the top deck and stood fascinated as they watched the ship's bow power into the Atlantic and the waves roll away and break up in the darkness.

It was a feeling like nothing he had ever experienced before.

CHAPTER TWENTY-SIX

Cruel Summer

Gleb Leapail and his wife Olga lived in Zvenigorod, fifty-three kilometres from Moscow, a city known for its wonderful fourteenth century Savvino-Storozhevsky monastery. At twenty-four Gleb joined the army for his twelve months National service and he immediately had a plan. He earned a reputation for his willingness to take on any task and was soon given access to weapons and trained in subterfuge. He knew he needed to cut his potentially lengthy military career short and faked mental illness. When he was discharged, he took a menial job showing tourists around the monastery and saw it as a way of learning other languages.

When Gleb and Olga failed to have any children of their own they were left with just one option - to foster. *Russians are not allowed to adopt children and can foster only from orphanages where they are known to be affected kids.* They decided not to take that option and soon split, divorcing a year later. At the age of thirty-five, Gleb moved to Sankt-Peterburg and using the name of Pavel, a man for hire, achieved immediate success with small assignments in and around the sprawling city. The Russian financial collapse in 1998 forced him to diversify and expand his work in Eastern Europe. His reputation grew and as he was much cheaper that western operatives and with his excellent reputation, he soon found himself in demand across Europe.

Gleb needed to be seen to be earning a legitimate income and found it easy to move on. His experience gained as a guide at the monastery set him up for the job as a tour guide in Sankt-Peterburg. Following several months of training he was set loose, initially on Russian visitors, and then on the foreign tourists. Every word of his two hour spiel was written for him and he repeated it perfectly. 'Sankt-Peterburg was the second largest city in Russia and lies at the head of the Gulf of Finland on the Baltic Sea coast. The city's name was changed to Petrograd in 1924 but was later changed back to Sankt-Peterburg in 1991. Widely regarded as Russia's cultural hub it is probably the most western of all Russia's cities. Sankt-Peterburg's historic centre and related collection of monuments have been declared a UNESCO World Heritage Site.' He soon had it word perfect in several languages and would describe how the city was once criss-crossed with canals and, with the land being marshy between April and September, it was home to thousands of mosquitoes. Some of the canals were then filled in and the long wide streets served well at the start of the Russian Revolution. He walked them to the riverside and onto the protected Aurora, a cruiser moored in the Neva. He told them. 'In October 1917 the ship fired the blank shot that served as the signal to storm the Winter Palace during the October Revolution.'

His pièce de résistance was always telling his intrigued audience how Hitler had invited his fellow commanders to attend a victory party at the Astoria Hotel when the city fell. 'It never happened,' he would say proudly. He always found the last part of his tour hard to complete and every time he had to swallow hard before he spoke. 'Eight hundred thousand inhabitants of the city died during the siege.' He lowered his voice. 'To survive... residents of the city boiled leather belts and shoes...' He always waited for the gasps of total shock to subside before he continued. 'They were mixed with sawdust to create something - anything to eat.' His demeanour quickly changed and at this point he always forced a grin. 'But we beat them!' he would say, punching the air with his fists and receiving tumultuous applause even from the German tourists. He also relished the tips in so many different currencies which he used to legitimise his savings.

He needed somewhere to live that maintained his anonymity, as much as was possible in Russia, and took his time to choose the fourth floor flat at Ulitsa Yakubovicha. It was on the top floor of the dull and uninteresting building, like so many in the city, which ran the length of the street mirroring the block opposite. The grey non-descript block was built in the early fifties and was close to the imposing university buildings, museums and the Nicholas Palace and only a short walk to the Moyka and Neva rivers. It was perfect for him to blend into obscurity when not working. Sankt-Peterburg was a huge contrast to Zvenigorod and its historic architecture mostly consisting of Baroque and neoclassical buildings of the 18th and 19th centuries, had been largely preserved.

He'd also chosen the three roomed top floor flat to enable him to look down onto the street below to make it easier for his escape should he ever need. He knew that the fire escape at the rear of the building was rusty but he could easily make his way up and along the roof to the fire escapes further along the building that weren't rusted out. Every few months he rehearsed his getaway and was confident that if he ever needed to avoid the police or the authorities, he knew he could escape.

The pigeons took shelter beneath the window box from the torrential rain, something that everyone living in the city knew on average occurred one in every three days. Hence the need for the deep and wide gutters and downpipes which frequently overflowed spewing gallons of water onto the streets and pavements below.

He sat and watched from his dining table as an old disabled misshapen woman, with a stick, stood precariously out of the rain and stopped to breathe in the fresh air, before shivering and hobbling the short distance to the front door of her block.

Gleb shook his head as he mumbled to himself. 'Another elderly spinster who will soon be returned to heaven unopened,' he muttered to himself.

The rain stopped and the orange eyed pigeons darted everywhere and scavenged for the smallest morsel. A magpie swooped and the pigeons scattered up into the thinning rain clouds.

His pride and joy was a window box which he had wired to prevent the pigeons damaging his colourful petunias and hanging begonias to brighten up the often grey Russian days. His right thumbnail was often green from the regular efforts he made to deadhead and tidy them.

In contrast, his flat was drab and sparse with only the basics that he felt he needed to live. He had no photographs or pictures on the walls and no television. He owned a radio and an archaic TYPW telephone which was in pride of place on the edge of his dining table, with one chair. In the corner was an armchair that he seldom used. The sole bedroom was just as sparse with a single bed and a wardrobe that was empty except for his one suit, a pair of jeans, blankets for the long dark and freezing winter months, a pair of grey trousers, a brown jacket, thick long coat and a raincoat, several shirts and plain grey tee-shirts, all of which were second-hand, bought in a bazaar. With the exception of his handmade suit, expensive shirts and shoes, he replaced his clothes every year and gave the old clothes back to the sellers.

Once a month Gleb would treat himself to dinner at the same luxury hotel on the bank of the River Moyka and followed the same ritual every time. He would take his time to get ready so, before shaving and showering, he would lay everything out on his bed. His pride and joy - his only suit, dark blue pin stripe and made to measure for him when he was in London in 1985, a crisp shirt, modern tie and handmade black leather shoes.

He was a well-known customer at the hotel and would sit at the bar and drink three glasses of single malt Scotch whisky before being shown to the same table in the restaurant. He would take his time to order whatever he wanted from the overpriced and extensive menu and, to ensure their undivided attention, he always tipped the maître d' and the waiters. He loved the self-indulgence and, with no partner, it was his only way of enjoying his money.

Once a year he would visit one of the few Beriozka stores that were located in carefully chosen select five-star hotels, usually on the second floor, and in airports. The Beriozka chain of outlets was set up by the Russian Soviet Federative Socialist Republic as a way of "collecting" foreign currency from tourists, visiting diplomats and businessmen. Access to these special stores was prohibited to all Soviet citizens who were legally forbidden to hold any foreign currency but high-ranking officials who became regular visitors were the exception. The stores would only accept foreign currency or credit cards but Gleb was different and, using his various guises, he was able to buy what he wanted - when he wanted. He would take his time to look at the smaller items, cufflinks, ties and sometimes a watch - he loved watches. Using one of his many forged passports from his collection and foreign currency earned from his very secret and illicit overseas "work" he didn't have any problems spending his ill-gotten gains. But even then, he always took care not to raise any suspicion from the ever present, eagle-eyed undercover State employees.

CHAPTER TWENTY-SEVEN

Grey Day

The rain hammered down again, overflowing the huge gutters and downpipes on what was to be the second successive day of rain in Sankt-Peterburg. Gleb sat at the table near the window, stripped down his Makarov pistol and took his time to clean it. He stopped briefly, stood and stretched and looked across the street at a shrivelled old man who was talking to his only friend, a bright yellow canary in a small cage, in front of the window. He smiled and waved across to him before shaking his head, sighing heavily and talking to himself.

He slid up his sash window and ignoring the rain used his thumb and forefinger to deadhead the petunias and trailing geraniums. He stopped briefly and lifted his head. He stood looking into the opposite block at a naked young couple standing in front of the window and kissing, totally oblivious of him ogling them.

The grey retro rotary telephone on the corner of the table clicked. He closed the window and waited.

It rang three times.

He stopped and gazed at it in anticipation.

It had been a while since it had rung three times.

The phone rang again.

After letting it ring several more times, Gleb reached across and picked it up. 'Da?' he said.

'How is the weather?' asked the caller, using the coded phrase in a matter of fact voice.

'It's raining once more,' replied the Russian, in a clipped tone while he flicked at his dark green thumbnail.

'I have a delivery for you. Are you available?' asked the caller.

The Russian chuckled. 'I'm always available. What is the job?'

There was a brief silence and exhalation of relief. 'OK. You have a fax, yeas?'

'Da.'

'How much?'

The Russian craned his neck, looked out of the window and down on the street at a teenage couple, sheltered beneath an umbrella that was much too small for them. 'Where?' he asked.

'Not far - Germany.'

'OK. Fifty thousand dollars - US - to box number two.'

'Of course, I'll–'

'Send me detail,' said the Russian.

He waited for the caller to finish and then spoke. 'Do you know when and where?'

'Yes, of course. I will get the details to you...'

Silence.

He pulled out a drawer, reached inside and flicked a switch to his fax. It was linked to his phone by a cable hidden behind the skirting boards which led to a false panel in the back of his wardrobe. Ten minutes later the fax clicked into action and spewed out a photograph of his victim, the subject of the call, along with his name and details of the location.

He tore the paper off of the roll and scrutinised every feature of his victim before he returned to deadheading his flowers.

A few minutes later the fax machine clicked again. He tore off the paper and grinned at the confirmation of the transfer of the money into his number two Swiss bank account.

*

Keeva sat waiting patiently at the breakfast bar. She poured her third coffee of the morning and looked out of the window at the unusually large Atlantic breakers that crashed onto the shore.

An hour after making the call De Groot was a changed man.

He closed his office door, slid back the large painting and walked into the kitchen. He gave her a massive hug and kiss on the forehead. 'It's done.' He dropped his shoulders and smiled to her. 'The bastard giving me the pain in my ass will soon be gone–'

'Really?'

'I've hired the best.' He said with the biggest grin in many months. 'And I mean *the best* in the business - never fails.'

Keeva expelled the physical relief followed by a huge smile and a reciprocal hug.

De Groot gently pushed her away. 'Come on… let's get changed. We'll go for lunch to celebrate at the Bodegas Rubicón.'

She was shocked.

'Do you *mean* that?'

'Course.' He raised his head smugly. 'Why not?'

'You must be happy.'

'I am,' he said, with a self-congratulatory shrug of his shoulders.

She loved the Bodegas Rubicón. It was her favourite restaurant on the adjoining island of Lanzarote. De Groot had taken her there for lunch twice before, the first time in January after leaving Amsterdam and the second on their anniversary to celebrate the day they met back in 1998.

The Bodegas Rubicón restaurant was located in the winery's oldest building with stunning views of the Timanfaya National Park and the leading wineries. The building had classic Canarian décor of painted timbers, smooth foot worn stone floors and olive wood chairs and tables.

When they arrived they were given the best table in a private alcove protected from the hot sun by the aged timber rafters trailing with vines and pink bougainvillea overlooking the surreal volcanic moonscape.

The maître d' knew Dieter Stange was important but didn't know how and didn't care. He passed him the wine list but was waved away. 'We'll have your *best*... and I mean *your best* champagne.'

'Certainly, Sir,' he said, with a smile that became broader as he walked away.

CHAPTER TWENTY-EIGHT

Moving On

Liam and Zita leaned on the handrail and were soon joined up on deck by other passengers who looked on with anticipation at the grey rocky cliffs that jutted high above the flats, shops and government buildings, flying the Union Jack. The ship guided, by the pilot, took its time to manoeuvre in the harbour and finally docked at the quayside.

Zita moved away from the crowd and looked out across the bay and the fuel carrying ships. She whispered to Liam. 'I did one of dose?'

'Ugh?'

Zita grinned broadly. 'Just one and a half hours to take down the attackers–'

'Attackers?'

'Yeah. There were six of dem.' She grinned and continued. 'I killed two...' She briefly closed her eyes as she remembered in detail and sucked at her teeth. She stretched out the fingers of both hands and waved them in the air. 'With my bare hands,' she said, her face displaying great satisfaction. She continued. 'And the third...' She grinned her satisfaction as she relived the moment. 'With my knife... *Very quick.*'

Liam shrugged and pulled away from her. 'Fuck.' He remembered her ripping out the throat of Erag, the Albanian, back in Amsterdam. 'Don't you ever take prisoners?'

Zita frowned. 'Why, should I?

Liam nodded. 'OK... yeah.' He hissed. 'Got it. Your assignment...'

Zita ignored his response and tugged at his arm. 'Come on, let's get ready... you can show me Gibraltar.'

A shocked Liam replied. 'Me? I've not been here before...'

'Isn't it part of England?'

'I suppose it is... but I got no idea what it's like.'

They left the ship from the third deck and walked down the gangway, onto the quayside and alongside the ship. Liam looked up and was still in awe at the sheer size of the 'small' ship towering high above him.

They followed the fellow passengers slowly through the terminal, sited at the North Mole of Gibraltar harbour, completed just a few years earlier in 1997.

She took Liam's hand and guided him along the pavement following the passengers that seemed to know where they were heading.

They walked past the tourists and ex-pats sitting outside the bars enjoying the sun while the Spanish residents sat huddled together and gabbled noisily in the shade beneath the trees and at tables inside.

A young boy trailed awkwardly behind his mother. They stopped every few metres and after grabbing his arm she dabbed roughly at the cuts on his knees and legs with a dirty handkerchief. He screamed out in pain every time she rubbed heartlessly at the bloody abrasions. She ignored his pained screams with a sadistic grin and continued to walk ahead of him as though he didn't exist.

Liam and Zita found it hard to contain their anger but, after agreeing there was little or nothing they could do without getting noticed, continued down the road.

Liam paused briefly to read the plaque near the front door of the large run-down mustard coloured building that housed the Flying Angel Club. He took a step back and looked up. For some reason it reminded him of the buildings in Casablanca, a film he had watched so many times when he was incarcerated. With it came the memories of his years in Wandsworth prison and the violent riot. He shook with emotion as he mentally revisited his alleged *brave* actions saving the lives of two prison warders from imminent death and the consequences of his ensuing horrific injuries that for some reason eventually affected his early release.

Liam pulled away from the club, wiped at his sweating face and neck and swallowed hard before looking around at the newly built seven storey blocks of flats along the roads looking towards Spain. Each of them was lined with trees and exotic pink, yellow and red hibiscus. Brightly coloured oleander swamped with bougainvillea grew everywhere and the exotic bird of paradise flowers with their orange and blue petals, resembling a bird's head.

Zita took in her surroundings and finally spoke. 'This is a very nice place. I don't ever get to England... is it *like* this?' she asked, with a smile.

He chortled loudly. 'It's nothing like *this*.'

'What is funny about dat?'

'No.' He said waving his arms. 'It's nothing...' He shook his head and continued. 'Like this.' He paused, thought for a split second before looking around. 'Well the post boxes are similar–'

'How?'

'They're red,' he said, laughing loudly.

Feeling embarrassed Zita pulled away from him.

Liam reached out for her hand and tugged her towards him. 'I wasn't laughing at you,' he said, with a forced smile.

179

Zita lifted her left shoulder and bit at her bottom lip. 'Alright,' she said softly.

The crowds from the ship had already thinned out naturally and the younger passengers were already on their way to the English named bars while the elderly passengers took longer to walk in the heat and would probably not make it much further than Marks and Spencer.

Zita and Liam stopped at a roundabout and while they waited for an elderly man who struggled to push his sick wife's wheel chair across the busy road, Liam eyed the bronze monument in the centre of the roundabout. Zita read the inscription, *Evacuation of Gibraltarians between 1940 and 1951*. 'Did you know dat, Liam?' she asked.

Before he could reply a red double-decker bus passed the monument and their view was briefly obscured. Liam read the words which ran the length of the bus - *Ministry of Transport*. For the first time in many months he was homesick and he could feel a lump in his throat. He rubbed at his watery eyes before shaking his head and taking his time to read the inscription. He sniffed hard. 'No idea. I didn't know anything about Gibraltar until today.'

Zita continued. 'This is in a very special position - the way into the Mediterranean for everyone and to so many countries.'

Liam shrugged his response and swallowed hard as he tried to come to terms with the strange surroundings of an unknown and distant part of England. An England so far removed from what he was used to back home.

They watched as a group of noisy and brash Americans laughed and drawled as they pawed over several young girls in tight tops, figure hugging jeans and leggings. An aging golden retriever limped as he weaved his way in between them and struggled to keep up with the elderly woman.

They walked in silence, enjoying the warm sun and sea air until Zita gently guided Liam alongside the aged marina towards a Spanish tapas bar with outside seating protected by an awning and a clear plastic screen. It stood between huge banana trees, their leaves swaying in the warm breeze, and multi-coloured geraniums that were more than two metres high.

Knowing that Liam would get sunburnt Zita chose one of the tables beneath the awning and walked inside to order a coffee and a tea.

He sat and watched two men with clipboards haranguing every tourist, for trips and island tours, as they nervously walked past. *He knew that if they had dared to harass him he would not have been so polite.*

The waitress arrived with their drinks and a small wrapped biscuit on each saucer. While they stirred their drinks, they watched the sparrows as they flitted between the legs of the tables and chairs searching and fighting over crumbs. A little girl sat at a nearby table and watched nervously as the sparrows tried to pick at the cake crumbs on her plate. She flinched as her mother aggressively waved them away with her serviette.

Without warning the little girl mimicked her mother and screamed at the tiny defenceless birds.

Zita swore under her breath.

A tall young man wearing a baseball cap entered the café accompanied by an elderly couple who appeared to be his mother and father. He shepherded them to a four-seater table nearest to the plastic curtain and helped them into their seats. They both dropped their hands into their laps and waited for his instructions. He picked up the menu and read it out to them. There was no response or even a glimmer of comprehension. The woman took a comb from her handbag and straightened her grey fringe, put the comb back into her handbag and joined her husband to stare out of the window.

The young man walked up to the counter and ordered three toasted tea cakes, two coffees and a Fanta before rejoining his parents. He attempted to make conversation but they continued to stare blindly out at the pedestrians and cyclists as they made their way up and down the busy pedestrianised area. As a dog passed, they both smiled simultaneously for the first time.

The waitress delivered their order on a tray and placed the drinks and toasted tea cakes on the table. The woman reached for the bottle but her son tugged it away and slid the coffee in front of her.

The young man buttered each of the tea cakes and slid the plates in front of his parents. They looked around and then down at the plates as though everything was alien to them.

His father noticed a man stop a few feet from them and speak into a mobile phone, he turned and spoke to his son for the first time. 'I want one!' he said, animatedly.

His son replied in a soft voice. 'Dad, you can't afford one of those.'

His father reached into his inside pocket and pulled out a crumpled five-pound note.

'Only a few people have the money to pay for them,' said his son. He reflected. 'Maybe in a few years we might all have them. Things always get cheaper... in time.'

Their son took his time to explain that there was a very expensive monthly rental charge. It fell on deaf ears. His father returned to looking out of the window and smiling inanely. Minutes later he turned to his son. 'So, *will you* buy me one?'

The woman turned to her husband and pointed to the man outside before she spoke. 'How do you know about that?' she asked, in a weak voice.

Her husband slowly raised his arm and pointed at the huge vinyl signs that covered much of the window of the newly opened mobile phone shop opposite. When she returned to look at him, he exuded a wide childlike grin.

Silence.

The young man's parents turned and watched the waitress deliver a large tray of cream teas to the next table. They looked on enviously at the pots of jam and cream and the plate of scones as she placed them strategically around the centre of the table. They both looked at their son's empty plate and the toasted tea cakes on their plates, gasped and sighed heavily before breaking down and sobbing uncontrollably.

'Poor bastards,' muttered Liam, under his breath.

'I know. Dementia is a terrible thing.' She paused, exhaled and continued. 'And it is becoming so common these days.' She reflected. 'Do you know we will soon have a village for that in Holland?'

Liam didn't hear her.

Instead he struck out at the flies that were annoying him. 'Can we go now?'

'You didn't finish your tea.'

Liam shrugged and stood up. 'Come on let's see more of this... This... *fake* England,' he said, grinning broadly.

The young mother placed her daughter in her push chair, took her time to meticulously collect the remainder of the crumbs from the table and dropped them into her empty cup and left.

Zita grabbed at Liam's arm. 'Wait a moment,' she said.

Reluctantly he sat down, crossed his arms, and glared at her.

She ignored his reaction and reached for the unopened biscuit in her saucer. She unwrapped it, broke it in half and then crushed it. She carefully cupped her left hand and tapped it gently with her right until the crumbs were in the middle of her palm. She held her hand out and waited. Within seconds a sparrow flew down and picked at them. This was followed by a second and third until they had eaten all of the crumbs.

Liam was impressed and smiled. 'I didn't know you liked birds.'

'I love all creatures.' She remembered the little girl and frowned. 'Why did her mother show her to do that? Now she will always hate dem–'

'What?'

Zita continued. 'Animals and birds, they are better than people. They have no anger in them.' She paused. 'Well... most of them,' she said softly.

Liam reached out for Zita's hand under the table and tugged it. She acknowledged him with a nod and they left.

While they walked along the quayside and back towards the ship Zita looked out across the run-down harbour at the yachts and small fishing boats as the fishermen unloaded their catch. She spoke without looking at Liam. 'There are plans for a new marina with shops and bars. It will be so much better.'

He shrugged. 'I hate them sort of places–'

'Why?'

'Dunno.'

'Really?'

'Bastards... with fucking yachts!'

He kicked out and dug the toe of his trainer into the pavement. 'They live in their own world of make believe.'

'Not all of them,' she retorted, defensively.

She looked around before slowly raising her arm and pointing to an elderly man in dirty white ill-fitting shorts and a grubby tee-shirt trying to clean the deck of his boat. 'Some people live on them. That's *all* they have,' she said, sympathetically. 'And remember, Liam.' She finally had his attention and he turned to her. 'We live on a houseboat now...'

Liam backtracked. 'Well.' He paused to think. 'Not them...' He said, shrugging his shoulders. 'Just the rich bastards...' He looked back at the elderly man and waved to him before turning to Zita. 'OK?'

As they walked towards the cruise terminal they passed what appeared to be an extended shop front but when they looked inside it was a day centre for elderly people. The residents made up solely of women sat around the perimeter of the room and feigned interest at the teacher. He wrote the letters: O.M.A.N on the nobo board with a thick red marker pen, underlining each letter as he repeatedly pronounced them. He then paused and after saying the word "OMAN," he added the letter "W" in front of them. He read out the whole word repeating the word Woman several times. The Gibraltarian women repeated it back to him but it was evident they had no interest in learning to speak English.

As they waited to board the ship a passenger immediately in front of them sobbed uncontrollably as she relived the terror of having been attacked by an ape up on the rock who stole the bag of presents she had bought for her family.

Zita looked at Liam and covered her face as she fought hard to hide her grin.

CHAPTER TWENTY-NINE

Hurt So Bad

Four days after receiving the call from De Groot, the Russian walked into his sparsely furnished bedroom and unlocked the drawer hidden at the back of his wardrobe.

He flicked through the various papers, notes and coins in several different currencies, and assorted identity cards, and laid it all out on the table. He shuffled the collection of forged passports from hand to hand before choosing one and grinning at the name on it. He threw a shirt, two plain white tee-shirts, trousers, socks and underpants into a small well-worn travel bag, along with the ripped plastic washbag that he always had ready for his work. The contents were the most popular part-used western brands. He rechecked his chosen passport and set about changing his appearance to match the photograph. None of his disguises took him more than a few minutes to prepare.

He changed into a plain white tee-shirt, counterfeit Levi denim jeans and brown ankle boots before pulling on his favourite well-worn dark brown leather jacket. He carefully placed everything in specific pockets, disconnected the fax and phone and checked that the back of his wardrobe was secured. He gave one last cursory look around the flat before closing the front door and double locking it behind him.

He took a tram to the port and bought a single ticket for the ferry to the busy Helsinki port.

Once in Finland he took the train to Helsinki-Vantaa Airport and boarded a plane landing at Hamburg's Fuhlsbüttel Airport almost five hours later. He passed through customs unhindered and took the U Bahn to St Pauli station at the top end of the Reeperbahn.

He let the crowd rush past him and took his time to walk up the stairs, to a world that was very different to Sankt-Peterburg and down the infamous Reeperbahn until he reached Talstraße. He took a leisurely walk past numbers 10-12 before crossing the road and looking back at the home of his target.

He crossed the Reeperbahn and bought a coffee and two slices of pizza from an imbiss before checking into the Park Hotel, opposite the infamous Große Freiheit, on the other side of a very busy dual carriageway.

He didn't want to waste the opportunity of tasting life in this legendary part of the city so he asked for a twin room on the second floor overlooking the Reeperbahn. He paid in cash and asked the receptionist where he could find the nearest gym. She opened a tourist map, and marked the three gyms in St Pauli, and he slid it into his jacket pocket.

He locked the door of his room and checked it was secure before throwing his bag onto one bed and lying on the bed furthest from the door. He took his time to memorise where the nearest gyms were and after a shower, he changed his tee-shirt and put on the same trousers and jacket and walked up the Reeperbahn as far as the police station, and crossed.

The first club was boarded up and the second was for teenagers and amateurs. He knew that his victim would be obsessed with training and he needed to be at the top of his game if he was to continue winning his fights. He crossed the Reeperbahn and turned into Taube Straße.

The St Pauli bars and clubs were very special and already buzzing with tourists and local people. Rock and disco music pumped out from the open bar doors and windows that were all vying for the same passers-by. Alluring girls of all shapes, sizes and nationalities stood outside and competed for business from everyone that passed, whether they were male or female.

He had rules.

Business first and then extreme sadistic pleasure after.

After completing his contract, he always had a lot of adrenaline to release.

He made a mental note of the bar he would return to before taking a left into Bernhard-Nocht-Straße. He walked the hundred or so metres until he reached Seeearten Straße. Nine minutes later he found himself in the tree covered cobblestone courtyard. He strode down the steps towards the partial red brick and rendered building, his only remaining option.

When he saw the words *Bewegung am Hafen* painted on the four-metre long canvas sign above the door, he grinned. It was a dojang, a training hall, where they taught Shinson Hapkido, a form of Korean martial arts. He immediately knew that this was where his target would train.

He walked into the immaculate and restful reception and took his time to read the posters advertising the many classes held there. What intrigued him were the posters advertising workshops for children and "self-defence classes for *women by women.*"

He acknowledged it with a thoughtful nod.

He heard the sound of noisy and heavy training and, after tilting his head towards the activity, walked up the stairs and into the first of several training studios. Even at that time of night, the large open softwood framed windows let in the last of the warm evening sun mixing with the coloured lights from the vibrant area that surrounded it.

It was weird to be in a place that taught such a calming and yet potentially violent sport if misused, in an area notorious for sex, drugs and violence.

He spoke to the young woman who was sitting near to the door. He told her he had recently moved to Hamburg and was considering joining. She offered him a seat and he sat down. She smiled and shook his hand. 'I am Ilka. You will love it here,' she said, gushing with enthusiasm. 'We have this club since1984.'

He looked confused.

She coughed. 'No. Sorry. It was in Altona... until we moved to here.

He didn't react. *He wasn't thinking about that. His mind was on his victim.*

Ilka continued. 'I know what you are thinking.'

He shook his head. 'Um?'

Ilka continued. 'I know it looks very new.'

He nodded.

She giggled. 'It is. We moved here only last year.'

'Ah.'

'We made this place.'

He turned his attention to the activity, which was feverish even for Shinson Hapkido with its teaching of inner and outer peace.

He eyed Toto.

Even though he was training, the Georgian was totally zoned in and didn't hold back. His three opponents didn't attempt to hide their discomfort and pain as his moves of even limited power still hurt them.

The Russian stood, thanked the woman and gave his victim once last glance before he left.

He took his time to walk back to his hotel. He was subdued as he thought of the best way to fulfil this contract. Toto was very different to anyone he had ever been hired to kill and, having watched him in action, he knew it would not be easy.

CHAPTER THIRTY

A Summer Place

The ship docked in Funchal, Madeira and after clearing customs Liam and Zita joined their fellow passengers on the courtesy coach that took them the short distance around the quay and into the centre of the beautiful town.

They strolled along the main street until Zita noticed the fountain on the left-hand side and the entrance to the Esplanada Jardim Municipal. It was a very special place with its exotic flowers, manicured lawns, flowering shrubs and unusual trees and plants. They took their time to walk along the narrow paths while she reacted enthusiastically to the wonderful plants and flowers until they reached the café which overlooked the impressive open-air theatre.

Zita chose a table beneath an umbrella large enough to provide shade to every seat. 'Isn't this a great place?' she said.

Before Liam could answer, a waiter appeared from nowhere. Wearing a crisp white shirt, bow tie, black trousers and matching waistcoat he stood erect and with his pen poised he waited patiently for their order.

After carefully eyeing the menu, Zita chose steak sandwiches and bottled water.

Liam looked around. 'It is like paradise.' He reflected. 'If paradise even exists...'

Zita smiled. 'I'm sure it does,' she said, wistfully. She closed her eyes and took steady breaths as she experienced her idyllic surroundings. She finally opened her eyes and smiled. 'There are many wonderful places in the world, Liam.' She lowered her eyes. 'Maybe…' she said, pausing to release a thoughtful smile. She looked around. 'Tell me Liam, did you ever expect to be somewhere as wonderful this?' She paused and looked directly at him and waited until she had his undivided attention. 'We *could* live here?'

He shot her a confused look. 'Us? Here? How?'

He took his time to look around and grinned. 'Tommy, the little bastard would love this…' He stopped abruptly.

She leaned into him. 'What's the matter?'

He let out a heavy sigh. 'Well, the last time I called home… and I spoke to him.' He breathed hard. 'I cut him short.' He rubbed at his throat. 'Didn't give him time to say…' He sighed. 'Not one… fucking word...'

The waiter arrived at their table.

Zita leaned forward, reached out and rubbed his hand. 'I'm sure he understood,' she said, softly.

Liam grunted.

The waiter took his time to place table mats, knives and forks neatly on the table. He set down the glasses and poured some of the water from each of their bottles into iced glasses and then added coloured straws.

Liam shook his head in disbelief. 'If they are like this… in a *park*… what the hell are the hotels like?'

Zita fidgeted in her seat. 'Maybe I will show you one day.'

He shrugged and pulled the straw from his glass, dropped it on the table and proceeded to empty the glass.

He took a huge breath and his blank face changed to one of sheer bewilderment. 'How did that Dutch bastard just disappear from here? It's such a small place and he couldn't stay below the radar.' He sniggered. 'It's not his style. He's so bloody arrogant. He'd want everybody to see him.'

Zita grinned. 'He did not ever come here—'

'What? But Ackerman said he did,' gushed Liam. 'Europol told him that too. Are they that stupid to make a mistake like that?'

Zita's eyes bulged excitedly as she sucked at the straw and took a drink of her sparkling water. 'I told you... he *never* came to here.'

De Groot did go to Madeira but in name only. When the plasterer's plane touched down, he took a taxi to Reid's Hotel where he enjoyed the five-star luxuries and the decadence of years gone by. The outdoor heated swimming pool, regular massages in the spa and when he was too exhausted to dress for his evening meal, he would order room service, while other evenings he would eat and drink in the bar. The plasterer had had his special bags packed for months, with clothes bought for him by De Groot, and hidden, ready and waiting should the time ever come when he was instructed to use them. De Groot had chosen him because he was single and could leave Amsterdam without drawing any attention to himself. The plasterer spent a week "living the dream" at Reid's Hotel and throughout his stay he was invisible and yet in plain sight.

The trail to De Groot ended as soon as he arrived on 1st January 2000 when the plasterer checked into the hotel using yet another fake passport and debit card given to him by De Groot. On the 8th of January he checked out of the hotel and took the short taxi ride from the hotel to the airport and used yet another debit card to buy a one-way ticket to Schiphol. After showing his fake passport at the departure gate, he flew home.

When he arrived back in Amsterdam, he was stunned to hear the news that his boss, Matthijs Kikkert and his wife, had died in the fire at the Love Shack. He soon learned of De

Groot's disappearance and knew he couldn't go to the police - he was implicated in his paymaster's deceit.

Neither of them spoke until they had eaten their steak sandwich and cleared their plates. After sitting back for a few minutes Zita picked up a newspaper from the adjoining table and read it before turning to Liam. 'Don't *you* like football?'

He shook his. 'Nah. Never seen it.' He shook his head. 'Never wanted to.'

'I thought all the English men liked football.' She paused and thought. 'Didn't De Groot say you were a football fan in your false documents?'

'He fucking did - Crystal Palace!'

She sucked at her teeth. 'I see.'

'Why did you ask that?'

Zita showed him the newspaper but he pushed it away with a shrug. *She knows I can't read foreign crap.*

She pushed it towards him again and tapped the large action photograph on the back page. 'Do you see this young footballer?'

He nodded and mumbled. 'Um.'

She turned back to the newspaper and read it. 'Well, his name is Christian Ronaldo. He was sixteen last February and they say he will become one of the best players in the world.'

Liam failed to react.

Zita continued with an excited screech startling the people on the adjoining tables. 'He was born here in Funchal!' She lowered her voice and continued in little more than a whisper. 'He already plays for Sporty CP and now lives and trains in Alcochete near Lisboa.'

'Lisboa?'

'OK.' She grinned. 'For you it is Lisbon.' She found it hard to hide her excitement. 'Isn't that fantastic for such a young man?'

Because of Liam's disinterest she deliberately took her time to fold the newspaper, laid it on the table and stood. 'Come on we need to go back to the ship.'

It was late into the evening when the ship left the quayside. They stood on deck and looked back at the street lights zig zagging up and across the hills and thought their own thoughts before kissing passionately.

CHAPTER THIRTY-ONE

Nowhere to Run

The following morning the Russian was up at dawn and, after making the most of the buffet breakfast at his hotel, he made his way down to the Landungsbrücken pier. It was a jetty for the tourist boat trips, a working port and ferry terminal, and even at that time of day the bars and cafés were busy. He walked away from the hustle and bustle and into a street with row upon row of chandlers and speciality shops selling everything needed by the thousands of employees who worked in the huge port. He bought a second hand pair of dark blue logoed overalls, safety boots, logoed jacket and safety helmet, a dented lunch box and tool bag which he filled with carefully selected tools. He wandered the street looking for a suitable victim and when he noticed a dockworker in his late thirties, he pushed past him and unnoticed snatched the ID badge from his jacket. He smiled to himself as his disguise was complete. He was now a bone fide employee of the large Norderwerft shipyard that had been part of the port of Hamburg for more than 100 years. The shipyard was regarded as one of the best in Northern Europe for its conversions and refits, as well as maintenance of commercial vessels, yachts and naval vessels. With three floating docks, quayside berth with ten docks, ten huge dockside cranes and gantry cranes he knew that he could lose himself amongst the hundreds of employees who lived in and around St Pauli.

He felt hungry and wandered unnoticed into a smoke-filled café. After drinking a coffee and eating two currywurst in crusty rolls, he left. He took his time to walk back to the Reeperbahn. Once in his hotel room, he slipped the *Do Not Disturb* sign outside the door, locked it and hooked the chain, stripped off and took everything out of the tool bag and laid it all neatly on the second bed.

He fell onto his freshly made bed and slept.

It was still light when he woke up. He made himself a coffee, took a shower and changed into his Docker's work-clothes, he chose his weapons, slid them into the tool bag and left. It took him ten minutes to reach Talstraße. He sat at a table in the window of the bar opposite Toto's building and ordered a coffee.

He waited.

And waited.

Two and a half hours after he had sat down, he saw Toto come out of his flat through the side door adjoining what was once the Mambo Schänke and now a Turkish restaurant. Despite wearing a handmade dark blue suit, crisp white shirt and polka dot tie, the Russian was still surprised how short he was.

Toto looked around, shrugged his shoulders, tugged his jacket and walked off in the direction of Simon-von-Utrecht Straße.

The Russian sniggered when he remembered how he had been so aggressive at the dojang and unless anyone knew the diminutive Georgian, they would have no idea what he was capable of.

He paid for his drinks and followed Toto at a distance.

He knew he would have only one chance of the hit and he had to get it right.

He followed him for fifteen minutes and wondered if he had any suspicion of being followed. As Toto walked through a narrow alley which led out onto Große Freiheit the Russian saw his chance - the one and only chance he had. He rushed up behind his victim and raised the hammer but Toto was expecting it. He jumped to one side, twisted his torso, pivoted ninety degrees, flexed his right leg and drove a punishing kick smashing the heel of his shoe into the Russian's left kidney. As he leaned forward in extreme pain, Toto ripped the hammer from his attacker's hand and smashed it into his right arm.

The Russian's instinct was to reach across to protect himself.

He failed.

Despite his attacker towering high above him, Toto was undeterred. He had fought much bigger opponents in many of his MMA fights and they always went the same way.

They were defeated and often left unconscious.

He launched a hail of heavy blows onto the Russian, pummelling his legs, arms and neck using his fists, elbows and legs until he fell heavily onto the cracked and uneven slabs. Toto didn't waste any more time. He brought the hammer down onto the Russian's right hand, breaking his fingers and knuckles and grinning at the sound of breaking bones and snapping tendons.

The Russian screamed out in agony and prepared himself for his execution.

It didn't happen.

Toto threw the hammer down the alley and it clattered as it bounced along the corrugated panels. He now checked the Russian's tool bag and when he found the pair of pliers, he grabbed them and pushed them as close as he could to his attacker's face. He peered directly into his defeated eyes and grinned. 'What did you wish to do with this?' he asked.

The Russian grunted.

Toto grabbed the Russian's left hand and as he winced in anticipation of the pain, let out a premature childlike squeal. He tightened his grip on the Russian's hand until the colour drained out of it and he slowly moved the pliers towards it enjoying the sheer panic and anticipation of his attacker's impending pain.

'Who was it?'

'What?'

'I said who paid you?' He shook his head angrily. 'To do this?'

He took a step back, briefly closed his eyes and clicked his tongue. He looked down at the damage he had caused to his attacker. 'Sorry, my friend.' He sniggered as he tilted his head. 'Can I call you my... friend? I mean... We are friends. Yes?'

Silence.

'Or did I make the wrong words?'

The Russian nodded and trembled knowing he had no alternative but to lie. 'Friends,' he said, in a painful and strained voice.

'So... I will ask once more. Who paid you?'

Toto knew who it was but wanted to know for sure. His face reddened as he screamed. 'The fucking Dutchman?'

Silence.

He cuffed the Russian around the head and then stamped on his ankle.

The Russian whimpered as he tried to ignore the pain.

Toto looked down at him. 'One more time, for luck,' he said, before faking a smile. 'Is that what the British say?' Without any warning Toto stamped on the Russian's already damaged ankle, and putting all his weight behind it, pushed his heal down and rotated it snapping his attacker's ankle with a loud crack.

As the intense pain shot through the whole of the Russian's huge frame, he gritted his teeth. 'OK. Da.' He was finding it hard to breathe and continued with a wheezy groan. 'Yes... It was *him*.'

Toto laughed raucously. 'I knew it...' He leaned into the Russian's face and continued. 'Did he pay you enough for this? The pain and...' He continued in a slow solicitous voice. 'Torture? Uh?'

The Russian chose not to answer.

He had already broken his code of silence.

Toto turned away, spun back and faked a look of deep remorse. 'Ah.' He grinned. 'This is the first time... You failed. Yes?' He paused to play with his bottom lip. 'I should be honoured.'

The Russian grunted humbly.

Toto took his time to study his attacker. 'You are such a big man,' he said, as he opened his eyes wide. 'A giant of a man.' He scoffed. 'But you should know that I have already learned that the bigger my opponents are.' He paused. 'And you are an opponent to me.'

'Um.'

'The harder they fall. Yeah?'

The Russian whimpered.

'Did I say the correct words?'

The Russian offered a slow reluctant nod in agreement.

Toto reached across and ripped the ID badge from the Russian's overalls, 'Who the fuck are you?' He looked at the photo and compared it to his attacker. 'That's not you. You are a khumroba...' He took a second to translate it. 'Yes. You are a joke.' He scoffed. 'A professional?' He scoffed. 'You're just a cheap rated amateur?'

A beat.

He straightened his tie and continued. 'How old are you?'

'Wha–'

He raised his voice. 'I asked how old...' He pointed at him and raised his voice. 'You?'

The Russian confused by the question screwed up his face and after taking a huge ragged breath reluctantly gave his garbled answer. 'For... for... forty-one...'

Toto ignored the reply and suddenly looked suspicious.

'You are Russian, yeas?'

The Russian lowered his head.

'And for sure it was the Dutchman who hired you?'

'Da.'

Toto spat at him, dropped the ID badge, raised his arm and threw the pliers down the alley. They clattered and echoed as they bounced against the wall of the block. 'We... Georgians... We hate Russia!'

The Russian tried to shrink his pained body into the wall.

'Maybe I should kill you? Yes?'

He waited a beat.

'I think it is your time to...'

He waited for the Russian to finish the sentence and react. He didn't and Toto continued with what was totally unexpected. 'Gadadges.' He paused. 'How do you say?' He closed his eyes while he mentally searched for the word. 'Retire... You should retire.'

The Russian murmured with relief.

Toto grinned. 'I want to know. Tell me why you did follow me into this place.' He looked up and down the alley. 'You had no chance... No chance at all. It was stupid of you.'

The Russian looked at him and tried to reply.

He couldn't.

Toto glared at him and screamed in his own language. 'Mudak!' He gave him one last kick in the ribs. 'You are an asshole.' He exhaled. 'I am about to lose my temper... So... Piss off!' He straightened his jacket and after cursing in Georgian, he hummed to himself as he walked away.

The Russian lay there for several minutes before struggling to stand.

The painful journey back to his hotel took him nearly an hour and once back in the safety of his room, knowing he couldn't go to the hospital, he bandaged his broken hand and ankle.

Once on the bed he watched the flashing neon signs and passing traffic lights dancing across the ceiling and he reflected. *He had enough money and having failed a contract, albeit only once, he made the decision that he would retire and perhaps open a souvenir shop.*

The following morning the cleaner found him on his bed unconscious and he was rushed to the hospital in Altona.

CHAPTER THIRTY-TWO

How Long

It was late morning when Keeva returned from her daily trip to Corralejo to buy De Groot's precious newspapers. She raced up onto the roof and, although she was out of breath, she couldn't hide her excitement.

Keeva, carrying a designer handbag and shopping, rushed out onto the sun terrace to De Groot. 'I think I saw them...'

'Who?' he snapped.

'You know...'

He didn't hide his impatience and screwed up his face.

'Them.' She shook her head. 'You *know*...' She appeared fretful and wriggled her fingers erratically. 'The Irish drunk.'

De Groot laughed at her. 'Aren't you Irish?'

'So!' She screwed up her face in disgust. 'It's not funny and... I'm not stupid!' She shrugged. 'I told you... I *saw* them–'

'Saw who?'

'Liam and Zita!' She kicked off her designer sandals and slumped onto the huge sunbed beside him. 'An hour ago... sat outside the bar near the ferry terminal... *here* on the island.'

De Groot sniggered. 'Listen. I've told you they're long gone.' He shook his head and smiled. 'They won't bother us again. You know as well as I do that all of them died in that fire.' He paused. 'The police wouldn't lie about that.' He settled himself on his sunlounger and checked his watch. 'Come on, let's have a drink.'

He reached out and poured two brandies.

She couldn't rest.

He emptied his glass and rubbed impatiently at his chin. 'If you're that sure, I'll make a call later.' He sniggered to himself until it grew into an outrageous full-blown laugh. 'How many times do I have to repeat myself? They're all long dead and buried.' He raised his voice. 'We both saw it on the television and you read it in the papers as well as I did. Didn't you?' he snapped.

She closed her eyes, reached out for his hand and squeezed it.

She felt his hands twitching. She knew he was desperate to get his hands on his newspapers. It was his daily ritual to lie on his own huge bespoke sunlounger on the sun terrace amongst the pots of large shrubs and plants and the fountain fanned by the light breeze which sprayed a very welcome fine mist across him.

As soon as she passed him the armful of newspapers he pulled out De Volkskrant, Amsterdam's morning paper, and immediately read the front page. She knew he would spend the next couple of hours reading all of them from front to back and perhaps read some of the pages for a second time.

'I need to get changed,' she said.

Reluctantly he lowered the newspaper. 'But you've only just got back.'

'I know, but I've arranged to meet Margarita down the coast this afternoon.'

'What?'

Keeva shook her head in disbelief.

'How can you forget? I told you last week that I was having lunch with her.' She grinned mischievously and lied. 'And... then I'm going for my second scan at the hospital.'

Although he didn't hear her, he still nodded and returned to his papers.

She raised her voice and repeated herself.

He finally grunted his reply. 'OK, maybe I'll come next time.'

She knew it was pointless arguing with him. Instead she seized the opportunity. 'I'll take the Mercedes. OK?' she said.

He turned the page and ignored her.

Keeva changed into a black and white polka dot long sleeved silk blouse and white figure-hugging shorts.

Ten minutes later she roared out of their private underground garage in the open topped Mercedes with the stereo blasting out Wham's *Club Tropicana*.

CHAPTER THIRTY-THREE

Daytripper

Zita had chosen the Euro 2000 final as a perfect and possibly the only time to be able to go undetected and dispose of De Groot with minimal suspicion, but it did take her a great deal of research to be sure she would be in the right place at the right time.

This was it.

When the ship docked in Arrecife they left with their backpacks and walked to the courtesy bus that took them to the harbour. After speaking to a waiter standing outside a restaurant, who gave her animated directions, they walked off and hired two motorbikes. After showing their passports, she paid in cash and they rode off towards Playa Blanca.

When they reached De Groot's large apartment block nestled on the mountain overlooking the beach and harbour, instead of riding up to the main entrance and the large car park, they rode along a track which took them high above the block.

Zita told Liam to wait in the shade of a rocky outcrop shielded by tall oleander and huge geraniums.

She made her way down to the building which was covered with the pink bougainvillea that had been carefully trained across the roof of the now neglected building. De Groot had bought the apartment block, of six apartments on three levels in 1988 when he sold on his first consignment of drugs from North Africa. He regularly used it himself and to entertain judges, politicians and dignitaries and anyone that would protect or further his illegal activities in Amsterdam.

Zita reached out and flicked the hidden remote control at the side of the building and the security doors glided open allowing her to walk into the underground car park. She glanced at the only remaining vehicle, a dirty white Seat Toledo, which she had used a few times as a decoy when De Groot had been threatened. She made her way up the secret staircase linked directly from the garage to De Groot's top floor apartment. He had only needed to use it once and even then, the problem was dealt with by her and Artem, allowing him to escape to the airport unscathed.

The top floor consisted of two identical luxury apartments, one of which was De Groot's and was still partially furnished with what was left of furniture that he had taken months choosing and spending a fortune. The kitchen worktops were littered with empty tins and packets of instant meals, dirty crockery and mugs growing thick fungus. She touched the kettle. It was still warm so she took her time to cautiously check out the other rooms. The once opulent lounge had been stripped of all the furniture except a badly split leather armchair and two side tables, one of which was used for the television which was playing to itself. She crept into the other rooms, finishing her sweep in the master bedroom. The bed had been recently slept in and stained with dirty bedding piled up in the centre of the filthy mattress.

She checked the remaining apartments once tastefully furnished for use by judges, politicians, government ministers, or business partners for as long as they saw fit to entertain their mistresses, wives or boyfriends. They had also been stripped bare and the ceilings were badly stained from rainwater which had seeped through the neglected flat roof. The rooms at the rear, with no sea view at all, were once used by Zita and De Groot's bodyguards, and they too had been stripped of anything of value.

As she left the last room, she heard a sound.

She stopped and listened.

She heard it again and waited behind a damaged door hanging from its hinges.

The wizened Spanish caretaker kicked at the door which threw Zita off her balance. As she fell onto the timber floor, he threw a handful of grit into her face which briefly blinded her. She tried to get up but he rushed towards her and smashed a chair leg across her shoulder. She countered with a raised elbow and recoiled before kicking out at him. He wasn't expecting it and as he fell to the ground in a heap his Alfa Defender, a relic of a gun made in Czechoslovakia in the seventies, slid across the floor.

She stretched her leg and kicked it well away from him.

Now she knew she would have the upper hand.

She didn't want to kill him yet but beat him mercilessly until he was barely conscious. She took his gun and forced him towards the staircase leading to the garage.

She was already thinking several hours ahead and wedged open the staircase door leading into the main house.

She jabbed his gun into the top of his neck and he stumbled painfully and awkwardly down the secret staircase into the double garage, lit only by the one functioning fluorescent tube. Once in the garage she pushed the gun into the small of his back and her eyes scanned the various DIY tools and gardening equipment hanging on the wall. She reached out with her left hand and grabbed a large rusty wrench. She jabbed the gun harder into his back and told him to pull his shirt over his head. It was her way of stopping or reducing any of his blood splashing onto her clothes. The Spaniard raised both hands and struggled to do what he'd been told. She jabbed him harder and as soon as his shirt covered his neck and head she smashed the wrench into his skull several times and, for good measure, as his body crumpled and began to fall towards the dirty floor, she pounded his spine with the bloodied weapon. She'd been taught not to leave anything to chance. It wasn't like a film where victims don't always die and miraculously survive and come back at their attacker when they are not expecting it.

She checked her watch and raced back up the hill, re-joined Liam and together they freewheeled down the track and into the open garage.

He gave the bloody Spaniard a cursory look and shrugged. 'You didn't spare his life then?'

'Why should I?'

'Fuck.'

She ignored him, flicked the boot lock and opened it.

'Don't you ever question what you do?' asked Liam.'

She replied without having to think. 'Probably not.'

'Fuck.'

'OK. So, you have your answer.' She paused and glared at him. 'Now come on.' She motioned to Liam to turn around and she opened the largest flap on his backpack, checked the initials and handed him a sealed plastic bag of clothes she had bought in Hamburg. 'Put these on and leave your other clothes neatly folded in the boot,' she said, firmly.

'Neatly? Why?'

She snapped back at him. 'Because they will be easier to put on if we don't have enough time when we come back.' *This was her mission and she wouldn't leave anything to chance or to anyone that could make her fail.*

When Liam opened his bag and saw the contents, he grunted his feelings and refused to move. Instead, he stood and watched as Zita changed into her clothes. She had deliberately chosen them to reduce any possibly of them being challenged by opposing drunken fans. For her it was an oversized tee-shirt with a full colour print of the non-partisan mascot of Benelucky - a pun on Benelux, Euro 2000; a smiling lion-devil hybrid with its mane having the flag colours of both host nations.

Liam looked at it, shook his head and scoffed. 'Fuck, are we wearing these for a bet?'

Zita continued to straighten her tee-shirt before checking her watch. 'Liam, we have to go. Now!'

She checked her watch again and screamed at him. 'Come on, Liam, can you put those on!'

He ignored her.

She breathed deeply and fired her anger at him before changing her tone. 'Please.'

He nodded and flounced childishly. Under obvious sufferance he removed his clothes and put on the faded XL tee shirt, with the same football logo, denim jeans and the regulatory white trainers.

And again, having deliberately chosen to hide her shapely body, she pulled on the oversized grey shorts. After finally pulling on her matching baseball cap, she threw one to Liam.

Zita was aware that brand new tee-shirts would stand out amongst the tourists and real fans who had probably been wearing theirs for weeks, and some well before the start of the tournament. So, she had already washed the tee-shirts several times and deliberately left them creased and unironed. They needed to blend in with anyone and everyone who had even a minimal interest in football. Most people, even the children, were wearing brightly coloured tee-shirts, linking them to their respective countries. Others wore new tee-shirts that had been hastily printed for, France and Italy, the finalists, identifying their recently converted "fans".

They drove down to the Playa Blanca ferry terminal, parked the car and, after pulling on their respective backpacks, they walked into a nearby bar. Zita ordered a bottle of sparkling water and a tea for Liam while they waited for their ferry to arrive.

The adrenalin was already building and minutes later they left the bar and their drinks untouched.

CHAPTER THIRTY-FOUR

It's All in the Game

While Liam waited for Zita who was queuing to buy the tickets from the booth for the Volcan Tindaya, the smaller of the Fred Olsen ferries, it brought back mixed emotions of his only visit almost a year earlier.

They were the last foot passengers to board and joined dozens of fans of all nationalities, all with the same purpose to watch the Euro 2000 final held in the Stadion de Kuip in Rotterdam on the afternoon of 2nd July. Although many were openly disappointed that their team hadn't made the final, they still wore their shirt with pride.

When the ferry docked at the quayside of Corralejo all the bars and restaurants were overflowing with fans already drunk with the euphoria of the impending final which was still almost an hour away from kick off. Liam and Zita left the ferry and walked to the roundabout and turned left onto the tree-lined road. Zita signalled to Liam to wait for her in the shade.

He looked around for somewhere out of the red-hot sun and chose a high stone wall with the branches of several huge orange trees overhanging it and casting a deep shadow across the path. He sat on the bench, and while he took his time to light a cigarette, he watched a scraggy white poodle with matted fur lying prostrate in the sun. Without warning the dog jumped up, rolled over and lay down again. Liam smiled to himself as he repeatedly took huge drags before stepping on the stub and kicking it into the deep gutter. An elderly man with a walking stick ambled precariously down the road and his equally old mongrel limped along beside him. Two elderly women stood looking at Liam wanting to share the seat. He slid along to one end and they each gave him a toothless grin and then, oblivious to the stranger, they continued to gabble to each other as they sat down.

Zita was on a mission. She repeatedly checked her watch and proceeded to walk briskly between the motorbikes that were parked haphazardly around the square. She took a few minutes eying the various motorbikes until she finally made her decision and chose two older machines that she knew she could fire up without keys. She chose a 1980 Ducati Bevel Twin 900 SS and a 1989 Yamaha YX 600cc Radian.

She checked that they each had enough fuel to travel the journey of fifty-six kilometres to De Groot's property and back to Corralejo, before making a mental note of the respective mileage, fiddling with the ignition and kick-starting each of them in turn.

She beckoned Liam to join her and pointed at the Yamaha.

He screwed-up his face and waved her suggestion away.

She pointed at the Ducati, he smiled back at her and she climbed onto the Yamaha.

Zita checked her watch once more and whispered to Liam. 'We have two and a half hours to do this - and to get back for the ferry.'

He nodded enthusiastically, revved up his powerful machine, let out the clutch and raced up the deserted street.

No one heard or cared.

Zita rolled her throttle and followed close behind him and down the coast in the direction of Puerto del Rosario.

They raced out of town and after travelling five kilometres they stopped at the side of the deserted road. Zita pulled a lightweight grey Adidas tennis tracksuit from her backpack and pulled it over her shorts and tee-shirt and handed Liam a black Puma track suit top.

They reached the obscure sign, visible only to those that knew what they were looking for, and stopped. It was almost a year since Liam last visited the island the previous summer, though Zita had made monthly visits with the laundered money from Amsterdam.

'Turn off your engine,' said Zita.

Liam obliged and she followed suit. They freewheeled in silence down the winding road, between the pink and white oleander bushes and lush grassy slopes, to the private car park and nearby beach.

Zita signalled to Liam with the wave of her hand and he pulled up fifty yards from the entrance. 'Stay here,' she whispered. She reached over her shoulder and into a side pocket of the knapsack and removed two pairs of latex gloves. She flicked a pair at Liam and motioned to him to put them on. She whispered. 'I'll come back for you when I'm ready.'

Liam nodded and hid the motorbikes amongst the taller shrubs.

Zita knew every inch of the complex; four luxury apartments built with no expense spared, and none of them could be overlooked by anyone else in the elite complex.

She slipped unnoticed through the large imported palm trees, shrubs and bushes, through the trade entrance of the plush building and into the basement garage. Within minutes she was in the control room with its state-of-the-art security system which she had helped to design and commission. She smiled as she checked the bank of screens that filled one wall and congratulated herself with a whisper. 'Perfect,' she said.

There was no sound or movement.

It was the second of July and she knew that it was probably too hot for most people. Their private pools and sun terraces were deserted as many were either having a siesta in their rooms, down on the beach under umbrellas, or watching the football using their collective illegal cards to access the many stations from their respective countries.

She saw De Groot on one of the screens, on his private roof terrace that ran the length of the building, lying on a huge sunlounger with an equally large umbrella to protect him from the strong afternoon sun. His nose was buried in his newspaper and the Euro football final on the television played to itself.

She smiled as she eyed the television and she knew it would make it so much easier to judge her timing. She reached into another pocket of her backpack and removed several metal jointing cables and clips and temporarily shorted out the cameras.

The screens immediately went blank.

She beckoned Liam to join her, secured the door from the outside and left.

When they were safely inside the garage and the alarm had been turned off Zita reached into Liam's backpack, and opened a supermarket bag and removed two bottles of water and two high energy fruit bars. She checked the labels and handed the still water and fruit bar to Liam. 'Eat that and drink the water. It will be very hot up there and we mustn't get dehydrated.'

Liam took one bite of the gooey bar.

His face displayed his distaste.

She opened hers, took a huge bite and looked at him as she chewed and swallowed it. 'Energy,' she said, before taking a huge bite and swallowing the remainder and putting the wrapper in the plastic bag.

He wasn't convinced and stood looking at it. 'You don't have to like it, Liam. It will give you energy.'

He screwed up his face and looked back at her.

'You will *need* it.'

She showed her impatience by looking at her watch and alternating the tapping of her right foot.

He bit into it and forced it down before handing her the wrapper.

After finishing the water, she put the wrappers and empty plastic bottles into an inner bag and slipped it into Liam's backpack. She opened a larger pocket and took out two sets of white lightweight coveralls supplied by the ship's engineer and similar to those used by forensics teams when examining crime scenes. She checked her markings on the outside packing and handed Liam his. 'Take off your clothes and put this on, and make sure you put on the shoe protectors and…' She watched him undress. 'But keep your gloves on.'

Liam struggled to put his coverall on. She helped to pull it over his shoulders and playfully covered his head with the hood.

He objected with a grunt.

'It's OK, this will give us the element of surprise and he will have no idea who we are until *we* decide to show him.' Liam understood with a grin. She continued and tugged at the hood. 'We can pull that down once we've surprised him.'

He grunted and nodded back at her.

'Now, we need to put on our backpacks.' She could see he was having difficulty and helped him to pull the straps over the coverall before sliding hers effortlessly across her narrow shoulders. She looked him up and down and smiled. 'OK. Let's go.'

She signalled to him to follow her through the escape tunnels that had been meticulously planned in the design of the building by Juan Marisco, the now missing, and presumed dead, architect.

They took the private lift and stopped at De Groot's fourth floor complex.

As the lift door opened Liam tried to take in the decadence that was De Groot's luxurious new world. He shook his head in disbelief as he moved from room to room until he had covered every inch of the penthouse. The complex was complete with individual infinity pools, a hot tub and jacuzzi, as well as fully automated security entrance doors to the individual secure garage to each apartment and access to separate lifts which were controlled via a fingerprint reader. Only Zita knew how to override it.

De Groot's apartment was the largest and most opulent. It offered a dining room with a table set to seat twelve, a large open kitchen, five bedrooms each with their own en-suite. There was also a billiard room, gym, separate dressing rooms with walk-in wardrobes and a fully fitted utility room. The highlight of the suite was the vast airy sunlit lounge with full height electronically controlled glass patio doors which looked out onto the jacuzzi and infinity swimming pool providing panoramic views of the Atlantic and the deep blue sky raked by high white fluffy clouds. Tinted roof lights that allowed the light to penetrate the inner areas of the lounge were carefully positioned across the ceiling. The decoration and furniture was a mixture of modern, clean lines and original Art Deco, with restored period furniture, lamps and other expensive accessories. Liam scoffed when he saw a white Fender Telecaster in one corner. The remaining rooms in the sprawling apartment consisted of a guest suite with a kitchen and bathroom. Other electrically controlled features included blinds, curtains, heating, a central audio system, and automated pool cleaning.

De Groot had a secure office behind a full height painting that was known only to him, Keeva and Zita, who had helped to design and plan it.

Above them the roof garden offered a true oasis for relaxation. The ornate fountain was surrounded by the professionally designed and carefully tended garden with lush greenery and exotic plants and flowers all exaggerated by the summer sun.

CHAPTER THIRTY-FIVE

Every Little Bit Hurts

Zita had helped to plan De Groot's office and, after sliding back the huge painting, she opened the door and took her time to search it. She checked the fax machine, pressed a button and seconds later a print out of all the dialled numbers spewed out from the paper roll. She grinned as she ran her finger down the list of numbers stopping at the code for Saint Petersburg. She checked the waste bin and carefully unravelled the first of the tightly screwed up pieces of paper. She placed it on the desk, held it with her left glove and ran the palm of her other gloved hand over it several times until it was flattened.

Her grin grew as she read the two words. They read: *All set*.

She was intrigued by the message and thrust her hand deeper into the bin and picked her way through the remaining tight balls of paper, unrolled them and taking care not to tear the paper she flattened each of them in turn and lined them up on the desk.

She scanned each of them and identified the three that were of interest.

Zita read the first fax. *Kill him in Hamburg - money transferred and confirmed.*

The second gave the Swiss bank account details of the Russian and De Groot while the third gave the name and address in Hamburg and, on a second page, a photograph of a man with the name Toto scrawled beneath it.

She took her time to fax the banks using details on the printouts and the codes and passwords in De Groot's notebook and transferred all the money from his and the Russian's bank accounts into those she had recently set up in various names in Switzerland, Germany, Ireland, England and Holland.

While she waited for confirmation of the transfers, she sorted out the fax pages and smiled as she re-read them several times before putting the pages detailing the bank accounts into her backpack. She screwed up the others into balls and threw them back into the waste bin. She picked up the telephone, tapped in a series of numbers she had memorised and used when she had worked for Mossad, which rerouted her location to Berlin.

After several rings the phone was answered. 'Hello,' said the Dutchman.

'Hi, is that, Detective Ackerman?'

'Yes. Who is it?'

She laughed. 'Hello, Piet, it's me... Zita.'

'Zita,' he said, sounding surprised. He paused. 'Where are you?'

'We're in Berlin,' she lied. 'I'm here with Liam.'

'Berlin?'

'Yeah, I did tell you.' She sensed he didn't believe her and smiled as she continued. 'It's a long story.' She paused. 'My mother was born here in Berlin–'

'Really?'

Zita sighed. 'Surprised eh?'

'Um.' He nodded erratically. 'Yeah, I am. How come?'

'That's a long story too.' She sighed heavily. 'Maybe one...' She stopped suddenly and tapped her index finger on De Groot's desk. 'I don't have long. We're about to visit East Berlin want to show Liam what it was like behind the wall.'

She looked furtively around the office checking if there was anything else that could be of future use to her, as she continued to talk. 'How's Ribeker?'

'She's not back at work yet' He sighed. 'It's hit her hard and I'm not sure if she will ever come back. We'll have to wait and see.'

'Are you any nearer to knowing who gave the instruction for the fire?'

Ackerman took a huge drag on his cigarette and continued. 'Off the record, we're not too bothered who it was...'

Zita coughed her frustration at the detective's lack of interest.

'But I reckon De Groot was behind it.'

'You aren't following it up?'

Ackerman tried to hide his mistake with a nervous cough. 'Well... I still have a man following up on the leads but so far we have nothing concrete.'

'Don't you see... it had to be De Groot?'

He gained time to think by taking two extended drags on his cigarette. 'Well... I'm sure you could be right but until we find him.' He sighed. 'You won't know the answer to that until we do.'

'Don't you have any idea where he may be?' she asked, with a grin.

'No, we don't,' he said, raising his voice in embarrassment. He coughed hard and continued in his normal unruffled voice. 'Not yet, but we're still looking.' Zita heard him drilling his fingers on his desk. He took a couple more drags of his cigarette and continued. 'We are no further forward than the report that he took a flight to Madeira on New Year's Eve–'

She feigned vagueness. 'Oh, yeah... Madeira.'

The Detective continued. 'Then...' He shook his head. 'Well... he disappeared into thin air after that.'

Zita faked a laugh. 'You'll find him sooner or later,' she said, as she lifted her head, rolled her eyes and grinned into space.

Ackerman spoke with a renewed enthusiasm. 'We found Tsotne Tabagari. You know, Toto, the cage fighter.' He paused. 'Well... the police in Hamburg did.'

Zita sighed before speaking. 'He may well have links to De Groot and I thought they may have been in contact with each other.'

'But guess what?'

'What?'

'You may be right. He was attacked in Hamburg it looks like someone put out a hit on him,' he said, forcing a feeble laugh.

'What was he doing there?'

The Detective sniggered. 'Apparently, he lives there.'

'Wow,' she said, as she sniffed loudly. 'Any ideas?'

'No, but it was a professional hit.' He cleared his throat. 'Well - he tried.'

Zita faked her surprise. 'Wow!

Ackerman continued. 'Being a cage fighter he's a fit bastard. Whoever tried to kill him met his match... That's for sure.'

'Any idea who it was?'

'The Hamburg police said they arrested a Russian who was wearing overalls from the Norderwerft shipyard. He bought them from a workwear shop in Landungsbrücken the day before. He also had a stolen ID badge on him and a screwed-up fax from De Groot with an address in Hamburg and a photo of Toto.'

'Right.'

'The police are pretty sure he's a hit man.'

'How did they get to find him?'

'He was unconscious in his hotel room on the Reeperbahn
- they have no idea how he manged to get there.' He sniffed
and continued. 'He was in a bad way... badly beaten up... a
smashed ankle and hand.' He paused. 'When they searched his
hotel room, they found a fake passport and Russian money.'
He paused and lit a cigarette. 'They took him to hospital. He
said it was a hit and run...' He laughed unsympathetically.
'But they know different. And guess what?'

'What?'

'Tabagari called it in–'

'Who?'

'I've just told you - the cage fighter.'

'How, and why would he bother?'

'Bravado?

'I can believe that.'

'He said he saw a dock worker attacking someone in an
alley off Talstraße.' He paused and laughed. 'But the police
couldn't find anything.'

'Isn't that a bit weird?'

'Yeah. It sure is but the Russian must be harder than Toto
thought to be able to make it back to his hotel with injuries as
bad as that.'

'Right,' said Zita, thinking ahead.

'We already had the Russian in our sights. He's come up
on the radar a few times before via Europol. But getting him
back here to face charges for his earlier hits is a very different
matter. The Russians don't help us unless there is someone or
something they want from us.' Ackerman paused, took a huge
drag on his cigarette then squeezed it into the overflowing ash
tray. 'But do you know what?' He looked at the smouldering
cigarette end and pressed it deep into the other dog ends until
it was totally extinguished. He continued. 'Something's not
right,' he said, as he scratched at his chin.

'Well?' asked Zita impatiently.

Ackerman continued. 'It is strange...' He took a deep breath. 'Too much of a coincidence.' He nodded. 'You may be right about this... Toto being linked to De Groot–'

'Really?'

'Yeah. Back in January we caught a glimpse of him watching the fire at...' He looked at the faxed photo of Toto. He deliberately lowered his voice and continued. 'At the Love Shack–'

'How?'

'He was spotted on the television - on the news–'

'Are you sure?'

'Oh, yeah. The television station gave us a copy.' He took another cigarette from the packet and lit it. 'It was definitely him.' He coughed. 'The Georgian has now taken over the lucrative end of De Groot's empire so maybe the attack was meant to be a warning.'

Zita grinned and nodded. 'I'm sure it was.' She paused. 'So, De Groot must still know what's going on there?'

'Yeah. I'm sure he does... Somehow. But the attack failed.' He took a drag on his cigarette. 'And everyone is still desperate to find him. Europol are working overtime to find the bastard.' He tipped the cigarette ash into the overflowing ashtray. He scoffed. 'If he so much as coughs we'll get him.'

'I'm sure you will,' said Zita forcing a laugh. 'We all know De Groot has too big an ego to want to stay hidden forever.'

'Um.'

Zita asked a question to which she already knew the answer. 'Okay. So, assuming it was Toto - why the hell would he arrange the fire?'

'Putting a marker down on De Groot.'

'He didn't waste any time, did he? Something like that would need to be planned.'

The Detective pursed his lips. 'Sure. Perhaps he knew something we didn't?'

Zita offered an empty reply. 'Yeah - who knows.'

'Maybe we'll know more by the time you get back.'

Zita tapped her watch. 'Sorry, I have to go. We'll see you soon. Give our love to Andrea.'

'Course I will... And... enjoy East Berlin.'

'Thanks.'

'Bye.'

She smiled as she clicked off the phone. She cleared the number and ripped it from the wall and smashed it along with fax.

Liam heard the noise and appeared at the office door and looked around. 'Everything alright?'

'Yeah.' She licked her lips. 'They have no idea where De Groot is.' She celebrated with a huge grin. 'But they know Toto is living in Hamburg.'

Liam ignored her. Having spent the last few minutes in De Groot's huge sitting room while Zita was on the phone to Ackerman, he had had time to think. He glanced around the walls and desk. 'Don't you think it's weird?'

'What is?'

'He's got no photos. His office in Amsterdam was wall to wall with 'em. Right?'

Zita's mind was elsewhere. She briefly closed her eyes and lowered her head. 'Maybe,' she said.

She slowly exhaled and signalled to Liam to leave her with a wave of her hand.

CHAPTER THIRTY-SIX

Let It Be

Within seconds, and with little or no effort, Zita was able to open De Groot's safe, taking whatever she felt would be of use and value, filling a second backpack that she had slipped into her outer backpack. She picked through the contents and carefully placed them in different pockets and zipped it up. In one of his office drawers, she found an electronic key and slipped it into a small side pocket in her backpack.

Liam was waiting in the huge open plan kitchen.

Zita walked in and he watched her, mesmerised at her deftness as she opened the huge American style fridge and removed a selection of food and a bottle of beer. She prepared the plate of tapas and, as she flicked the cap off the beer, Liam looked on enviously licking his lips as the froth oozed out of the top of the bottle and onto the tray.

Zita shot him a condemning look of her disapproval and, as she tutted, waggled her forefinger at him.

Liam signalled his agreement with a knowing nod. *He knew alcohol would kill him if he ever dared to drink again.*

Zita took an Am-Tech box cutter from her zipped pocket and passed it to him. Still holding it, he walked back into the enormous expensively furnished lounge with its leather four-seater settees, designer tables, mood lighting, wall to wall electric patio doors and a huge television on one wall. He stood and looked at the swimming pool and Jacuzzi and out across the sparkling Atlantic before flicking out the blade and thrusting out at an invisible assailant.

Minutes later, Zita returned with the tapas and beer on a raffia tray.

She whispered to Liam. 'He's on his own and we need to surprise him.'

Liam nodded and wiggled his fingers as the tight latex gloves began to cause his large hands to sweat.

Zita made her way up to the roof terrace and the perfect blue sky and occasional white clouds. She tiptoed silently across the large terrazzo paved patio between the raised beds of shrubs and plants. Liam followed a short distance behind her and waited apprehensively.

Although the television was on, De Groot had muted it so the only sounds on the roof, with its lush plants and shrubs, were the wind chimes that tinkled softly in the light afternoon breeze and the water trickling down the fountain.

Zita stood out of sight immediately behind De Groot and spoke. 'Hola, Senor.'

De Groot didn't look up from his newspaper, preferring to grunt his acknowledgment.

Zita continued. 'Tapas y cerveza, Senor,' she said, as she took the contents from the tray and placed them on the low table beside him.

As Zita flicked the newspaper to gain De Groot's attention Liam simultaneously grabbed the huge umbrella and slashed it with the razor-sharp blade.

De Groot immediately lowered the newspaper. Was zum teufel?' he said, in German.

'Hello, De Groot,' said Zita, speaking to him in Dutch.

He shielded his eyes from the sun and took a moment to see who it was. He shook his head and then stuttered with a combination of shock and surprise. 'I thought you were *dead*.'

Zita sneered at him. 'We are,' she said, cockily.

'We?' said De Groot.

Liam let out a huge belly laugh. De Groot twisted his head to look towards the second voice who, with a theatrical wave, he slowly flicked back his hood.

The Dutchman pulled back shocked at seeing Liam alive and having the nerve to venture into *his* territory.

He replied in German with the perfect Hamburg dialect. 'Ich bin, Dieter Stange.' He sneered at Zita. 'De Groot ist schon weg - für immer verschwunden,' he said, forcing a painful cocky grin. 'Er starb in Amsterdam.'

Zita smirked and turned to Liam as she translated what De Groot had said. 'The sick bastard really believes we will accept that De Groot is dead - gone forever.' She turned to De Groot and replied in German. 'Aber es gibt keinen Körper, der es beweisen kann.' She told Liam what she'd said forcing a staged laugh. 'But there isn't a body. Is there?'

De Groot answered her in Dutch. 'There are many bodies still to be found - any of them could be me...'

Liam cut him off. 'None of that matters now. We knew you were still alive and would be here.' He grinned back at him. 'Why do you think we're here?'

De Groot narrowed his eyes and carried on the pretence, smirking at the strangers. He slowly shook his head before speaking. 'I don't know who you are but... I don't have anything of value here... and...' He paused briefly and continued in a raised voice. 'Be careful who you mess with.'

Their response was silence.

He had no option but to acknowledge that his subterfuge was over.

He looked at Zita and feigned sadness. 'Out of all *my* people you were the only one I trusted–'

'That's crap! Total crap!' she said. She glared at the Dutchman and their locked eyes seared into each other.

De Groot gave an ironic smile and winked at Liam. 'It's red hot up here. I bet you could do with a bier?'

Liam shook his head and forced a sarcastic grin before he walked over and slashed the second umbrella leaving it to flap in the breeze.

De Groot knew he was very vulnerable and what the immeasurable outcomes could be if he tried to fight back.

Zita walked around the sun lounger and fixed a stare on De Groot.

Liam pushed the blade menacingly into De Groot's penis and testicles.

De Groot gasped and took a huge nervous breath as he attempted to regain his composure. 'You're both still on the payroll, you know,' he said, attempting a grin.

'I know,' said Liam, flippantly.

Zita looked at him and sneered.

De Groot looked back at her. 'OK, so what do you want?' he asked. He looked across at Liam who appeared to be getting agitated so he returned his gaze to Zita. 'Can't you sort this bastard out?' he said, hurriedly.

Zita ignored him.

Liam glared at him. 'You have nothing *we* want.' He took his time to look the Dutchman up and down. 'You've put on weight.' He sniggered. 'You ought to watch yourself or you'll probably die from a heart attack.' He poked and prodded De Groot's stomach with the handle of the box cutter and continued with an intimidating whisper. 'If you're *not* careful.'

De Groot shook his head and watched in horror as Zita walked across the roof and, although the CCTV was turned off, she methodically turned each of the cameras around to face away from the roof, into the shrubs and bushes and at the infinity swimming pool which glared back up at her with the reflection of the bright sun.

De Groot took the opportunity to speak to Liam and pointed at the lush plants and shrubs. 'It's changed a bit since you were last here?'

Liam took his time to take it all in. He noticed a lizard resting on a rock warming itself in the sun and smiled to himself. 'I don't like gardening. Never have.' He sniggered. 'We don't have nothing like this where I come from.'

Pleased with her actions Zita walked back to him and whispered into De Groot's right ear. 'We need nothing *more* from you.' She grinned inanely. 'We already have it all.'

De Groot attempted a shrug and chose to turn his attention to Liam, hoping he would break down. 'You've both got such short memories.' He paused for effect. 'You're a fucking *loser...*' He grinned at him. 'Little more than a useless drunk...' He sniggered. 'When the police took you away... Have you forgotten I got you out of jail?'

'Really,' screamed Liam, as he stomped around the huge sun lounger and pushed his face into De Groot's. 'You had innocent people killed and... and for what?' He didn't give De Groot time to answer. He continued. 'Greed? Power? To save your fucking reputation?' He grabbed at De Groot's throat and dug his finger nails deep into the loose and saggy skin. 'Why?'

De Groot struggled and gasped for breath.

Zita shouted at Liam and reluctantly he released his grip with a hefty shrug.

De Groot looked at Zita and took a while to catch his breath. 'What's your real reason for coming here, eh?'

'Fuck you,' she raged.

De Groot turned to Liam. 'What about you, eh? Does *she* know why you were there?' He scoffed. 'I told you. Anyone with something to hide ends up in Mokum!' He turned his head towards Zita and continued. 'You... like that bastard had

230

nowhere else to go.' He glared at her, his bright red face exuding intense anger. '*Did you*?' he screamed.

His scathing words clearly hit her hard and as she turned away, she growled incomprehensibly back at him. She took a huge breath and glared down at him before she replied. 'Working for a tyrant and bully like you came at a price! A PRICE LIKE NO OTHER!' She shook her head and lowered her voice. 'Watching how you treated *innocent* and vulnerable people.' She faked a deep urge. 'Young girls...' She took a deep breath. 'And boys.' She spat her contempt at him and continued. 'Was beyond contemptible. And... and for what?' She screwed up her face visibly expressing her disgust. 'Money!'

De Groot enjoyed their anger and responded. 'You're both amateurs - nobodies!'

Zita glared at him. 'There will never be any redemption for you, De Groot,' she said. 'Or, whoever you *believe* you are!'

De Groot opened his mouth wide to exude a huge grin exposing his nicotine stained teeth. 'Touched a nerve did it?'

Zita ignored him, otherwise occupied, and responded with an ineffectual wave of her open left hand. She slid the backpack from her shoulders, laid it on the table and reached into one of the numerous side pockets and pulled out an assortment of cable ties.

De Groot knew what was about to happen to him and he offered only token resistance. Nonetheless, Zita smacked him hard around his head followed by the thrust of the blade deep into his stomach from Liam, causing blood to gush from the deep wound and soak into his white designer shirt. De Groot knew it was futile to offer any resistance and lay motionless while Zita stretched his arms and legs out much wider than normal to reach the edges of the expansive sun lounger. She bound his arms at the wrists and feet at the ankles, pulling the

231

cable ties as tight as she possibly could without stopping the circulation.

Once their victim was secured, she motioned to Liam with a flick of her head.

Liam pulled off De Groot's Commodore XLT designer leather deck shoes and threw them as far as he could across the roof. When he saw his rolled down socks he stopped. 'Zita, look at this.'

She pulled at the socks each marked separately with port and starboard, identifying which foot the wearer had to put them on. She faked a loud laugh. 'Decadence beyond belief and… I bet he doesn't even sail,' she said.

She looked at Liam. 'Do it.'

He tugged at the top of the first sock, sliced it down to the toe and ripped it off. He then concentrated on the other foot and threw them both across the roof.

Liam now turned his attention to their victim's clothes. He thrust the blade towards De Groot who squirmed and breathed erratically as Liam took his time to affect a theatrical performance of his handiwork. He sliced off the buttons, one at a time, from the bloodstained white cotton shirt and flicked them across the roof, in the process exposing De Groot's matted chest hair. He then turned his attention to the olive linen trousers and haphazardly sliced through them, cutting into De Groot's pale skin. Blood ran onto the sun lounger before dripping onto the hot terrazzo paving and fizzing as it dried. Liam finally reached De Groot's undersized silk boxers, overhung by his expansive stomach, and cut through them exposing his shrunken penis. Liam flicked it with the razor-sharp blade and De Groot shuddered. *He knew what may be coming next. He and his henchmen had regularly meted out lengthy and painful psychological torture to his enemies in order to maintain his total control in his Amsterdam.*

CHAPTER THIRTY-SEVEN

Hot Hot Hot

While Liam was taking his time to slash through De Groot's clothes, Zita removed some of the contents from various pockets of the backpacks and laid them out on the defaced hardwood table. The deep gouge in the table was the result of Liam's anger the previous summer, the last time he was on the island. He had violently refused to succumb to the revolting advances of Francesco Raphael, the greasy, overweight, gay pervert and partner of De Groot's architect. He had stabbed him, pinning his podgy hairy hand to the table.

Liam sat at the table and dug his finger in the gouge but stopped suddenly. He swung around and looked down at De Groot. 'Did you expect us all to die in that fire?' he asked.

'*Fire*. What fire–?'

'Fuck!' screamed Liam.

Zita spun around and glared at him. 'Do you really want to play dumb with us?'

De Groot swallowed hard. 'Yes, yes... Yes. I know about the fire in that fucking shit hole.' He looked directly at Liam. '*Your* shit hole!' He slowed and smirked. 'I watched it on the television.' He reflected. 'Very impressive.' He grinned. 'Pity that.' He blinked and shook his head faking a flick to remove the invisible tears. 'But it wasn't me...' He struggled to breathe. 'Why the fuck would I destroy my own property?'

Zita pushed her face into his. 'If it wasn't you... then *who* did it?'

'It could have been that cage fighter - the Georgian dwarf?'

Zita grinned at him. 'Really?'

De Groot suddenly took the offensive and twisted his head painfully to look at Zita. 'What about my fucking takings over Christmas and New Year?' he snarled.

Zita stretched out her arms and pushed her tongue up into her top lip and flicked it out. 'M O N E Y?' she said, exaggerating every letter. She turned to Liam. 'Do you know anything about *his* money, Liam?' she asked, pointing at De Groot mischievously.

Liam screwed up his face and nodded frenetically. 'No idea?' he said, glibly.

Money was De Groot's life. How he got it was immaterial. He exploded with rage. 'You're a fucking, whore. I can't wait to see what Erag does to you!'

She ignored him but Liam tensed and clenched his fists and made to move towards him.

Zita shushed him away. 'Relax, Liam... *Please.*'

Liam ignored her and snarled at De Groot. 'Erag's *dead*. Zita ripped out his filthy throat with her bare 'ands!'

De Groot closed his eyes and nodded. 'There will be others. Whatever you do to me - you will always need to watch your backs.' He swallowed. 'You'll never be safe.'

'Um,' mumbled Zita. She lifted her head and grinned. 'I think we can take that chance, don't you, Liam?'

'Yeah, course we can,' he said, and underlined it with a slow calculated nodding of his head. 'Sure can.'

De Groot opened his eyes and watched her as she opened the third pocket of the backpack and removed a chamois leather and a handful of the wafer-thin leather studded straps, she had carefully chosen in the most extreme Amsterdam sex shop, before leaving for Hamburg and the cruise.

She walked across to the fountain, dropped everything into the clear sparkling water and left it to soak.

She returned to the table and flicked at the flies before picking up the plate of tapas. She sat down on the huge sun lounger beside De Groot and smiled. 'I hope you're hungry,' she said, evocatively.

He grunted.

'This is your last meal - so I suggest you enjoy it.'

He couldn't reply as she forced a large piece of raw squid into his mouth and then continued to force more and more of the tapas into his ever-expanding mouth. He swallowed all of it, urged and immediately vomited. The undigested food ran slowly down his chest and onto his stomach.

Zita looked at him and faked pity. 'Ahhh, you poor bastard,' she said, softly, 'you've been sick. Maybe the food doesn't agree with him? She turned. 'What do you think, Liam?'

'Fuck 'im.'

Her face suddenly reddened with unbelievable anger as she remembered how he had treated her when she first arrived in Amsterdam. 'You stink!' She pretended to vomit. 'You're such a vile, pathetic bastard!'

Liam, driven on by her unusually angry outburst, something he had never seen from her before, moved close to De Groot and gloated hideously before pushing his face into the Dutchman. 'You're a fucking pig! You stink!' he screamed.

Zita returned to her normal calculated disposition. 'I expect he's thirsty, Liam.' She turned to De Groot. 'Would you like something to drink?' she asked. She answered her own question and grinned at Liam. 'Of course, he's thirsty after *all* that delicious food.' She grabbed his hair, pulled his head back and forced the beer bottle into his mouth, cutting his bottom lip.

De Groot squirmed as he spluttered and emptied the bottle.

Zita released her grip on his hair and threw his head forward. She poured a bottle of olive oil onto the empty tapas plate to sit in the red hot sun. She returned to the fountain, wrung out the leather studded straps and chamois leather and walked back to De Groot.

She motioned to Liam to grab De Groot's head.

He obliged with a grin and spread his large open hands around the sides of De Groot's head before tugging at it and stretching his fat neck. Zita carefully wrapped the wet leather straps tightly around the Dutchman's neck, leaving him to resemble a Kayan woman - a giraffe woman, of the Ndebele people in South Africa.

De Groot swallowed hard before he spoke. For the first time he was clearly disturbed by what was happening to him. 'Surely,' he stuttered and trembled, 'can't we be civilised and come to an agreement?'

Liam glared at him. 'Civilised? Have you ever done *anything* that's *civilised*?' He spat at him. 'Do you even know what that means?' He spat again. 'You're a fucking animal - nothing less.' Liam lowered his voice and replied in a menacing tone. 'If it was one of *us* laying there you wouldn't think twice about what you or your cronies did to us... Would you?' He stamped his feet and turned away. He clenched his fists and turned back to look down at De Groot. 'Would you?'

De Groot sucked at his bleeding lip, forced a grin and let out an unintelligible reply.

Zita gently moved Liam aside and looked De Groot in the eye. 'Why?' she scoffed.

She glanced across to Liam, who was taking great pleasure in painfully removing the remaining shreds of De Groot's vomit covered clothes.

Liam paused briefly and pushed the blade hard into De Groot's engorged neck. 'You've lost your grip on Amsterdam... You're fucking Mokum. You're last year's news. You're *forgotten...*' He screamed. *'Gone! History!'*

De Groot wanted to explode with rage but as he felt the blade cutting into him, he tried to hold his breath until he was left with no option but to take small distressed gasps. 'I'm still in control of *my* empire.' He struggled for breath. 'The dwarf has been dealt with...'

Liam replied. 'That dwarf... as you call him, is taking everything... everything you ever had.'

De Groot offered a wide mouthed toothy grin. 'You are wrong, my friend. Toto is dead. Murdered in Hamburg... *Yesterday,*' he grinned. 'And, I *still* have my control.'

Zita laughed loudly. 'He's not dead. Your *Russian* failed. That's more of *your* precious money wasted.' She turned to Liam. 'Do you think this *idiot* will ever learn?'

Liam shook his head. 'Never.'

She took her time and exaggerated the shaking of her head. 'No. Course he won't,' she said.

Unable to control his anger Liam raised his voice. 'It's gone... All of it!' He glared at De Groot and moved threateningly towards him. 'And *you* destroyed *my* Love Shack.' He stamped his foot. 'What the fuck was that all about?'

De Groot's face hardened and his whole demeanour changed as he felt the leather thongs ever tightening around his neck. He knew he was a trapped animal and all he had were words to verbally attack his torturers. 'What a shit place that was?' he said, as he struggled to breathe through his constricting throat. He pulled back and spat at Liam. He

237

continued. 'Do you honestly believe anyone will miss that scheiss loch?'

Liam understood the German phrase, he'd heard Zita use it when she was angry. He replied. 'I will,' he said, in a faint, sad voice.

De Groot shook with anger. 'You both knew I wouldn't let it go.' He took a laboured breath. 'Did you expect me to let you idiots ruin ME!' he raged. 'It's piffeldang man.' He huffed at Liam and took a moment to think. 'Um.' He raised his head painfully in defiance. 'That's all you were...' He snarled. 'A fucking waster.' He continued to stutter his obscenities. 'It's all you were good for - an *amateur* trying to run a tin pot fucking bar.' He continued to insult him in German. 'You're no more than *Klaus Klappstuhl,*' he screamed.

Liam had no idea what he meant but as his face contorted with renewed anger, he clenched his fists and stepped towards him.

Zita flexed her arms and held him back. 'We can't mark his face,' she said, softly. She clicked her teeth and her face broke into a very unusual childlike grin. 'This has to be a vendetta.' She paused and continued in a whisper. 'From someone... somewhere on the island,' she said, as she looked out across the calm sea.

Liam shrugged his anger away, nodded and reluctantly relaxed his fists. He turned to De Groot and smiled.' So, what is it with the guitar?'

De Groot forced a sarcastic smile. 'It's not too late to learn to play something, is it?'

Liam scoffed. 'It *is* for a bastard like you. And... I wouldn't place any bets on it either.'

De Groot struggled in vain and with every attempt at freedom the cable ties tightened and cut into his wrists and ankles. 'I'll stop you. I still have influence here... on the island–'

'What the fuck use is that?' said Liam. 'You're already a dead man–'

Zita interrupted Liam and dived towards De Groot pushing her face into his. 'Well... Not yet, Liam.' She grinned inanely. 'But he is *dying*.'

De Groot offered a shrug.

'Trust me.' Zita licked her lips and grinned mischievously. 'You'll be beyond saving by the time anyone finds you up here.' She took a step back, shot Liam a weird look and sniggered.

De Groot looked at Liam and lowered his voice provocatively. 'If you look in that cool box...'

Liam reached down and removed the lid.

De Groot shot him a self-gratifying smile.

Liam took out a bottle of bier, opened it, sniffed at the froth, partially closed his eyes and blew it towards De Groot.

Zita stomped towards De Groot and smacked him across the face. 'Fuck you.'

De Groot raised his voice. 'Course, he'll drink it. Drunks always have a weakness. That's how they get where they are... at the bottom of the fucking food chain.'

Zita's face twisted with revulsion as she glared at Liam. 'Go on then...' Her hand shook with anger as she pointed at the bottle. 'Yeah...' She bit hard on her bottom lip. 'Kill yourself!'

While Liam blushed, De Groot chuckled hideously.

Liam looked at Zita, lowered his eyes and nodded slowly. He turned to De Groot and grinned inanely as he emptied the bottle over his sweating red head. He delved back in the box, pulled out a bottle of water and drank it all. He threw the bottle at De Groot but he dipped his head painfully to one side and avoided the bottle that smashed on the terrazzo.

239

De Groot mocked him. 'Fuck you.'

Zita returned to her backpack and took out a small plastic spray can and filled it with the warm olive oil from the table.

'Don't you know this will burn me?' said De Groot, in Dutch.

Zita grinned and nodded as she sprayed every inch of his exposed pale freckled skin. She took her time to reply in Dutch and then for Liam's benefit spoke in English.

Liam screwed up his face. 'You bastard,' he screamed. 'Isn't that what you wanted to do to us?'

De Groot grinned back at Liam.

Zita turned to De Groot and sprayed a second burst of oil over his already reddening body and scratched roughly at the dried blood before violently rubbing the oil into him making sure she inflicted as much pain and discomfort as she could.

She stood back with Liam and watched and waited while it soaked into his body. She then reached into another pocket of her backpack and removed the small plastic bottle containing the clear liquid she had obtained from the ship's engineer.

Liam looked on with baited breath.

She flicked the cap and making sure De Groot could see it, she poured a few token drops onto the terrazzo flooring.

It sizzled and bubbled.

She watched De Groot squirm wildly and grinned back at Liam. 'Now you know why we came back to visit you,' she mumbled.

Liam mouthed to her. 'Wha…?'

As De Groot felt the leather thongs tightening around his neck, he stopped squirming and lay there breathing hard.

Liam sat at the table and returned to finger the deep cut that he had made with his knife a year earlier. He grinned to himself and wondered if the architect had gotten rid of his gay minder after he had stabbed him and pinning his hand to the table.

He slid the large fruit bowl across the table and removed the butterfly food dome before picking at the fruit. He tried everything in the bowl: apples, pears, mangoes and bananas, taking only token bites from each.

Zita turned and noticed what he was doing. She huffed at him and took the plastic bag containing the empty water bottles for Liam's backpack. 'Put all of that in there.'

Liam gave her a curious look.

She repeated herself in a stern voice. 'All of it.'

'Your DNA will be on all of *that* and they may be able to trace you.' She sighed and continued. 'Okay?'

Liam did as he was told and took his time to empty the fruit bowl before sliding it into the bag.

She looked across to him. 'Tie it up,' she said firmly.

He obliged with a shrug and tied up the bag.

'Now put in back in there,' she said, pointing at his backpack.

She reached across to her backpack and pulled out a bag of cotton wool and crammed as much as she could into De Groot's mouth.

She walked across to the fountain and pulled the chamois leather from the water, lightly wrung it out, and then placed it across his red face tracking his profile slowly and evocatively.

De Groot moaned with sadistic pleasure.

Liam watched her. 'What will that do?' he asked.

'It will slowly tighten up the skin on his face and cause horrific pain.' She sucked at her teeth and continued with an exaggerated single word. 'Pain,' she said, with a slow extended breath.

She pointed her fingers and struck De Groot forcefully in his bloody stomach.

241

All that came out of his crammed mouth was a heavily muffled scream. She grabbed the chamois and a self-gratifying smile crossed her face as she walked back to the fountain where she briefly soaked it. She picked up the chamois and, ensuring De Groot could see what she was doing wrung it out before she walked back and laid it on the table. She picked up the clear plastic bottle from the table, removed the lid, lifted it as high as she could and dripped it onto the even hotter terrazzo. Once again, it immediately bubbled and fizzed but this time much quicker.

She looked De Groot in the eye for the final time and spoke, slowly and calmly in Hebrew. 'ממז ,להתראות,' she said. 'Auf wiedersehen... you bastard.'

She placed the damp chamois on his face and this time she meticulously followed every contour of his face until it formed a detailed imprint, like a piece of clay waiting for the sculptor to make any final touches to their work. Using the box cutter, she reached across and dismissively cut a small hole for his mouth allowing him enough of a gap to breathe before she took her time to pour the liquid onto the chamois.

De Groot's potentially earth-shattering pained screams through the cotton wool were little more than a muffled shriek as the liquid burnt into his face. All the while the thongs around his neck were tightening and as they continued to dry it resulted in more muffled agonising squawks.

While Zita sprayed the last of the hot olive oil onto De Groot's naked body, Liam picked up anything that might incriminate them.

De Groot expended all his energy as he let out a series of muffled sustained shrieks.

Zita cuffed De Groot with a heavy precise backhand to the side of his head.

He rasped in agony.

It was mid-summer, the hottest time of the year and, after checking the direction of the sun, they dragged De Groot's lounger around to face directly into it.

Zita took one last look at De Groot's covered face and already overheating body. She thumbed her lips and looked across at the television. 'One and half hours...That's all the time you have left,' she said, confidently, with a wide grin.

De Groot made a token show of bravado but it was clear his will and energy was deteriorating as the olive oil heated by the sun began to bubble and continue its torturous work.

Zita passed the second backpack to Liam and told him to get the bikes ready.

Liam tilted his head and slowly raised his open palms. 'Okay,' he mouthed derisively. He pulled it across his shoulders and gave De Groot's grotesque blistering carcass one last glance before he made his way across the roof and down the emergency staircase.

Zita checked the roof garden and picked up anything missed by Liam, slipped it into her backpack, reset the CCTV and ran down to join Liam. Zita pushed their forensic overalls and shoe covers into her backpacks and changed into her football tee-shirt and shorts and Liam, his jeans and football tee-shirt. They fired up the bikes and took their time to ride up the private road. Once on the main road they stopped briefly to take one final look at the view and they grinned to each other as they considered the red-hot sun beating down onto the roof terrace and De Groot's body.

Zita passed Liam his baseball cap. 'You need to keep this on.'

He grimaced.

'It's okay, I'm wearing mine too.' She pulled a second cap from the backpack and pulled it on. 'Do you want to burn again?' she said, as she remembered Liam's painful sunburn the previous year on Lanzarote.

They disappeared as quickly as they had arrived.

They both felt exhilarated as they raced along the main road having finally dealt with their most hated nemesis.

CHAPTER THIRTY-EIGHT

It's All Over Now

They drove along the coast and turned inland until they reached the outskirts of Tuineje, a village set high in the hills. Zita slowed down and her eyes searched for the large covered communal rubbish bins. She stopped and waited while Liam lifted the lid of one of them and dropped the plastic bag containing the partially eaten fruit, plastic water bottles and energy bar wrappers into it.

Liam stopped before climbing back onto his motorbike. 'Fuck, did you really spray him with acid?'

'My evil "twin" would have done that....' She bit her bottom lip quirkily. 'But I didn't.'

'Twin?'

Zita laughed loudly. 'I have no twin. It was only my alter ego.' She waited for Liam to digest what she had said and continued. 'No... I switched the containers... I used water - just water.' She grinned mischievously. 'But he didn't know dat... and would *never* know it. He was so frightened at the very thought that *anything* would have had the same effect.' She paused. 'To frighten him... almost to death.'

'Fuck.'

Zita continued. 'I would *not* have used acid on *his* face.'

Liam shook his head enthusiastically and faked a laugh. 'Oh... that is *very* thoughtful of you,' he said, patronisingly.

Zita chose not to hide her annoyance. 'It is barbaric and used by certain weak or jealous men...' She raised her voice. 'Who are vile *animals and cowards.*'

Liam pulled his head back and shared her disgust as he sighed heavily. He abhorred the action practised by some men and shot her an agreeable look.

Zita continued. 'There was another reason. A very good reason,' she said, sternly. She paused and waited until Liam was looking directly at her. 'If I had used acid, he would not immediately be recognisable and...' She paused and waited for Liam to understand.

It took a minute before it registered with Liam and then a smile slowly crossed his face. 'Ah.'

Zita continued. 'It would make it so much more difficult to identify him and... I wanted him to be recognised...' She sucked in air. 'This day... And... as *De Groot.*'

'Why?'

'Because the police are so much more interested in the football this day that they will be lazy and... This time.' She grinned impishly. 'I want to make it so very easy for them.'

They pulled into a layby and Zita checked her watch.

She smiled.

'We're ahead of things,' she said, confidently.

When they arrived back in Corralejo every television in the bars, houses and flats blasted out with the manic sports commentators screaming out their commentaries in varying languages and the very drunk euphoric fanatical fans being carried along with them.

They returned the motorbikes unnoticed to the spaces from where they had briefly borrowed them and Zita took a couple of minutes to reset the milometers. After checking her watch, they walked hurriedly along the street. When they arrived close to the ferry terminal Zita motioned to Liam to sit

246

on one of the many empty tables outside of the bar and out of sight of the television screen.

She forced her way through the crowded bar and returned with two coffees.

They sat in silence, sighing and grinning at each other for a few minutes as they mindlessly stirred their coffee, before turning their attention to the few tourists and parents with their young children who, although they had no interest in the Euro final, many of them were still wearing their country's logoed tee shirts.

Liam picked up his cup and held it close to his mouth but didn't drink. 'Phew, we've done it,' he said, as he slowly exhaled.

'Yeah.' Zita looked out across the port. 'It took a while but, yeah... We did it.'

Liam's demeanour changed. 'You know, that bastard is like a fucking disease... just got inside our heads.'

'Not mine, so much,' said Zita.

'Are you sure?' quizzed Liam.

Zita failed to reply and sucked at her bottom lip. 'He won't anymore.' She grinned widely. 'Trust me.'

'Can I ask what you did in his office?'

'Do you really want to know?'

Liam shrugged and finished his coffee.

'Maybe later,' she said, as she watched the ferry dock at the quayside. She stood and listened to the televised football commentary blasting out of the bar and smiled. She grabbed her backpacks. 'Come on. Let's get back on the ferry, eh?'

Liam tilted his head with a silent question.

'There is extra time,' said Zita. Her smile broadened. 'That is fantastic.'

Liam turned up his nose. 'Is it?'

The celebrations of the drunken crowds inside the bars continued to fill the air as Liam and Zita made their way along the empty street and onto the almost empty ferry except for the same tourists with their children waiting to make their way back to the Playa Blanca terminal in Lanzarote.

During the short journey, Zita dropped the box cutter into the sea and twenty-five minutes later they were once again in the Seat. They both let out heavy sighs as Zita drove back to De Groot's neglected apartment block.

She drove the car close to the left-hand door of the double garage door and stopped. She told Liam where the remote-control button was and as soon as he pressed it the door slowly rose. Zita wound down her window and shouted to him. 'Be careful.'

He wasn't expecting what awaited him inside.

He pulled back in shock, retched violently and vomited as the smell of the Spaniard's body, already decomposing in the heat, hit him. He was overcome by the buzzing cacophony of the thousands of bluebottles vying for their part of the rotting carcass and the female flies as they laid their eggs on the inviting host. Fat beetles scurried under the body and wasps buzzed madly in and out as they fought for their share. Trails of ants made their regimented way back and forth along the bloodied concrete floor between the unexpected feast and their nests.

She drove the car into the garage. They pinched their noses and tried hard to ignore the gruesome feeding frenzy playing out in front of them as they raced to take off their football clothes, grabbed their original clothes from the boot and changed.

Once dressed she opened the storage cupboard, disconnected the racks of gas bottles that supplied the apartments and, with little or no effort, carried them across to the car placing them strategically inside and beneath it.

She opened every pocket of Liam's backpack and took her time to meticulously place their incriminating clothes, forensic overalls and shoe protectors, latex gloves, shorts, jeans, track suits and trainers, the faxed details of the various bank accounts and lastly their football shirts, on the seats and in the matwells, knowing that if they were not totally destroyed and found by Europol they could be traced back to them. She emptied a can of petrol targeting the gas bottles as well as the clothes and seats and then ran a petrol trail to the outside of the garage finishing it with a petrol-soaked cloth.

Liam kicked his hire bike into life and rode part way down the private road and waited.

Zita partially closed the garage door, leaving a small gap beneath it, checked her watch and smiled to herself as she lit the cloth. She watched the burning petrol track beneath the door towards the car before riding away.

She joined Liam and they waited.

Nothing.

Liam looked towards the once luxury apartment block and then back at Zita, silently quizzing her.

She shook her head in disbelief and questioning of her ability. 'Fuck, you,' she said, defensively.

Seconds later there was an almighty explosion as the fuel in the car ignited, the gas bottles exploded one after the other and the flames raced through the open door of the secret staircase, deliberately left open by Zita earlier when she killed De Groot's caretaker, and up into the main building.

Zita twisted the throttle and raced away leaving Liam far behind. In defiance, she let out an almighty banshee yell. 'Yeehah!'

De Groot's property would soon be a burnt-out shell and with the local authorities unable to contact the owner, would be left derelict.

CHAPTER THIRTY-NINE

Go Now

After their initial acceleration, they slowed down and took their time to enjoy their ride back to Arrecife, returned their hired bikes and thanked the proprietor. He was so engrossed in watching the celebrations of the French team who had beaten Italy 2-1, following golden goals, that he thanked them with a blind flourish of the cigarette in his hand.

They walked back onto the cruise ship an hour and a half before their planned departure and, after having their cruise cards checked, Zita guided Liam in silence to their cabin. Once inside they finally released the pent-up frustration and resentment they had for De Groot or his alter ego, Dieter Stange, and made the most passionate love either of them had ever experienced.

While Liam was in the shower Zita checked that the cabin door was locked before tipping the contents of her backpack onto the bed. She took her time to meticulously go through the contents she had removed from De Groot's safe.

She couldn't hide her excitement and shouted out to Liam through the bathroom door. 'Do you realise that bastard did have a totally different name with... with *everything* to back it up.' She held up his driving licence and his passport, then details of his property in St Pauli in Hamburg. She raised her voice excitedly and forced a laugh. 'Do you see what I've discovered?'

Liam was still drying himself when he left the bathroom and scratched at his bristly chin. 'No.'

She continued as she picked her way through the remainder of the contents on the bed. She shot Liam a look of total shock. 'The bastard really has been leading a double life.'

Liam shrugged. 'So?'

There is nothing here that belongs to or identifies him as De Groot.' She paused and grinned. 'Nothing.'

She opened the other pockets and thick wads of money in different currencies fell out. She gave the backpacks a final shake and a photograph fell onto the bed.

She picked it up and stared at it.

She was unable to speak.

'What is it?' asked Liam, curiously.

'Remember you mentioned there were no photographs at De Groot's place?'

'Yeah, course.'

'Have a look at this.'

She passed the photograph to him.

He reluctantly took hold of it, nervous at what he was about to see.

He was stunned into silence.

It was several minutes before he could speak. 'What is *she* doing with *him*?'

Zita pursed her lips and held her breath. She removed a passport from the side pocket, flicked through the stamped pages and passed it to Liam. 'She's been there for a long time.'

Liam finally exploded. 'Fuck!' He shook his head violently and after calming down, he continued. 'Since she left the Love Shack.' His face reddened with rage. 'Back in April... Last fucking year...' He tugged angrily at his wet hair. 'A few days before we opened.'

He paced the cabin kicking out at the beds as he moved around. 'Fuck! Fuck! Fuck!' As the pain in his damaged throat shot through his body, he stopped, grabbed at his throat and exhaled deeply before he was able to speak. 'Why? How?'

Zita stood up and wrapped her arms around him. 'Desperate people do desperate things. Are we any different, Liam?'

He swallowed two painkillers and cleared the pain in his throat, mumbling as he tried to shake the confusion from his head.

'Come on, Liam we're not are we? You know dat.'

He slumped onto the bed, closed his eyes and exhaled heavily.

Zita moved close to him, kissed the back of his neck and traced the scars on his back. He rolled over and propped his head on his arm. She reached across and stroked his bare chest. 'Do you think De Groot may not have destroyed the Love Shack?'

Liam screwed up his face and squinted at her. 'How could he?'

'Easy.'

She shrugged. 'It was just that Ackerman wasn't too sure.'

CHAPTER FORTY

Running With the Night

It was almost six o clock when Keeva drove along the coast with her 1998 Madonna CD *Ray of Light* blasting out on the deserted road.

Life was good. Very good.

She stopped briefly, turned up the music to an almost unbearable level and gazed out across the Atlantic. The sun was still red hot and she pulled her sun hat down to protect her delicate Irish skin and fantasised.

Life was indeed - great.

She and Margarita had had a wonderful and unexpected extended lunch and afternoon drinks at the wonderful Cofradia De Pescadores restaurant. The usually quiet restaurant had been overtaken by the football fans and the drunken euphoria of the final which was further highlighted by the exciting event of the golden goals.

Keeva had drunk too much but was still in control when she left the restaurant. She knew the local police officers and that they, like almost everyone else, would have been watching the exciting Euro final.

She drove into the garage, turned off the alarm and took the lift to the fourth floor and kicked off her shoes as soon as the door opened, removed her sunglasses and hung the car keys in an ornate brass hook beside the door.

She walked into the kitchen, turned on the CD player then walked away. After a few short steps she returned to turn up the volume and let it fill the huge apartment through the speakers hidden in each room. She had bought Frigadellen and kartoffelsalat, Bram's favourite, from the German delicatessen in town and planned for them to eat on the roof terrace and watch the late summer sun go down. She placed the plastic bag on the middle shelf of the huge American fridge before reaching up to the top shelf and letting her fingers dance along the rows of magnums of champagne. She stopped at the fifth bottle and took it out without reading the label - she knew they were all the most expensive vintage, something that was really immaterial to her or even De Groot but he insisted on buying the most expensive whether or not it tasted any better. She unwound the wire and undid the foil. She knelt down and took out two iced champagne flutes. De Groot liked the idea of drinking from iced glasses. After all he had spent a great deal of his time in Germany and had got to enjoy his beer and more recently champagne served in iced glasses. She popped the cork and giggled as she filled both glasses then held one of them in the air and for the umpteenth time that afternoon toasted France for winning the Euros.

Bram hated the heat and always had a sleep in the afternoon. He still found it hard to call it a siesta preferring to refer to it as his afternoon rest.

Keeva sang along with the music as she danced her way towards the bedroom, taking another sip from her glass before placing it on the side table while she turned the handle. She gently pushed open the door with her left foot and called out. 'Hi, darling I'm back.' She faked an apologetic grin. 'Sorry I'm so late.'

Silence.

She giggled. 'Surely, you're not still asleep, darling?' she purred.

A beat.

She now sensed something was wrong - but what?

Nervously she walked into the bedroom and suddenly became apprehensive when she noticed that the curtains were still wide open and De Groot wasn't in the huge bed. She placed the champagne glasses on the ornate table, rushed into the lounge and looked out onto the pool and jacuzzi.

Both were empty.

Her mind raced as her alcohol blurred mind tried to take control.

Something was wrong.

Very wrong.

But what?

She walked out of the lounge, across the landing and up the stairs leading to the roof. She climbed the first of the thirteen steps but when she reached halfway, she winced as the hot tiles burned her feet. She cursed as she rushed back down the stairs and slipped on her designer leather sandals before racing up onto the roof.

When she saw the grotesque red and blue bloated naked body of De Groot, her lover, she stifled a scream.

She was too shocked.

She edged towards him but stopped. She tried to take in the horror but found it surreal. She covered her mouth before retching and choking on the vomit. She coughed and coughed until she was able to breathe and trembled out of control. She grabbed at her hair and tugged it hard until she realised the self-inflicted pain. She stamped on the hot terrazzo tiles until she flipped and broke into a frenzied maniacal laugh. 'Is this for real?' She screamed. 'What the fuck have you done to me?' She moved nearer to the body and looked down at De Groot in disgust. 'You're such a selfish bastard!' She wiped the perspiration from her forehead and walked towards the fountain. She grabbed a handful of the warm water and rubbed it across her face and then scooped up a second handful and threw it over her head. As she shook her head to release the water, she talked to herself. 'Think. Think. What do you do now?'

She gave De Groot's bloated body one more glance and raced down the stairs.

She grabbed two Louis Vuitton designer suitcases from the dressing room and filled them with her most expensive jewellery, favourite clothes, shoes and bags. She flicked the painting and the door slid open. She walked into De Groot's office and soon realised that everything had been taken including her Irish passport. She returned to the bedroom and flicked open the bedside drawer, reached deep inside and took out a handful of De Groot's "pocket" money. She quickly counted it and smiled at the wad of mixed foreign currency equivalent to almost five thousand pounds.

De Groot had bought her a flat in Puerto del Rosario and her own car, a Seat Ibiza Mk 2, when she left Amsterdam and moved to Fuerteventura, a year earlier. She knew that with the money in her hand and what she had managed to steal from him and saved from her very generous monthly allowance, she could survive until she had the baby and then she would decide what to do. She still had the Dutch passport that he had arranged for her before travelling to the island.

For her this was a bitter sweet moment.

In one way she felt relieved that he wouldn't be around when the baby was born.

She threw the cases in the boot of her car, reset the alarm and drove up the private drive and onto the main road. A few kilometres along the coast road she stopped, chose a George Michael CD and pushed it into the player. As the sound of *Careless Whisper* filled the car, she gently rubbed her stomach and sang to herself as she gazed out onto the mysterious horizon.

She had a plan that would change her immediate future.

To have an abortion.

She always had an escape plan but it was much sooner than she had ever expected. She knew that De Groot couldn't escape his violent past forever and that one day someone would eventually come for him.

At seven the next morning the Spanish gardener whistled his way up the rear stairs at the far end of the terrace and took his tools from the shed. He walked slowly across the roof garden checking his favourite shrubs. He looked up and stopped and stared in disbelief at the grotesque sight of the dry blackened blood splattered terrazzo flowers and plants. He moved closer until he saw a mass of dried and twisted bloody entrails of De Groot's mutilated and distorted body spilled over the sun lounger and onto the terrazzo. Although his body would have attempted to control the change in temperature, the extreme heat had caused the gases in his stomach to explode prematurely.

The gardener rushed off and picked up the phone in his shed.

It was dead.

He raced down to his car and, in shock, drove the thirty kilometres to the police station in Corralejo.

CHAPTER FORTY-ONE

Wonderful Tonight

Liam and Zita, walked arm in arm, past the swimming pool and onto the upper deck. He turned to her. 'Do you ever question what you do?' he asked.

Zita replied without having to think. 'Probably not.'

Liam grunted and replied with an extended. 'OK.'

'So, now you have your answer. Come on. Let's go.'

They both stood on the top deck and having killed their hated nemesis they watched as the ship guided by the pilot left the port of Arrecife and pulled slowly away.

Zita turned to Liam. 'Do you think De Groot may not have destroyed the Love Shack?'

Liam squinted and looked through his narrowed eyes at her. 'How could he?'

'Easy.'

Liam leaned on the handrail and looked out to sea. He turned to look at Zita and his concerned face revealed his fear.

'What is it, Liam?'

The photographers were out in force again, snapping everyone, but again they didn't approach them. It confused Liam. 'These photographers are taking pictures of everyone… Everywhere. Again.' He turned to her. 'How come they are avoiding *us*?'

Zita grinned. 'I spoke to them when we came on board and paid them *not* to take photographs.' She giggled. 'Remember, I told Ackerman we are in Berlin...'

Liam tilted his head to one side and closed his eyes while he thought about what she'd said. His face built to a huge smile. 'Yeah.' He nodded slowly. 'Yeah... got it.' He sniggered wryly. 'Yeah, good call.'

They each lay on a bed, Zita read a magazine while Liam fiddled with the remote control and tried in vain to find an English-speaking station.

Zita dropped the magazine on the bedside table, stood and pulled on her leggings and Liam's denim shirt. 'I'll be back in a few minutes. Why don't you have a shower and shave while I'm gone.' She waited for him to respond.

He grunted.

She continued. 'Liam, this evening is very special.'

Reluctantly he slid off the bed, walked into the bathroom, showered and shaved.

Zita returned with two bulging suit covers and hung them in the wardrobe.

When Liam walked out of the bathroom, she ran the back of her hand across his chin and dreamed. 'Smooth and silky - I love it.'

Liam blushed.

Still smiling, she stood. 'Come on. Put on your dressing gown.'

'Wha–?'

'It's alright. I've booked us a massage at the spa–'

'Massage!' He stood back aghast. I've never had one. Aren't they dodgy - for fucking pervs?'

Zita tugged at his hand. 'No. Liam. These are real massages. They are wonderful. Come on. Try it.'

He did and when they returned to the cabin they lay on Zita's bed and enjoyed the most wonderful sex.

Zita finally got up and passed him one of the suit bags.

Liam looked at her and mumbled his tired response. 'What is it?'

'Tonight, it is formal clothes. It's a dinner suit–'

'Where the hell did you get that from?'

She grinned. 'Yours came from one of the singers and mine is from Sylvania, the violinist.'

He cursed even louder.

She continued. 'I will help you when I'm ready. Relax,' she said, softly.

She stood at the bathroom door and watched him as he took his time to remove the hanger holding the jacket and trousers and laid them on the bed. He pulled out the white wing collared shirt.

'No way am I going to wear a fucking monkey suit. I've never worn or dreamed of wearing that - never have and never will!'

She looked at him and pleaded in silence.

It didn't have any effect.

'You will look wonderful in that... Come on,' she pleaded.

She left him and took her suit bag into the bathroom.

Liam picked up the shirt undid the black ceramic buttons and put it on. He then turned to the trousers and struggled to fit the braces. He cursed to himself and threw them onto the bed.

Zita heard him and grinned as shouted from the bathroom. 'Is everything alright, Liam?'

He pulled the trousers on again and after grabbing the braces managed to clip them to the trousers and pull them over his shoulders. He tried to clip the elastic pre-tied bow tie beneath the winged collar but he found it impossible and threw it onto the bed. He picked up the cummerbund and after battling to clip it in the front he managed it and slid it around his waist. He then sat on the bed and put on the black patent shoes.

As the bathroom door opened Liam sighed with relief. But when he saw Zita step into the room he pulled back in astonishment, shell-shocked and unable to speak.

She wore a body clipping red satin and lace dress and red high heeled shoes. Her shoulder length hair had been curled and she wore eye liner and eye shadow. Her alluring lips were emphasised with deep purple metallic lipstick.

'What is the matter, Liam?' asked Zita.

'You are so beautiful...' His voice tailed off and he held his breath and took his time to admire her. He saw her looking like this for the very first time. 'Beautiful...' he repeated.

He blushed as she stood back and looked at him.

He looked back at her.

She leaned over and kissed him gently on the cheek.

He pulled her close to him and spoke as he exhaled. 'Wow. You look fantastic.' He gazed at her again. 'Absolutely beautiful,' he said, romanticising.

She giggled while she helped him to adjust his bow tie and straighten up his braces, adjust his cummerbund and his jacket, and all the while he found it harder and harder to keep his hands off of his new look lover.

After rearranging his hair, she stood back, turned him to face the full-length mirror, stood beside him and they both gazed into it.

'We are a handsome couple, ja?'

Liam blushed. He had never seen himself look like that and as he gazed into the mirror, he shook his head. 'Fuck...' he said softly. 'Yes, we fucking are.'

She tugged at his arm. 'Come, young sir. Would you take me to dinner?'

She stopped at the door. 'I forgot something I bought for you.'

'What?'

She reached into the drawer took out a small bag and opened the small bottle of aftershave.

Liam pulled back.

He had never worn aftershave.'

She reached across and he pulled back. 'Just a little, Liam. It is a very special occasion.'

He tilted his head forward and grimaced as she dabbed it on his chin and cheeks.

'Now we *are* ready for dinner. Yeas?'

Heads turned as they walked into the restaurant and Liam noticed that the waiters and many of the husbands ogled Zita. For the second time in his life he experienced jealousy. Zita felt him put his arm tightly around her and smiled a knowing smile.

Over dinner and much to the annoyance of their wives, most of the husbands were raving about the Euro final and the golden goals. Zita and Liam chose to nod and smile when spoken to but otherwise they enjoyed the food, gazed into each other's eyes and grinned giddily.

After their celebratory dinner they walked out onto the deck and past the ship's pool which was covered, for safety, with a tightened net. The starry sky and the warm summer air were perfect and the soft jazz music drifted across the open deck from the ceiling speakers.

Liam looked up at the moonless sky and the blanket of stars. 'Is this for real?'

Zita grinned back at him. 'Oh, yes, it is,' she said, before kissing his cheek. 'Isn't it wonderful?'

He nodded. 'Yeah, I just can't...' he said softly. 'I can't believe I've never experienced anything like this?' He continued. 'I was always drunk. You know I have missed so much.' He sighed. 'Simple, but unbelievable things.' He looked towards the starry sky. 'Beautiful things... that were there all the time.' He shook his head wildly. Fuck. I have been such an idiot. Wasting my life!'

She placed her arms around his neck. 'Shall we dance?' asked Zita softly.

'I can't dance.'

'Have you ever tried?'

'No. I've never needed to.'

She moved close to him, pulled his arms around her narrow waist and gently shuffled him across the deck.

Zita kissed him and held him tight. 'You know I asked you earlier what was wrong?'

'Yeah.'

'So?'

He shook his head and covered his face with his open hands and spoke through his fingers. 'What the hell are we going to do with the rest of our lives?'

'That is good that you say that. You mustn't worry about the past. That is gone. It's over. Now we worry about the future.'

'So, what are we going to do?'

She reached out and lowered his hands. 'Do you want me to be honest?'

His whole body shuddered. 'Yeah, of course.'

'I don't know, Liam. I really don't.' She sighed. 'What do you want to do, eh?'

He didn't reply.

When they arrived back in the cabin there were two towel animals hanging from the curtain rail: a monkey and sheep peering at them.

Zita grabbed the monkey and threw it playfully at Liam.

She looked at him and tilted her head. 'So, tell me, sir. How did it feel to be a gentleman?'

He grinned. 'I liked it. I never felt like that before.'

She giggled. 'So did I.' She pointed her finger and flicked his bow tie. 'We will do this once more before we arrive back in Hamburg.

He took a second to think. 'OK. I know what you want me to say.' He paused and waited and grinned at her. 'I can't wait.'

'Come on we need to put this on hangers and get it the back to the owners,' she said.

The early morning sun reflecting on the sea shone through portholes, filling their cabin and creating ever changing shapes as it raked across the cabin ceiling.

There was a light tap on the door.

Zita took her time to walk towards it and apprehensively she partially opened it to reveal the same smiling female steward carrying a tray. 'Breakfast,' she said, with yet another smile.

Liam lay in bed and thought. 'That Pito has it easy, don't he?'

Zita shook her head. 'He works sixteen hours a day so deserves some time to sleep.'

She buttered the toast, poured Liam's tea and her coffee, and they sat up in his bed giggling to each other.

'This is very nice, yeas?'

Liam grunted with pleasure.

When they'd finished Zita placed everything back on the tray and put it outside the cabin and closed the door. She sat at the dressing table and brushed her hair.

Liam knelt on his bed and looked out of the porthole towards the distant horizon and the never-ending sparkling sea. 'Zita, come and look at this,' he said, unable to control his excitement.

'What?'

'The sea shine.'

Zita stopped brushing her hair. 'Liam, how did you remember that?'

Liam grinned at her. 'It was the first thing I heard you say when we arrived in Lanzarote last year.'

Liam returned to the porthole and spoke without turning around. 'You know... this is the nearest we will ever get to riding on a magic carpet.'

She laid the hairbrush on the dressing table, tilted her head towards him and waited inquisitively.

He continued. 'You know... We go to sleep... And wake up... in another place - another country.'

'Yes. I never understood it like that. But you are correct.'

She smiled to herself, flicked her hair and walked towards the wardrobe.

She held Liam's denim shirt up against her perfect naked body. 'Shall I wear this today?'

He smiled at her. 'Yeah. I like you in *my* shirts.'

CHAPTER FORTY-TWO

River Deep Mountain High

While Zita spent her daily two-hour session in the gym Liam stood on deck and watched as the ship made its way slowly up the Tagus River. He wiped the early morning dew from the ship's rail with his sleeve and leaned on it. While he waited for the ship to tie up at the Lisbon cruise terminal in the historical district of Alfama he watched in awe as the crane swung out over the quayside and above the cargo ship. They clamped giant claws to each end of the huge container lifting it with such ease and loading it directly onto the back of nearest queuing lorry.

Lisbon, the capital of Portugal, was a beautiful coastal city, as well as being breath-taking with its World Heritage Listed monasteries, exquisite Moorish castles and medieval towers. There had been a massive earthquake on the 1st November 1755 which decimated the city and demolished more than ten thousand houses. It was also All Saints Day and many people were in the churches which were unable to withstand the earthquake and consequently more than sixty thousand inhabitants died. The quake was followed by a tsunami which wreaked even more damage and caused more deaths.

While they were waiting to go ashore, Liam and Zita leaned on the handrail and watched as a group of German passengers rode off on the ship's logoed bikes.

Liam cussed and pointed to the quayside, 'Look at that lot. Only Germans would do that.'

Zita gave him a look of indifference and grabbed at his arm. 'Come *on*... let's *go*.'

They left the ship and ran the gauntlet between the waiting taxi drivers, and owners of brightly coloured tuk tuks, all touting for business and row upon row of tour coaches parked in the terminal car park waiting for the passengers who were booked on guided tours.

They crossed the busy dual carriageway and forced their way through the bustling crowds of passengers heading in and out of the Santa Apolónia Railway Terminus, the oldest railway station in Portugal, built in 1865. To the left of the railway station and just a few metres away was the Militar de Lisboa. With a huge collection of artillery and war-related artefacts which included guns, pistols and swords. The building also had rich Baroque decoration and ceilings with 18th century paintings on military themes and battle scenes and tiled panels, highlighting the most historic battles since the Christian Reconquest period and up to World War One.

Although Zita could feel Liam pulling her in that direction, she guided him towards the Farol café.

'Why are we stopping here?' he asked.

'The coffee in this café is the best?' said Zita, with a beaming smile. She pointed at the only free table on the edge of the pavement, sheltered from the sun by a large colourful umbrella.

Liam sat down while she went inside to order.

The few minutes later the waiter brought their drinks and pastel de nata.

Zita looked up and spoke in perfect Portuguese. 'Obligado,' she said.

Liam sipped at coffee and grinned. 'Yeah, you are right... But... I do prefer tea.' He picked up one of the cakes and peered at it. 'What are they?' he asked.

'Portuguese custard tarts, made with crisp pastry.' She goaded him. 'Go on, try it, they are delicious.'

He took a tiny bite and then chomped at it.' He grinned as he finished the last piece. 'Great,' he said.

Having demolished the first tart, he looked enviously at Zita's. She smiled at him. 'It's okay, you can have mine too. She grinned at him. 'I bought them for you,' she said.

Liam picked it up and ate it in two bites.

He sat back and scrutinised the thronging travellers, with backpacks and cases, who had all migrated towards the same café and were milling around them looking for a seat. 'Do you wonder who they are and where they are going?' he asked.

Zita nodded and briefly closed her eyes before speaking. 'Often,' she said, 'it was *my* work.' She grinned and continued. 'I can tell you about them in a few seconds.'

Liam screwed up his face. 'How?'

Zita signalled to Liam and lowered her hand beneath the table and pointed towards a young couple with brightly coloured suitcases. She grinned to Liam. 'They are French and travelling to Madeira on the ferry - two and half hours from Lisboa.'

Liam was clearly stunned.

Zita giggled. 'It's easy...' She pointed at their luggage labels. 'Look at the labels... They are for the ferry.'

He moved his head until he could see them.

'Okay. So... how?'

'They are ferry labels and have details printed in French. They leave here for Madeira.' She giggled. 'So, you can see why it was–'

An elderly man with a walking stick hobbled uncertainly past them. He slipped on the uneven wet white and black mosaic tiles and fell heavily.

Zita stopped speaking.

She jumped up her metal chair legs grating on the pavement as she rushed to join him. She pulled a red check cloth from the nearest table, rolled up his trousers and wiped at the bleeding gashes on his leg. She helped him to her chair and sat him down. She waved to the waiter who was clearing a table and fired instructions to him. He returned with glass, a jug of water and two towels. She poured some of the water from the jug over the gashes and after checking that the towels were clean, she wrapped one of them around the damaged leg and before turning her attention to his head wounds. She took her time to bathe them with the second towel and wrapped it around his head.

The 734 bus to Santa Maria Hospital made one of its scheduled stops outside the station. When Zita saw it pull up, she helped the injured man onto the bus, told the driver what had happened and handed him the man's walking stick.

Liam had felt totally helpless and could only sit and watch until the bus pulled away and Zita returned to their table.

Almost immediately, a young boy came out of the café with a mop and bucket and slopped soapy water over the blood-stained terrazzo paving. He was followed seconds later by the owner carrying a tray. He spoke to Zita. 'Thers são para você - em casa.'

The manager removed the empty cups and plates and replaced them with drinks and two more custard tarts.

Liam looked on in astonishment.

'Muito obrigado,' she said, nodding her appreciation. Zita grinned at Liam and pointed to the custard tarts. 'Go on,' she mouthed.'

269

While Liam demolished the custard tarts Zita walked into the café past rows of tables covered with red and white check cotton clothes occupied by excited people of all ages. Halfway up the left-hand wall were shelves displaying aged bottles of port and wine stored behind sealed glass panels.

Zita picked up the receiver and called Detective Ackerman's office in Amsterdam.

It was picked up before the second ring. '*Ribeker.*'

'Hello. It's Zita. Good to hear your voice, Andrea,' she said brightly. 'How are you?'

'A lot better now, thanks. Light duties - answering the phone,' she said, with a gentle laugh. She continued. 'So, Ackerman told me you were in Berlin.' She looked across her desk at Piet Ackerman, pointed at the handset and mouthed Zita's name. 'How is it?'

'Fine. We love it.'

'Really,' she said. She paused and tried to stifle a yawn. 'Maybe I'll visit one day.'

'You must.'

'Um.'

'Any news?'

'Well. We have and we haven't.'

A beat.

'Well nothing conclusive but we believe we now know who arranged for the fi...' Her voice faded as she remembered that fateful night. She took a huge breath and continued. 'That dreadful night of the fire and the destruction of the Love Shack.' She shook briefly and paused. 'Wasn't it terrible?' she said, her voice quivering as she tried to clear the horrific memories from her head.

Zita sighed she remembered it all so vividly. 'Yeah… terrible,' she said. She caught her breath and continued. 'De Groot,' she gushed

'No!' The detective shook her head to her invisible caller. 'That's what we all thought.' She exhaled slowly. 'In fact, we were sure it was him.' She paused to take a shuddering breath. 'But–'

'But, what?'

Ribeker grinned into the receiver and after checking herself continued in a stern voice. 'If I told you it wasn't De Groot would you have any idea who it might have been?'

'Come on, Ribeker. Cut the crap and just tell me!'

'Everything points to the cage fighter–'

'Toto?' Zita looked blindly around in disbelief. 'That bastard,' she cursed. 'I knew that they hated each other and he had his sights on De Groot's empire but not that soon.'

Ribeker continued. 'But do you know what?'

'What else?'

Detective Ackerman reached across the desk and took the phone from her. 'Hi Zita.'

'Hello, Piet.'

'De Groot was murdered in Fuerteventura.' He took a deep breath. 'And pretty gruesome at that... I've seen the pictures...'He paused and took another breath and then spoke as he exhaled. 'Horrific... blood and guts everywhere.' He sucked air. 'Even by Mokum's standards.'

Zita feigned shock. 'Go on...'

'Of course, any of his *many* enemies could have done it.'

He remembered the photographs of his bloated and sunburned body on the sun lounger. He shook his head with revulsion and continued.

Ackerman continued. 'But not in that way,' he said, taking yet another deep breath. 'It's not been confirmed officially but we believe it was the Georgian.'

'Ah.'

'And do you know De Groot was also known as Herr Dieter Stange, a German... supposedly born in Hamburg.'

271

'What?'

The Detective sucked at his lip. 'All I can say is he had it coming to him–'

'I suppose he did.' Zita paused. 'Have the police on the island caught anyone?'

'No... But whoever did it planned it with military precision. Just like a court martial sentencing a convicted murderer to a torturous death.'

'Really... Do you have any idea who could have done it?'

'All I can say is that now we're all looking for the Georgian.'

'Everyone?'

'Yes, Europol are on it too.' He paused and Zita could hear him talking to someone else in her office. He returned to the phone. 'Sorry about that.'

'That's OK. I'm sure you're really busy with this one.'

'Yes, we are.'

Ackerman continued. 'As I said it was planned. I mean.' He extended the next word. 'W... e... e... ll planned.'

Zita wanted to know more about De Groot's double life. 'So, how did you find about this... Dieter? And De Groot?'

'Well we have some developments–'

'Developments. Like what?'

Ackerman raised his voice, the excitement clear as he continued. 'There was a problem a little way from Centraal Station and it was necessary to remove the railway track and excavate into the arches beneath it.'

'Okay,' she said, guardedly.

'Guess what they found?'

'I've no idea.'

'A secret chamber!'

'What?'

Ackerman couldn't hide his excitement. 'They called me to have a look and we discovered De Groot's secret bolt hole... And...' He took a deep breath. 'And fitted out with everything! It was like an air raid shelter! Food, bed and a shower... He had everything he needed to live down there for weeks on end.'

Zita paused to catch her breath as she remembered the electronic key she had taken from De Groot's office in Fuerteventura.

'And... *two* cars! One of them was the one we always see him in.' He paused. 'Sorry, I mean we saw him in. And... and strangely we found De Groot's passport, driving licence and his papers hidden in a secret compartment in the boot.' He lit a cigarette and slowly expelled the smoke before picking up his now cold coffee and spitting it out.

Ribeker reached across the desk and took his mug off of him and made her way to the kitchen.

Ackerman continued. 'The second car was a Mercedes with Hamburg plates registered in the German name of Dieter Strange... at an address in St Pauli, the Red-Light district.' He coughed a deep chesty cough. 'That's how we traced him. It seems he led a double life–'

'What?'

'Yes, he regularly commuted to Hamburg and took on the persona of Dieter Stange.'

'What? But how could that be?'

'Well, he's been doing it for such a long time that no one has noticed. Apparently, he's been living there for more the fifteen years and...' He laughed. 'And even paid his taxes.' He paused. 'He never put a foot wrong not even a parking or speeding ticket. Everything about him was clean as hell.' Ackerman laughed loudly. He stifled a yawn and continued. 'Mind you De Groot did serve six years in Untersuchungshaftanstalt prison, in Hamburg, before moving back to Amsterdam and building his filthy empire. So perhaps he planned it as far back as that.'

'But how could he keep that a secret for so long?' asked Zita.

'No one in Hamburg was ever aware. They said he was an upstanding member of the community.' Ackerman could hear that Zita was totally shocked at what he was telling her. He continued. 'If Toto did kill him on that island... then we'll find the bastard. It's only a matter of time.'

'Really?'

'Well that is unless someone else gets to him first.'

'Oh, yeah.' She could sense his excitement and smiled. 'You remember him–?'

'Toto? Course I do. Andrea told me.' She sighed. 'How could I forget him?'

'Well...'

He paused a beat.

'Remember I told you a Russian attacked him in Hamburg...' He took one last extended drag of the cigarette end before stubbing it out in an already overflowing ash tray. He continued. 'Tried to kill him.'

'Right,'

'He's still in hospital but we know everything about him now.' The Detective sniggered. 'It was a professional hit.' He cleared his throat. 'Well, as I said - he tried.'

'Off the record, we're not too bothered who called it but I reckon De Groot was behind it–'

'But Andrea said you'd found him in the Canaries?'

'Um.' He forced a laugh. 'I'm keeping an open mind. Until I get cast iron confirmation it was really him, we'll keep looking.' He sniggered. 'Who knows after the Hamburg debacle he could still be alive.' Zita heard him strike a match and light another cigarette. He took a couple of drags and continued. 'All we have is the report that the bastard took a flight to Madeira on New Year's Eve–'

Zita faked shock.

The detective continued. 'Then...' He shook his head. 'He disappeared into thin air.'

Zita laughed. 'If it wasn't him on the island, you'll find him. His ego is too big to want to hide forever.'

'Erm. Yeah, I agree with that.'

'OK. But assuming it was him in Madeira, how the hell could he just disappear?' asked Zita, with a question to which she already knew the answer.

'Maybe by the time you get back we'll know.'

Zita tapped her fingers on the receiver. 'Sorry I have to go. We're off to visit the zoo. We'll see you when we get back.'

'Enjoy it.'

'Thanks.'

'Bye.'

Zita replaced the handset, cleared the number and walked back to their table. She sat down and exhaled before speaking. 'Liam... we've killed the wrong man,' she said, faking concern.

'What?' he asked, with a loud puzzled laugh.

'Ackerman reckons it was Toto...' Liam squinted at her. 'You know... Toto, the cage fighter... they reckon he arranged the fire.' She paused. 'Remember he said they saw him on TV... watching the fire.'

Liam shook his head and sniggered loudly in disbelief. 'How can you say we've killed the wrong man?' He slowly scratched his chin while he tried to reconcile what she had just said. 'De Groot was a real bastard and the world's well rid of him. Everybody is.'

'Yeah. I agree with that.'

Liam reflected. 'So it was Toto, that fucking midget?

'Yep.'

'So, what now?'

She checked her watch. 'We have two more hours. Let's explore.'

As they left the Farol café, they passed an elderly woman who was filling a plastic bottle from a tap on three-metre-high ornate fountain in the centre of the wide pavement.

Zita took her time to read the large defaced sign above it and translated it to Liam. 'It says that it is for human and animals.' They both shook their heads before getting onto a tuk tuk.

Ten minutes later it shuddered to a halt outside the Restaurant A Valenciana, in Rua Marquês de Fronteira. She paid the driver and guided Liam inside. The restaurant was virtually unknown to tourists and was packed with local people who enjoyed its speciality chicken piri piri, the most popular dish in Lisboa. The waiter smiled as he showed them to their table and handed them both a food and drinks menu. Zita grabbed at Liam's and immediately gave them back to the waiter. Without looking at her menu she ordered their meal with two bottles of water, one sparkling and one still. They were served in less than ten minutes with side dishes of crispy French fries and a fresh salad of lettuce, tomato and onion which provided the perfect complement.

Their food was wonderful and left Liam drooling.

Trams clattered noisily past them as they walked along the wide pavements lined with trees laden with oranges. Liam reached up and picked one and rolled it in his hand. 'Why the hell don't people pick these?'

'An orange tree with a distorted figure eight leaf is sour and tastes very bad.' She pulled off a leaf and showed him. 'They don't eat that. They are grown for decoration at the side of paths and roads all over Europe.' She looked around before reaching up and after checking the leaves of several trees picked an orange. 'Single oval leaf is good.' She peeled it and passed a segment to him. 'Taste that.'

Zita pushed a segment into her mouth and screwed up her face in disgust. 'These are not the best oranges but it is a little better than yours,' she said, as she spat it out. 'When I was in a kibbutz,' she faltered. 'Sorry. A kibbutz is where we work and grow fruit and vegetables and share everything. At the beginning it was for Jews, and not gentiles.' Having suddenly realised what she'd said she lowered her head in embarrassment. 'I'm sorry, Liam,' she said softly 'But it is not like that now... Anyone can come and work on them.' She smiled at him waiting for his forgiveness.

He shrugged his shoulders with indifference. 'Who gives a fuck? I don't know what it means anyway.'

She took his arm and they sat on a seat sheltered from the hot afternoon sun. She smiled and whispered. 'Sorry. I really am so sorry.' She flicked the rest of the orange into a waste bin and continued. 'I lived and worked in Beit She'an Valley, the valley of the springs and warm weather even in the winter. We grew oranges and they are the best in the world.' She closed her eyes and imagined it. 'We have natural springs and...' She turned to him and her face beamed with sheer pleasure 'Fantastic food and fruit.' She smiled with pride. 'Do you know the Jaffa orange?

He shook his head.

'I believe you have eaten them, many times.' She paused. 'From Israel... Not Palestine?'

He shrugged.

Zita's mood darkened. 'A few months after I was there... something strange happened–'

'What?'

'Well, I was at the kibbutz picking avocados when the estate manager called my name over the tannoy. She asked me to go to the office.' She paused, as she remembered that

277

morning. 'When I got into the office two women were standing there. They looked scary... *Very scary.*' She grimaced and her body stiffened, remembering the fear she felt at that time. 'I thought I had done something... very... very wrong. But then one of them smiled and asked me my name. I was confused. I looked at the manager and told her she had just called my name. After looking at each of the women in turn... the manager nodded and gave me a false smile.' Zita became animated and spoke quickly. 'You know when someone doesn't mean it but still tries to do it?'

Liam grunted. 'I've seen enough of that.'

'Well, they told me I was leaving... I couldn't believe it. Where were they taking me? I was only seventeen - seventeen! They didn't say a word. I told them I needed to get my things... mind you I only had a small bag. The manager grunted and pointed to my bag that was already packed on a chair beside her desk. They put a black bag over my head and pushed me into a... a... vehicle. I think it was a car but I'm not sure.'

'Fuck.'

'When they took it off me, I was in a bare unpainted room with a desk and two chairs and armed women standing at each side of the door. They pushed me into one chair and a woman in uniform walked in carrying a folder. She slammed it on the desk and said nothing. She sat in front of me and just glared at me for ages. Then she opened the folder and asked me everything about myself. She even knew my mother had been *raped* in Berlin. I was so frightened. I asked them why I was there. She gave me a terrible look.' Zita breathed raggedly. 'She asked me everything about myself - every detail: the names of my friends in Germany and at the kibbutz and then after interrogating me for hours–'

Liam gasped. 'Wha...?'

Zita continued. 'Then I had to take a polygraph test–'

278

'What?'

'A lie detector test, we all have to do it - sometimes every year,' she said. 'After that the women closed the file, picked it up and left.'

'Fuck. That is heavy duty shit, Zita.'

Zita nodded. 'It was.' She bit her bottom lip. 'A few minutes later two women soldiers came for me and took me to a small cell with a bed, table, toilet and basin to wash.' She grinned at Liam. 'They didn't lock the door and... I was given food and coffee.' She licked her lips. 'Nice coffee.'

'So?'

'The next morning, they came for me and, Noa, a girl who was probably the same age as me took me to a dormitory and showed me my bed. She explained that I was at a very special training camp; the Medrasha near the town of Herzliya, for HaMossad leModi'in uleTafkidim Meyuḥadim - The Mossad,' she said softly.'

'Fuck.'

'We were all given code names and only using real names on a "need to know basis."'

'What was your name?'

'Sorry, I can never tell that to you.'

She anticipated his disappointed reaction and tilted her head to one side. 'I'm sure you do understand.'

Liam nodded. 'Yeah. Course I do.' He reflected and continued. 'So, do you consider yourself to be Jewish?'

She smiled. 'Sometimes.'

Liam stared at her and waited.

'So, where is home to you?'

She shook her head. 'Nowhere,' she said, curtly. She briefly looked away from him and continued wistfully. 'They trained us for months, teaching us to read and speak languages; as many as we could.' She grinned at Liam. 'I learned six.'

'Um.' He chuckled wryly. 'Six. Is that all?'

She ignored his condescending manner. 'The exercise regime was gruelling. They said it was harder than *your* SAS.'

Liam screwed up his eyes and squinted. 'Don't ask me anything.' He shook his head. 'I don't have any fucking idea.'

She continued. 'They taught us how to shoot, break down and clean a rifle and hand gun, survival, close combat, martial arts and...' She looked directly into Liam's eyes. 'Torture... and... to *kill*,' she said, savouring the last word.

'Fuck. So that's how you—'

'Yes. It was.' She swallowed hard. 'Each day there were less of us until one day there were only two left.' She smiled. 'They chose, Noa.' She took a huge breath. 'She was very pretty and...' She paused and her face flashed the widest possible grin. 'And then... they chose...' She nodded tersely and screeched. 'Me!'

Liam lowered his head and reached into his pocket for his daily cigarette but instead of lighting it held it in his hand.

'After that, I travelled around the world as a key asset for them.'

'So that's how you know all these places?'

'Of course, it is.'

'Were you never worried about getting shot?'

She laughed and tapped the table twice. 'Do you know what?'

Liam grunted. 'What?'

'They told me that if I heard the shot it wasn't meant for me.'

CHAPTER FORTY-THREE

How Can You Mend a Broken Heart?

They both left the ship at the Southampton cruise terminal and walked to the nearest telephone boxes.

Zita made several calls while Liam phoned his father.

He tapped impatiently on the glass while he waited for someone to answer.

'Hello... Who is it?'

'It's me, Liam–'

'Why are you phoning now?' His father raised his voice to a scream. 'You've got a fuckin' nerve phoning me after all this time–'

'Didn't you get the money?'

'Yeah...,' his father said, tersely. 'Do you think that makes fings alright?' He paused. 'Money don't solve anyfing.'

'Well...' Liam took a huge breath. 'I did what I could–'

'Well it's not fuckin'... *good enough.*' His father sniffed and sighed heavily.

Liam briefly fought back his emotions until he broke down and wiped at his tear-filled eyes with his sleeve. 'Look, Dad, it's been bloody hard. Don't you remember the fire?'

'Who gives a fuck about a fire...? You certainly don't. You've ruined this family. Do you know that?' He squeezed the handset and shook it in anger and tried to choke it. 'Your mother's got fucking dementia. Her brain's gone to mush. She don't know what the fuck is going on from one minute to the next.' He took a huge gulp of air. 'Almost set fire to the house - left the bloody gas cooker on...' He picked at the stubble on his chin. 'Most of the time she don't recognise any of us...'

A beat.

'Don't you understand? Your mother is nothing more than an empty... living shell.'

Liam choked back the numbness and collected his thoughts. 'What about Kath... and the kids?'

'Ugh. They've moved on... Better off without you. Michelle and Sally, they're doing really well... and Harry... I don't know where they got it from - *not you* anyway - but they may make something of 'emselves.' He sniffed. 'Kath is happy now.' He thought hard before continuing. 'Got a new fella and its working out–'

'Fuck,' said Liam, kicking out at the floor as he found it hard to take in so much guilt.

'I know you, son. You're trouble - a fucking jinx on this family. Always have been.' He let out a huge sigh. 'Do yerself a favour and keep the fuck away.'

Zita tapped on the door and without looking directly at him, covered her head and signalled that she would meet him back on board.

Liam made a pathetic attempt to acknowledge her and, as she raced away, he made to punch the glass but thought better of it and instead took his time to stare blindly at the heavy rain lashing the almost deserted quayside. 'How's Tommy?'

'He DIED–'

'DIED! What the fuck!' He broke down and let out a bloodcurdling scream that reverberated around the inside of the phone box. 'Tommy's... DEAD?'

While he tried to massage away the pain in his throat, he heard his father take a lengthy shuddering breath, before continuing in almost a whisper. 'Suicide.'

'What?'

'Months ago, now...' He sniffed hard, wiped at his watering eyes and tried to clear his head by shaking it from side to side. 'You're such a bastard; you know you broke your brother's heart.' He sniffed. 'He *adored* you and *you–*'

'Me?'

'*Yeah*. You let him down–'

'So, why are you blaming me?' Liam tilted his head back and waited for an answer.

'The last time y*o*u phoned... you cut 'im off... You shut out the only one who worshipped you!' He paused. 'Fuck knows why?' He swallowed hard. 'You didn't say more than a few words.' His father tried to control himself. 'That's why.'

'Yeah, but–'

'Yeah, but what? Don't you see? You fucked us all over. Me... Your mother... poor Tommy... Kath and them kids.' His father paused for a moment. 'And, now I've got fucking prostate cancer!'

Liam sucked in the shock and breathed raggedly.

His father continued. 'Did you fink sending that fucking money... would be enough?' His father punched the air with his huge fist. 'You must have *shite* for brains!'

Liam shook his head and wiped at the tears as the stark realisation began to sink in at how serious his drunken actions had been and the repercussions that had now caused so much destruction to the whole of his family.

For the first time during the conversation his father felt some remorse and continued. 'So, where the fuck are you this time?'

Liam looked around him at the tourists leaving the terminal for their excursions and running towards the coaches as they tried to avoid the rain. He shook his head. 'I've no idea where I am,' he slurred.

'Son, can I give you some advice? And make sure you take it in and... Act on it!'

Liam began to breathe erratically.

'Don't come the fuck...' He stuttered with a combination of emotion and anger until he could hold back no longer. 'We don't want you back 'ere! We can all manage without ya!' He paused and continued in a more restrained voice. 'Well... it's too fuckin' late for Tommy and... and... and your mother.' He coughed. 'Maybe me too...'

Liam dropped the phone. He didn't hear his father as he continued to release his pent-up anger ending with four tough words that he had been wanting to say but couldn't. He finally shouted them into the receiver. 'DON'T PHONE US AGAIN!' He wasn't sure if Liam had heard them. Part of him hoped that he hadn't but it was already too late to change anything.

Liam, his back hunched and shoulders slumped, walked out into the grey afternoon, his tears masked by the torrential rain.

Zita watched with apprehension from the deck as Liam, the downpour hiding the torrent of tears, ambled blindly towards the ship.

She cried too.

CHAPTER FORTY-FOUR

Kiss Me in the Rain

As the ship slowly pulled away from the quayside Liam and Zita stood on the windswept top deck and ignored the rain beating down on them. Instead, they both looked back at the grey city of Southampton as the lightning flashed across the sky and the thunder rolled overhead.

Zita knew Liam was battling with his conscience and carefully chose her words. 'Did you want to go back?' she asked.

He wiped at his tears and tried to choke back his despair. 'What is there for me to go back to... now?' He slumped forward and leaned heavily on the handrail and looked into the distance through his tears as the city slowly dissolved in the mist and heavy dark clouds.

Zita wrapped her arms around him and kissed him softly on his neck. As the torrential rain continued to soak them through there was another deafening crash of thunder.

Neither of them noticed.

She reached up and whispered into his ear. 'I've lost you, haven't I?'

Liam, overwhelmed by what his father had said to him, ignored her.

He pushed her forcefully away and stormed off.

He crossed the deck fighting the ferocious wind and stumbled awkwardly down the open staircase, gushing with deep water, and into the nearest bar.

It was deserted.

He ordered a double whisky but as he put the glass to his lips Zita reached out gently pulled his arm down and took the glass from him.

Liam broke and sobbed uncontrollably. 'HELP ME!' He took a few seconds to catch his breath and continued in a voice more strained than usual. 'Help me... help me *please*.'

She placed the glass on the bar, nodded to the barman, and walked Liam to a deserted sheltered area on deck. She held him firmly in her arms and hugged him while he sobbed out of control. 'Close your eyes, Liam.'

He ignored her.'

She whispered. 'Please.'

As he closed them, he shuddered and breathed raggedly, wiping at his running nose with the sleeve of his already sodden jacket. He looked at her through his wretched bloodshot eyes and released a distorted childlike grin.

'You are now living your worst nightmare, aren't you, Liam?'

He nodded soulfully.

'I will help you...'

He sniffed hard.

'If you really want me to.'

He mumbled an incoherent reply.

'Liam, do you?'

He replied in a pained and fading voice. 'Yes... Help me... Plea... ease.'

'I will,' she said, softly. She put her arm around his shoulder and guided him inside.

Liam managed a strained breath. 'I don't know if I want to go *back* to my old world... and ways...' He wiped away the last of the tears. 'I've seen too much with you.'

Zita gently touched his shoulder. 'What about your family?'

He sniffed. 'Everything and everyone is fucked!'

'Is it really so bad?'

'Oh, yeah. It is...' As he looked across at her his face changed and broke into a venomous stare. He spat into the air. 'And Tommy... my young brother... Died–'

'What–?'

'The poor sod committed suicide,' he said, as he shook his head violently.

'Liam, I am so sorry...' *She held back her tears as she remembered helping Liam to get Tommy to hospital after taking bad drugs when he was the roadie with a rock band playing in Amsterdam a year earlier.*

'I can't believe it.' He stamped his feet. 'I let him down.' He struggled to breathe. 'Everything is my fucking fault.'

'Liam... Liam, listen to me... You didn't.'

He ignored her.

He trembled and sobbed uncontrollably. 'They're better off without me,' he said, his weak voice breaking. 'My father said I was poisoning my family. Can you believe that?' He looked at Zita for an answer.

She didn't reply. Instead she offered him a soft caring smile.

He didn't see it through his tears. 'Me... poisoning them!'

'What?'

'Yeah, I know. It's unreal.' He looked at her, his obvious confusion visible on his tortured face. 'Can you believe it?' he said, shaking his head.

She wouldn't reply.

'My own father said that…' He shrugged and wiped at his new tears. 'I don't care what *he* says. Fuck 'im. I'm gonna *send it* anyway.' He shook briefly before his whole body stiffened. He continued. 'I just don't understand it. Tommy… my brother… dead!' He pounded his chest.

Zita, unable to give any helpful advice, covered her mouth and pinched hard at her lips.

'Why the fuck did he go and do that?'

She sucked at her lips, held him tight and rubbed his shoulder. 'We cannot be responsible for everyone, Liam.'

He grunted.

Zita continued. 'We all have choices.' She looked around as she took a deep breath. 'You don't know what else was going on in his life.' She looked into his pitiful red and swollen eyes. 'Do you?'

He sniffed hard.

'You know, Liam… sometimes it is good to consider yourself,' she said, firmly.

'Is it?'

'*Yes*, it is.'

He sniffed again. 'But, Tommy… Why?'

'You cannot blame yourself for everything that happens to others in your life.' She reconsidered and coughed. 'We all do things we may sometimes regret but it is *your* life too.' She sighed. 'Please remember dat.'

'So, am I to blame?'

'You have been away a long time now – more than a year. Yes?'

He sniffed and nodded slowly in agreement.

'I said that you didn't know what else was happening to Tommy… in his life. Right?'

'Yeah.'

'So what happened is *not your* fault.'

He sighed heavily.

'Liam, you must still send the money home to your family.'

'What–'

'Would your father tell you if he had problems with money?'

He sniffed forcefully. 'But he said he didn't want me to send anything...' He coughed. 'Ever again.'

'Um.' She paused and took a breath. 'I'm sure your father is a proud man.' She nodded slowly before she continued sympathetically. 'But he is getting older.'

Liam grunted.

'And I'm sure his many times in prison have taken his energy. And... and despite what he said to you...' She turned Liam's head and looked directly into Liam's eyes. 'They may need it.'

'Really?'

'Yes.'

He gazed at her and slowly understood her reasoning.

'You can do that... or...?' She tilted her head and let a gentle smile cross her face. 'Or...?'

He looked at her expectantly and waited for her to continue.

'Or... You can go back... and take it with you,' she said supportively.

He forced a smile.

'Do you want to do that, Liam?'

He shook his head and wiped at his sorrowful eyes. 'I dunno.' He shook his head violently. 'I... I... I really don't know.'

'This may help you to make that decision.' She reached into an inside pocket of her leather jacket and handed him a debit card and bank slip.

He wiped at his eyes, read it several times, and exhaled shakily. He looked back at her, the confusion evident in his tortured face.

She motioned to him to reread the bank slip.

His hands trembled as he read it again. 'When?' He flexed his hand and clenched them. 'How did you do that?'

'I just did.' She shrugged her shoulders. 'It's what I do.' She closed her eyes, slowly opened them and looked directly at him. 'Sorry, but I couldn't tell you.' She forced a half smile. 'I hated lying to you but–'

'Have you seen how much that is?'

She grinned. 'Of course - I did it *for you.*'

She tried to help him catch his breath by breathing with him.

She waited patiently until he had calmed down before speaking. 'When we were in Amsterdam, I opened several bank accounts at De Groot's 'special' bank.'

He grunted.

'They knew me and accepted my reasons for opening them.' She tapped at the card. 'You can send that to your father in England.' Her face took on a solemn look. 'But you must send the pin code, separately,' she said, emphasising separately. She continued. 'And your father can draw out money for your family as often as he wants.' She stopped abruptly. 'Well, if he wants to - until it's gone.' She smiled. 'But I'm sure he will take good care with it.'

Liam was still in shock.

He nodded and shook his head at the same time.

A desperate and confused man stricken with guilt.

Zita reached into another pocket, took out a second debit card, bank slip and a passport. She handed it to him. 'This is *yours...* OK?'

He wiped at his sore eyes and read the figure. He swallowed hard. 'Is that for real?' He opened the passport and paused as he checked the name and details on it. 'This is my original... It's my *own* fucking passport!' He stuttered. 'How?'

'That bastard had it in his safe in Amsterdam... I took *everything* when I cleared it.'

He looked at her, his eyes waiting for so many answers to his silent questions.

'I know what you are thinking, Liam.'

She reached across and touched the hand holding this passport.

He grunted his irritation.

'I know you are angry with me for not telling you before this time but I wanted to be able to help you when you *really* needed it. She smiled at him and continued in a gentle voice. 'And... I believe that the time is now...'

He raised his voice and directed his anger by pointing and waving his finger towards her. 'So, *you*... you made the decision to deliberately let me go through all this shit... When...? When you could have helped me?'

She tilted her head and spoke in an unusually subdued voice. 'Liam.'

He grunted.

'Liam, would you have done different things if you had this?' She tapped his passport. 'Earlier?'

He shook his head while he thought and took a huge pained breath. 'Erm...'

She forced a smile and hoped it would help him. 'Would you?' She sighed. 'Liam, would you have done something else?'

He took his time to exhale through his pursed lips.

Zita waited.

He looked into her eyes, paused and spoke. 'No... No I wouldn't.'

He wiped his eyes, read and reread the figure on the bank slip.

She touched his arm. 'Maybe that will help you make your decision, eh?'

He reread the figure. 'Fuck. I've never seen so much money. Is it for real?'

'Yes, it is.'

He closed his eyes and trembled before opening them and peering inquisitively at her. 'So, I can go... where I want...?' He waved his passport. 'When I want?'

She gently pushed him away from her and looked into his wretched eyes. 'Yes, Liam.' She paused and forced a guarded smile. 'But... Maybe...' She paused. '*We* can...' She took a deep breath and licked her bottom lip. She spoke as she exhaled. 'Go... *together...*' She watched and waited for his response. There was none and she continued in a soft calculated voice. 'If that is what you wish?'

His reaction was immediate and, as the grin spread across his face, his whole body relaxed and he gulped a huge breath of relief.

She reached out and pulled him towards her. 'You've come back to me,' she said, wiping at her tears of joy.

They held each other tight for several minutes before she gently pulled away and grabbed at his arm. 'Come on, when we dock in Hamburg,' she said, excitedly. 'We are going to Tallinn... in Estonia.'

He stared back at her blindly. 'What?' He shook his head. 'Did you know I would agree... all along?'

She replied firmly. '*No, Liam.*' She shook her head. 'I didn't.'

He chose to ignore her reply and continued. 'Where the fuck is that... and why?'

'You'll see.' She grinned. 'Come on.' She reached out and grabbed at his arm. 'We need to get changed for dinner.'

CHAPTER FORTY-FIVE

Everyone's A Winner

Toto was ecstatic when he received the call from his agent and the offer to fight in Tallinn, the capital of Estonia.

He always liked to be seen with pretty girls on his arm and he flaunted them at every opportunity. He immediately called his massage parlour in what was once the Love Shack and invited Osekll to join him. He met her at Hamburg Fuhlsbüttel airport and they flew on to Tallinn.

Twenty-two year old Latvian, Osekll, was beautiful with a perfect figure, petite with long blonde hair and a pale complexion. She like so many young girls had arrived in Amsterdam with promises of a great job and a way to get out of the poverty at home. Toto found her in one of the seedy brothels, rescued her, and moved her to his massage parlour. She soon became the most popular masseuse and in less than six weeks progressed to the job of manager and now only massaged the richest clients.

Once the cruise ship docked back in Hamburg Zita and Liam began the eighteen hundred and ten kilometre coach trip from Hamburg to Tallinn. They stopped overnight in Berlin at their rooms in the Aparthotel before taking the morning coach. They travelled for twenty-one hours through Poland before finally stopping at Riga, Lithuania, for yet another change.

Although Liam was exhausted when they stopped Zita could see there were questions behind his tired eyes.

'Okay. So, what do you want to know?'

'Your life...' He was stuck for words. 'The things you did. Do you call them missions?'

'No, they are assignments. It was my job. It's what I was paid to do.'

'So... why the fuck are we going to a place I've never heard of?'

She grinned. 'We're going to see a UFC fight on Saturday evening...'

'Wha–?'

'To see Toto... *Fight.*'

'How?'

'I called his agent in Hamburg.'

'How can you arrange that, it's a macho sport - for men? You're a woman?'

She glared at him before breaking into a puzzled cynical laugh.

Liam blushed. 'Sorry.'

Her glare slowly turned to a grin. She flung her right hand flippantly to one side and continued. 'He was so greedy. He wanted five thousand dollars to arrange it.'

'So, you paid him?'

She nodded.

'How?'

She giggled. 'I told him I was the assistant of a wealthy Estonian cage fighting fan and wanted to arrange for Toto to fight there.'

'And?'

'As I said - I paid him... And he agreed to it.' Her grin grew even wider. 'De Groot has *put up* the prize money for his fight at the top of the bill.'

'How the fuck can that be? He's dead!'

'You know. I cleaned out all of his bank accounts as well as the money in his safe in Amsterdam and on the island.' She paused. 'And... the bank account of the Russian.' She shot Liam an impish grin. 'I moved it all into new accounts... Some of them in Switzerland... in Germany, Holland and even in England.' She chuckled. Something Liam had never seen her do. She continued. 'The prize for the winner is *30,000* US dollars.'

'Why so *much*?'

'Because I wanted to be sure that Toto will be in Tallinn when we are there.'

Now it was Liam's turn to grin. 'You are such a clever and devious bastard.' After realising what he'd just said he blushed and swallowed hard. 'Oops. Sorry, I didn't mean it like that.'

'Who cares?' She leaned into him. 'I am *myself* and it is *my* life.'

The call came over the tannoy for passengers to board for the final four and a half hours of their exhausting coach journey.

Tallinn, the capital and largest city of Estonia, is situated on the northern coast of the country on the shore of the Gulf of Finland. It is the oldest capital city in Northern Europe and the biggest and most developed cargo and passenger port in the Baltic region. It is also the best preserved medieval city in Northern Europe and had close links with the traders in the hanseatic city of Hamburg for centuries. The city boasted gothic spires, original winding cobblestone streets and enchanting architecture, scattered with medieval churches and imposing merchant houses, barns and warehouses, many of which date back to the Middle Ages.

The bus station was close to the town and offered all amenities for passengers, including bus, tram services and train connections, but unusually for Zita, rather than walking, and knowing Liam was tired, they took the nearest taxi for the short journey to his insignificant guest house in Munga Street.

Zita paid the driver, grabbed their backpacks and handed Liam his. 'I'll come back in half an hour and we can have something to eat and for you...' She stroked his face and continued. 'A well needed sleep.'

Liam lifted his tired head and shook it before walking apprehensively towards the tiny entrance. He stopped and turned back to Zita, querying if it was the correct place.

She forced a tired smile and a slow nod of confirmation.

Zita took her time to walk to her backpacker's hostel in Lai Street. It was her way of stimulating her brain and to give her the time to complete the details of her plan and the one and only opportunity of it succeeding.

Her backpacker's hostel was a fifteenth century building that had been completely renovated a few months earlier. Situated in the widest and quietest cobbled street in the heart of the old city, it was a unique location only one minute on foot from Town Hall square, the heart of the Bottom Merchant City and close to the fifteenth century fortification.

She walked into the welcoming lobby and picked up a leaflet while she waited for someone to check her in. She took a few minutes to read it aloud. 'Where the old spirit goes with a modern design - spacious light rooms, noise proof windows, a parquet floor, the modern bathrooms and WC rooms, in accordance with the European standard. All rooms are provided with the new wooden eco furniture. Apart from sleeping rooms we also have a kitchen provided with all necessary facilities and a rest room furnished in an ancient pub style where guests can eat, drink beer, talk to their old and new friends and immerse in the old Tallinn colour.'

The door behind reception eventually opened and the young blonde receptionist with a name badge - Rea - smiled, signed her in, took payment and handed Zita the key to a three bedded room. 'For the first two nights you will be alone in the large room,' she said, with a smile.

Zita nodded. 'OK, that's fine.'

Rea blushed before she continued speaking. 'The rooms are mixed-gender.' She paused and waited for Zita to react. She didn't. So, she spurted out the rest of her words. 'Is that a problem for you?'

Zita shrugged her shoulders, raised her eyes and smiled sassily. 'Is anyone booked already?'

'Not at this moment,' replied Rea.

Zita shrugged. 'It's not a problem for me. I'm a big girl now.' She grinned broadly. 'Thanks.'

After a shower Zita took her time to make her way the short distance to Liam's guest house. She was in awe as she walked slowly through the twisted medieval cobbled streets beneath the walled city and red roof tiled buildings that towered above her.

When she met Liam they crossed the street and walked up the hill to the steak house in Vaike-Karja and sat outside on the raised seating enjoying a glass of the locally produced iced apple juice. When she felt the time was right, she spoke. 'Liam, I will need your help if we want to kill him.'

He shrank back. 'Me... Help? Doing what?'

She laughed. 'Don't worry.' She tapped his hand to reassure him. 'I will show you. This is the one mission when I do need a second person.'

'Mission?'

'Yes, of course it is a mission. It is *our* mission and not an assignment.'

He was still thinking about what she might want him to do to help but he eventually shook his head.

'You know why we came so far? Have you forgotten what happened to your dream?'

'Dream?'

She spoke slowly in almost a whisper, to emphasise every word. 'Yes... *Your* Love Shack... *Your* dream.'

He closed his eyes and sighed heavily. 'How will I ever forget *that*?' He bit at the side of his mouth until he could feel the warm blood on his tongue. 'And...' He sucked at his lip and wiped the blood with the back of his hand. 'Matthijs...' He sniffed. 'And Fenna, his *wife*.' He raised his bloody hand, made a fist and brought it down heavily onto the table. 'Bastard! The bastard!'

Zita waited while he took a huge breath of the warm summer evening air.

He looked at her with a tortured face. 'Course, I'll help you,' he said softly.

He coughed and cleared his throat. His mood suddenly altered and he chose not to hide the change in his attitude. He looked at her decisively. 'Never push anyone to a point when they *don't care* anymore.'

Zita was shocked at the change in him and pushed her chair back onto two legs. 'Wow,' she said, before carefully choosing her words. 'So, you're on a mission now?'

'Yep... But remember... I'm used to working on my own too.'

'I know. But you will be fine. We are a team, yeas?'

He flicked his head to one side before slowly turning to face her. 'Yes... We are.'

The following morning Zita was up early, walked to Munga Street and waited for Liam outside his guest house. When he closed the door behind him he still looked tired but, after forcing him to drink a double espresso with three sugars and a croissant with thick plum jam in the café across the street he seemed so much better.

They took their time to wander through the already bustling cobbled streets pushing their way between the excited tourists who were enthused by the medieval buildings, photographing everything in sight. When they reached the Viru Gates Tower, one of several exits and entrances to the old town, they walked through the arch and stopped in front of the first stall of what was a flower lover's nirvana The long row of stalls all displayed huge selections of summer and brightly coloured exotic flowers on their stalls divided by stone walls and pillars that supported the roof. It was extended with brightly coloured awnings that reached out over the pavement and would protect their buckets and bowls of cut and potted flowers from any rain or snow.

Zita left Liam struggling to retain his place in the square amongst the thronging tourists, while she walked from stall to stall taking her time to inspect the long-stemmed roses on all of them. Once she found what she wanted she bought a single pink rose, pushed her way back through the crowds and handed it to him.

'Fuck,' exclaimed Liam, wincing before dropping it and sucking hard at his bleeding fingers.

Zita turned away and smirked as she murmured under her breath. 'Perfect.'

She left Liam nursing his bloody fingers and spent time talking to the woman who stood beside her horse drawn carriage waiting for her next fare. She was immaculate in a black bowler hat, black turnout, with a white high-necked silk blouse and pearl pin, a red waistcoat, black leather gloves and riding boots. While Zita continued to talk to her the woman stood proudly alongside her shiny, four-wheeled traditional open topped carriage and stroked her horse, an Orlov Trotter, one of Russia's most popular horse breeds, renowned for its gentleness and demeanour amongst crowds.

After reaching agreement with the woman and furtively sliding payment to her Zita thanked her and walked back to Liam.

'What the hell was that all about?'

She grinned, picked up the rose from the ground and held it without giving any discernible reaction to the thorny stem, tugged at him, pulled him along with her and walked between the high stone towers.

'I will tell you later when we can find somewhere quiet.' She lowered her voice to a whisper. 'Where we can be alone and talk.'

The deep furrows in his forehead tightened and were highlighted even more than normal. 'You are so fucking mysterious... aren't you? A surprise a minute.'

To avoid the tourists' cameras, they took the shaded side streets, which were less busy and more relaxed with local people oblivious to anyone passing by. They strolled the short distance to the most central shops on Laikmaa Street, between the Tallink Hotel, the Viru Centre shopping mall and the nearby Sokos Hotel. Zita had specifically chosen the high-rise hotel, built in 1972, for Toto and his guest because it was one of the few hotels in the city that had its own gym and high-end shops. She knew that Toto would want to flaunt his importance and the high fee for his fight to his girlfriend and this was ideal.

Leaving nothing to chance, Zita had already pre-booked and paid for the top floor suite before leaving Hamburg.

They walked into the recently remodelled reception and she motioned to Liam to sit at a table near the window. She wandered across to the reception desk and picked up a copy of the hotel's brochure.

She had already read about the hotel so when she reached the table, she passed it to Liam. She ordered coffee and two portions of kringle cinnamon braid bread, a favourite in Estonia for breakfast or a mid-morning snack, and returned to the reception desk. After speaking to the receptionist, she handed Zita several letterheads and envelopes. She slid them carefully into her bag and returned to join Liam. While she poured the coffee, she watched as Liam flicked through the brochure pages without looking at them, underlining his total lack of interest, until he reached the final page which informed the reader that there was a KGB Museum in the building.

She saw his reaction out of the corner of her eye and smiled to herself.

He looked up at her. 'So?'

'Yes.' She nodded and answered his silent question. 'Yeah, Estonia was part of Russia - the USSR until 1991. Nine years - not so long ago is it?'

He couldn't hide his nervous shock.

'So, you see why that museum is here. Do you want to see it?'

He shook his head erratically. '*No*... *No way* do *I* want to know anything about those bastards.'

Zita accepted his answer and continued. 'But since that time there is a problem, unemployment is very high - almost fourteen percent. That is very high but...' She paused and took her time to look around the modern reception. 'It will get better in some time ahead.' She clicked her tongue. 'Maybe one day they will join the EU.' She shrugged. 'Who knows?'

They finished their drinks and Zita stood.

Liam followed suit but as they left he reached down and grabbed at the last piece of braid bread on Zita's plate.

After leaving Liam to rest at his guest house Zita returned to her hostel and used the retro typewriter in reception to type her messages on the Sokos Hotel letterheads. The typeface had to be untraceable in case the letters were ever seen by the police and analysed by their forensics team or, if they felt it was serious enough, Europol.

She checked the time on the reception clock and returned to the hotel. She handed two envelopes and a handwritten note to the receptionist, asking her to be sure to give them to Mr Tabagari when he arrived.

The receptionist checked her register and Zita watched while she slotted them in the pigeon hole alongside the key to Toto's suite awaiting his collection upon arrival.

Zita knew that thankfully Liam was exhausted so she used the time to plan the next part of her deception. She visited the Telliski flea market in Kalmaja, in what is referred to as the beating heart area, and held every Saturday between 10:00 am and 3:00pm. During the summer months the market was held outside but in the winter inside the Roheline saal - the Green hall. The flea market was a place where everyone came to sell their unwanted clothes and tools.

She knew exactly what she wanted.

The first thing she bought was an old ripped navy-blue shopping trolley. She spun the wheels before paying the old man who told her it was his late wife's. She thanked him and then turned her attention to specific clothes, picking her way from stall to stall, meticulously scrutinising everything before she bought it and dropped it into her trolley.

Toto and Osekll flew into Lennart Meri, Tallinn Airport - just 4 km from the city centre, on late Friday afternoon and took a taxi to their hotel booked and paid for by the sponsor of his fight.

Zita was already waiting in reception and watched as Toto was handed the key to the penthouse suite and the envelopes left by her containing the agreed fifty percent of the fight fee and a welcome message from the "sponsor."

Toto squeezed the thicker envelope and smiled to himself and, while the receptionist instructed the porter to collect their bags from the taxi, he slid it into his leather jacket pocket.

Zita couldn't resist getting close to the subject of her mission and brushed past them as they walked towards the lift and their top floor suite.

CHAPTER FORTY-SIX

Killing Me Softly

Toto spent the morning of his fight toning up his already honed physique in the hotel's gym while Osekll shopped in the nearby arcade. After a light meal in their room at six o'clock they left the hotel and were picked up by a taxi and driven to the multi-purpose arena built to seat 3,800 people.

Zita changed into a colourful dress and Liam changed into his second hand designer jacket, shirt and trousers before having dinner at the Peppersack in Vanaturu Kael, one of the oldest restaurants in Tallinn. The building was situated in the south side of the old town in a four-storey building with old beams and passages separating the different seating areas. The waiters all wore traditional costumes and once inside it was as though they had gone back in time. Once again Zita read the menu to Liam and after much deliberation chose his food. She ordered him chicken breast in a cream sauce with potatoes and for herself a chicken salad with dried tomatoes, greens and parmesan and to share, a side dish of freshly made bread. To drink she ordered two large glasses of super fresh apple juice and finished off with two cappuccinos.

At nine fifteen they took up their VIP seats in the third row of the sold-out cavernous arena outside of town. Like so many sports arenas across Europe they often doubled as ice rinks and were incredibly badly ventilated and the heat in the building was overbearing.

Toto's reputation of no losses in twenty-three fights ensured that as he made his slow walk from the dressing room the tumultuous applause, shouts and whistles built to an ear-shattering crescendo as he stepped into the cage.

Liam leaned across to Zita and shouted in her ear. 'Have you been to one of these before?'

She shouted back at him. 'No!'

They took their time to eye the diminutive fighting machine at the peak of his fitness. For such a tiny man he was bursting with confidence and the obvious free hand tattoos in the Cyrillic alphabet, carved into his muscular sculpted back, reinforced his menace. Even his shorts made a statement: the holster and gun embroidered on each side of them, to send a silent and threatening message to his opponents. As he strutted around the cage, he repeated an action that had now become his trademark. He raised both hands and formed a finger gun - mimicking two handguns and pointing them threateningly at his opponent. He stood in the middle of the ring, tensed his muscles, crossed his arms and screamed at him. 'I will take your head off! Do you still want to fight me?'

Liam leaned across to Zita and grabbed the few seconds of respite from the noisy crowd to speak to her behind his hand. 'What a frightening bastard.' He shook his head in disbelief. 'No wonder he sorted out that Russian in Hamburg.'

Zita studied the fighter and, in her mind, reviewed her plan for the following afternoon.

As Toto, with his fighting nickname of *Poster Boy,* was introduced by the overly enthusiastic master of ceremonies Zita thought to herself. *Not a problem. I know your weakness.*

Toto's opponent was a much taller, local fighter who had also never been beaten. Despite being given a massive standing ovation accompanied with loud cheers when he was introduced, Toto knew he had the edge.

Not surprisingly, the fight was short lived, lasting less than two minutes, and after an unbearable and continuous onslaught from a pumped-up Toto he made a concerted non-stop attack on his opponent. Toto didn't attempt any takedowns instead used his advantage by inflicting a series of unorthodox strikes. After a big knee to the Estonian's chin and a spinning high kick to the side of his head he crashed onto the bloodied mat unconscious.

Toto jumped manically around the cage before climbing up it. He raised his arms in triumph to the whistles, hoots and screams of adoration from the thousands of his new Estonian fans.

The master of ceremonies rushed into the ring followed by a young girl in traditional Estonian costume who stepped nervously towards Toto and handed him a bouquet of pink roses, along with an envelope from his sponsor agreeing to meet him for dinner at his hotel the next evening when he would pay him the rest of his fee.

Toto revelled in the tumultuous pop star treatment from the hyped-up crowd posing theatrically for the bank of photographers and journalists all vying for an interview.

On the other side of the cage the doctor and his opponent's trainers were desperately trying to resuscitate yet another of Toto's victims.

Early on Sunday morning under yet another clear blue sky and with the streets already bustling with tourists, Zita and Liam sat at a pavement café and watched the entrance to Toto's hotel from the opposite side of the street.

Liam fiddled with his spoon.

'What is troubling you? Ask your question,' she said.

He sighed. 'I'm confused.'

'Confused? About what?'

'It just seems weird. We always wear second hand clothes. On the cruise... in Lanzarote and now here.'

Zita's face broke into a grin before she raised her hands, covered her face and laughed. 'Is that why you are... *confused*?'

Liam turned away.

She sensed his embarrassment. 'That is an interesting question.'

He forced an exaggerated smile.

'It is easy.'

Liam sank back in his chair and visibly relaxed while he waited for her to explain.

'If our bags and cases were checked by customs whenever we travelled and our clothes were new... they would see something was not correct.' She paused. 'And, they could trace where and when they were bought.' She grinned. 'Smell a rat... Yes?'

Liam grinned back at her. 'Yeah, I see.'

She laughed. 'They all need to look lived in - never new.'

Toto and Osekll finally left the hotel and Liam and Zita followed them, keeping their distance as they took their time to look at the sites of the beautiful medieval city, finally reaching the cathedral of Saint Mary the Virgin, built in the early thirteenth century. It had been rebuilt several times since then with a mixture of architectural styles with elaborate interior decoration paid for by the elite German nobles. Toto effortlessly climbed the Baroque bell-tower, dragging Osekll behind him, and looked out across the beautiful city before finally stopping for lunch at the newly opened Balthasar Restaurant in the building of the Town Hall Drugstore in the heart of the Old Town.

Two hours later Toto and Osekll left the restaurant arm in arm, kissing and cuddling as they walked slowly towards the waiting carriage. As arranged with Zita, the coachwoman ensured Toto sat to her right then helped Osekll into the seat on the left side of the carriage.

With a token flick of the whip the horse threw his head back and cantered away.

Liam, wearing faded jeans, a light blue shirt and trainers all carefully bought for him by Zita at the flea market, sat on his bed in the guest house. He repeatedly checked the watch Zita bought him from a supermarket the day they arrived for ninety-two kroon. He tried to remember the last time he'd worn one. He'd never had a real job and had never needed a watch, his occupation as a criminal didn't rely on time, just opportunity and sometimes calculated risk. A shiver shot down his spine as he remembered the last time he had worn a watch. He'd won a Rolex - not a fake - in a card game and wore it to antagonise the original owner the night when they both drank at their local. It was the same night he'd accidently set fire to his home when he was in yet another of his drunken stupors. He'd been beyond help for more than two years and it had caused a major breakdown in his young family. He had considered going to AA but couldn't build up enough courage to enter the room at the Dellow Support Centre, Wentworth Street. He'd smashed his watch while he was rescuing his wife Kath and three children from the devastating fire which completely destroyed their house. Despite the newspapers and media hailing him a hero, his father knew the truth. He told Liam that he would not divulge the truth providing he would agree to go into rehab and upon release attend AA every week. With the threat of being exposed hanging over his head, Liam had no option but to agree.

During the following dark months, he had no need of a watch to control him and his life and even when he arrived in Amsterdam in March 1999 and living and working at the Love Shack, he still didn't need one. He could open when he pleased; generally, after having a shave, shower and breakfast. There was no specific opening or closing times in much of De Wallen - the Red-Light District. It was down to whether there were enough punters around still eager to continue to spend their money on the three vices: drink, drugs or sex.

He was getting fidgety now. He flicked back his jacket sleeve and tapped his watch.

At 3:18 precisely he carefully checked his pockets and left his room.

Having walked the route several times the day before and again that morning with Zita, he knew every building, tourist shop selling fridge magnets, flags and postcards, busker, street vendor, café and bar. The bars and cafés were different now. The price of drinks and food had suddenly become more expensive but nevertheless they were jam packed with noisy tourists from the cruise ships and Finnish people who had come over for the weekend to buy food and goods that were all much cheaper than their country. They loved to enjoy the alcohol in Estonia so they made the most of their time while they were there. Zita had told him that Finland was incredibly expensive. But the cost of the frequent, two and half hour Tallink ferry ride from Helsinki to Tallinn, which varied depending on the time of year, was not that expensive. It was often treated as a day out and an adventure for any kids who travelled with their parents on school holidays during the extended two and a half months break from June.

As he passed the post office, he checked his watch again. 3:21. Perfect timing.

Before meeting Zita Liam had never worked with a *professional* but having seen the slick execution of her work made him nervous and to feel like an amateur. Although he had learned a lot he was still learning and fast. When he was on his own in London, he could choose whether or not to carry out a robbery up until the last minute and if he felt it may not come off or achieve the outcome he was expecting, he would walk away. He remembered the failed robbery he and fellow petty criminals George, Harry, Matt and Dick had planned at the Mount Pleasant Sorting Office. He knew from the start that they didn't have the bottle to carry it through but they still went ahead. Surprisingly their part of the robbery was a success but he was drunk, blind drunk. Alcohol was the sole cause of the unprovoked attack he meted out on two innocent men who would never recover from their horrific and unnecessary injuries. He knew that by rights he should still be locked up in Wandsworth serving the remaining ten years left of his life sentence but his selfish actions to save himself, accidentally saved the lives of two prison warders who were taking cover in his cell. This was seen by the parole board as some sort of heroic action by Liam.

He shook his head and murmured to himself. 'Twice! The stupid bastards have been taken in twice... and... and... I never said a *word*.' He grinned. 'Me... Me...' He stabbed his fingers at his chest. 'A fucking hero? What bloody idiots.'

He checked his watch. 3:38. Perfect.

He continued to walk at the pace Zita had told him that he had to adhere to.

He checked his watch. 3:41. Great.

He knew he was getting nearer and for a split second he shuddered.

He muttered to himself. 'Pull yourself together. *Come on.*'

He checked his watch. 3:47. Excellent.

He turned the corner and began to walk up the steep hill before turning left, crossing the road and past a row of bars packed with rowdy tourists.

Even *he* could tell a tourist now.

He checked his watch. 3:55. Almost there.

Now he *was* nervous. Not for himself but not wanting to screw up Zita's meticulous plan of action and let her down.

He reached the top of the hill and checked his watch. 3:58. He was a minute ahead of Zita's schedule.

He leaned against an old weather worn timber gate post for one minute and checked his watch. 3:59. Time was almost up.

He looked around the almost deserted street and spotted the carriage making its way regally up the hill. He walked across to his designated spot, turned and looked at the reflection of the road in the empty shop window.

For the first time he actually felt nervous as he prepared himself for his one and only part of Zita's meticulous plan.

His removed the plastic cover from the scalpel and slid it into the bottom of the left-hand pocket of his jeans and then watched and waited for the signal.

Thirty-six minutes since leaving the Virus Gate the carriage arrived on cue at the location agreed between the coachwoman and Zita. It stopped to allow the excited children from the music school, carrying their instruments on their backs in brightly coloured cases, to race past them. As the last few stragglers made their way down the hill and past the carriage an old woman appeared holding an enormous bunch of pink roses. She had carefully forced the roses to open unusually wide earlier in the day before carefully placing them in her shopping trolley.

With her face hidden behind the roses the old woman stepped towards the carriage and up to Osekll. She pushed the unwrapped roses into the young girl's face and, completely blocking her view, put one foot in the carriage.

'These are for you,' she said, in German.

Toto turned and flashed a quizzical glance before forcing a smile and replying in German. 'Danke,' he said.

The old woman thrust the roses towards him giving him no choice but to reach out and grab them.

Toto quickly guessed that things were not as they seemed but, with restricted movement, he realised he was trapped in the confined space of the carriage. As the thorns penetrated deep into his hands, he dropped the roses into his lap and pulled his arms back in shock. He looked down and stared in disbelief at his stinging and bleeding palms.

Liam appeared out of nowhere and sprang unnoticed towards the carriage. He reached in, slashed through Toto's jeans and sliced deep into his right thigh severing his femoral artery.

Toto didn't immediately feel the scalpel and the roses partially hid the blood that was now pumping from his body.

The old woman tapped on the side of the coach and as arranged the carriage pulled away. While Osekll quivered with shock and confusion the carriage trotted further away from the nearest hospital and deeper into the narrow medieval streets of the city, leaving a snail trail of blood as Toto's body drained of life.

The old woman turned, and still pulling her trolley, made her way slowly and unsteadily down the hill.

When Liam saw her, he was gobsmacked. He stopped, shook his head and talked to himself. 'Fuck me, she's invisible…' He shook his head. 'She can do anything.'

He checked his jacket sleeve for any signs of blood as instructed by Zita during their trial run. There wasn't any and he congratulated himself with a guttural snort. Feeling the adrenalin still pumping through his veins he maintained his distance and followed her on the other side of the road but while he stopped to light a cigarette, his daily ration, she disappeared.

Minutes later he saw an amused Zita appear from an alley, making her way towards her hostel. As he exhaled and looked at her through the thick cloud of his cigarette smoke, she looked ethereal.

Zita had meticulously planned their attack on Toto to the nearest second. Visiting the locations with Liam and timing the journey of the carriage from the entrance of the Viru Gateway to where they would be waiting in the street in front of the music school. She left nothing to chance and spent hours teaching Liam how to carry out his part of her planned attack. She had him use a pen to simulate the scalpel, and with herself as a guinea pig, taught him to identify the exact position on her right thigh and the angle needed to penetrate deep enough to sever Toto's femoral artery.

Preferring to add an element of surprise to their assassination she made the decision not to tell Liam about her disguise.

CHAPTER FORTY-SEVEN

Home

After killing Toto, Zita and Liam left their hostels and joined the Finnish shoppers on the Tallink ferry for the two-and-a-half-hour journey to the West harbour ferry terminal in Helsinki.

Liam sat back and watched the passengers while Zita read a magazine. He waited for her to close it and then tapped it. 'Tell me something. How did you know Toto would take that horse and cart ride?'

She replied abruptly. 'It's not a horse and cart - it's a horse and carriage. That is *very* different.'

He huffed.

She continued. 'After the fight I left him a message at his hotel. As the sponsor I congratulated him on his win and as a token of my appreciation offered him the free carriage ride and a bouquet of roses for his companion.'

His screwed-up face held a silent question.

She immediately sensed it. 'Ah.' She raised her head and grinned at him. 'You are thinking of all that blood... in the carriage?' she said, glibly.

Liam smiled. 'Yeah, I *was* thinking about that.'

'It was all taken care of,' said Zita. 'The coachwoman was very well paid to do it.' She paused. 'And to clean her carriage.' A smile slowly spread across her face. 'Unless forensics and the police cleaned it for her... After they finish their botched investigation.'

Liam grinned. 'De Groot's money, eh?'

'Of course.' She giggled. 'We are only travellers...' She tightened her grip on her battered backpack and looked around at the other passengers. 'With little money.'

Liam shook his head and grinned back at her.

'You like this don't you?' she asked.

He closed his eyes and nodded.

She smiled at him mischievously. 'Coffee would be nice,' she said.

Reluctantly he stood and returned a few minutes later with a coffee, a tea and two chicken sandwiches.

'Very nice. Thank you, kind sir.' She grinned back at him as she bit into her sandwich. 'Now we *can* relax, can't we?'

When they arrived at the Helsinki ferry terminal, they took the number 45 bus to Vantaa International Airport and flew back to Berlin. They stayed in their suite at the Adina Apartment Hotel for a few more days, the final time before flying on to Schiphol.

Once back in Holland, Zita and Liam took the shuttle train from the airport to Centraal Station. Zita found it hard to hide her excitement as they left the station and hopped onto the number 17 tram to Westermarkt and walked the four hundred metres to her houseboat. She unlocked the door, pulled back the brightly patterned curtains and the roof light blinds, allowing the summer sun to stream in. 'This is so nice - isn't it?'

'Yeah... It is,' said Liam, nodding his agreement.

While she waited for the coffee to blend, she opened all the windows.

Liam grabbed the green watering can from the tiny cupboard at the end of the deck, filled it and poured the clean water into the bird bath, then sat down. Almost immediately a brown speckled female blackbird landed and, after three dips of her beak, lowered her body. After ritually fanning her feathers, dipped repeatedly in and out of the water spilling it onto the deck before flying onto the roof.

He watched her preen herself and smiled as he remembered watching Zita feeding the sparrows in Gibraltar.

Zita carried the tray up onto the deck, placed it on the small ceramic topped table and poured it into their favourite mugs.

Liam told her about the blackbird and while he sat sipping at his tea he watched Zita moving between the pots overflowing with plants and flowers.

She brushed her hands through a lavender bush, cupped them and held them over her nose. She closed her eyes, took a deep breath and inhaled the aroma before walking across to Liam and doing the same.

'Isn't that fantastic?' she purred.

He shook his head in disgust. 'Smells like a fucking pansies pocket,' he said, curtly.

She didn't totally understand what he meant but she guessed by the tone of his voice and, as she turned away, swore at him in Dutch. She reached down and cut a handful of white roses, laid them on the table and rushed back inside. She returned with a clear glass vase and took her time to arrange them before positioning them in the centre of the table.

Once she was happy with her handiwork, she sat next to Liam, grabbed her coffee and took her time to take in everything around her.

She turned to Liam and pointed at the vase. 'Roses... I bet you like them now?'

He grinned and subconsciously rubbed his fingers together. 'I like *those* because *you* picked them.' He lowered his voice. 'But I didn't like that smell you shoved up my nose.'

She smiled at him. 'No problem. But I *do*,' she said, in a whisper. 'I love all flowers.' She finished her coffee and after placing her empty mug on the table she sighed softly. 'Shall we stay here for a while?'

'Yeah,' he said, 'we've done enough travelling to last a lifetime.'

Detective Piet Ackerman walked along the canal humming to himself. When he saw Zita and Liam sitting on the deck he waved and joined them.

'Hello, you two.'

'Hi. You must have some news if you're coming to see us?' asked Liam.

He smiled. 'I wasn't coming specifically to see you but as you're here. I do have some news. I really do.' He grinned. 'And it's tied up so many loose ends.'

They grinned back at him.

He looked at the empty mugs.

Zita grinned mischievously. 'Would *you* like a coffee... detective?' she said.

'That would be very nice...' He paused for effect. 'Only if *you're* having one?' he said, flippantly.

She winked at Liam as she picked up the tray and disappeared below deck.

The detective took huge drags on his cigarette blowing smoke rings into the warm summer air and watched as Liam took his time to light his only permitted cigarette of the day.

Neither of them spoke, instead they jointly enjoyed the perverseness of their debilitating habit.

Zita returned a few minutes later with two mugs of coffee, a tea and a plate of peanut koekjes.

She looked at Liam's cigarette and fired him a concerned look before shaking her head in disgust and turning to pour the coffee. She adjusted her cushion and sat back. 'OK. So, tell us the news, Piet.'

The detective kept them in suspense while he took his time to light yet another cigarette. 'Well...' He took a long drag and continued. 'Tsotne Tabagari.' He coughed. 'Toto... the Georgian?'

They both nodded.

He continued. 'He's been murdered.'

'Murdered?' gasped Liam.

'Where?' asked Zita.

'How?' asked Liam.

Ackerman took another huge drag on his cigarette. 'He was killed by a *hit man*.' He pondered while he looked at the glowing end of his cigarette and smiled to himself. 'Well... *Possibly two*.' He exhaled an extended cloud of smoke up into the warm still afternoon air. 'Very clever...' He took his time, closed his eyes and released a slow considered nod before he continued with a smoky murmur. 'Very clever indeed... It was a master class in how to commit a murder.'

How?' asked Zita.

The detective continued. 'I mean so... oo... oo.' He looked at Liam and he lowered his mug in anticipation. He took a sip of his coffee and congratulated Zita with a smile and then returned to look at Liam. He continued. 'How do you say - *Bloody clever*?'

Liam nodded and then smirked back at him. 'Really?'

Ackerman took another drag and his whole body seemed to relax into what looked like utter euphoria. 'In and out,' he hissed. He partially closed his eyes and sighed lazily. 'And... nobody... Not *one* person... saw... *a thing*,' he drawled.

'Where?' asked Liam.

'Tallinn.'

Liam faked a confused look.

'Estonia,' said Ackerman, with a well-informed gratifying nod.

Liam maintained his phoney bewilderment.

'Estonia is in Eastern Europe - miles away,' said Ackerman. He grinned. 'All I can say... is whoever did it... deserved a medal.' He paused. 'Or... medals,' he said, flippantly.

Liam grunted and looked at Zita and then back to Ackerman. 'OK. If you say so...' He paused. 'Then do you know who *they* were?'

Ackerman didn't answer. He took his time to rub his chin as he studied the white roses in the vase on the table. He paused and with his hand still on his chin he rubbed his thumb up and down flipping his bottom lip before turning to Zita. 'Do *you* like roses?' he said, with a smirk.

Zita knew exactly what he was thinking. 'Course I do. All women *l... o... v... e* roses,' she said, showing just how much by extending each letter of the word. She continued and deliberately pushed her luck. 'But... I prefer *pink.*'

Ackerman missed his opportunity. He was busy exhaling and forming smoke rings, his speciality when he had a captive audience or felt inclined.

Zita tilted her head and looked at Liam as she spoke. 'But no one... has ever given them to me.'

Liam shrugged. *He was a man and wouldn't be seen with any flowers let alone roses and he had no intention of ever buying them.*

Ackerman lacked all motivation to follow up his crazy off the bat hunch. Instead he picked up his mug and emptied it. He licked his lips. 'Nice coffee... Delicious,' he said, with a slow salacious smile.

'The best,' said Zita, with a grin. 'Always... Here.' She winked at him. 'And *you* know it?

Ackerman turned to Liam. 'So, Liam, how's your throat?'

Liam shrugged. 'Not too bad,' he said, with a pained grimace.

Zita looked at him her face contradicting his answer.

He turned away and looked down the canal as he remembered the day Skipio inflicted the revenge on behalf of De Groot and carried out the irreparable injuries to his throat. He forced a cough to clear it before continuing in a strained voice. 'It will always be a problem,' he said, as he reached into his pocket and squeezed the small plastic bottle of painkillers - his sole lifeline to managing his pain.

Ackerman, still holding his empty mug, offered his sympathy with a slow nod before placing it neatly on the tray and adjusting the position of the handle. 'The Tallinn police have investigated and interviewed Osekll.'

They both fired him a blank look.

'His Latvian girlfriend...' He shrugged. 'But she was a mess... and a blubbering wreck.' He shook his head. 'I saw the video of her interview.' He scoffed. 'She said she saw nothing... nothing but... *roses*.' He looked at them. 'Can you believe that? Her boyfriend is murdered and all she can say is that she saw... roses. Verdomde hel!' He shook his head in disbelief. 'Roses! How is that possible?'

He paused and looked down at the roses on the table and mumbled to himself. After subconsciously taking his time to scrutinise Zita and Liam in turn, he continued. 'Well, the police said they had tried to contact a mystery couple–'

'Mystery couple?' asked Liam, feigning curiosity.

The detective nodded. 'That's what they said but the bastard's girlfriend is so shocked and... As I said they couldn't get any sense out of her. So, it looks like... Case closed.' He flicked the last of his cigarette into the canal where it briefly fizzed before being swamped by the passing tourist boat. He watched it glide by and waited until the

320

guide's tannoy that was filling the air around them faded before pushing another cigarette into his mouth and lighting it. 'I don't believe we'll ever know. And...' He took a huge drag. 'Do any of us care?' He looked at Zita and then Liam. 'I mean do *you* care?'

She shook her head. 'No. Neither of us do.' She turned to Liam and winked. 'Is that right, Liam?'

'Yeah that's right. Who gives a fuck?' He snorted. 'But I bet De Groot would be pissing himself if he was still around.'

'Um.' Ackerman checked his watch and stood. 'Well, I'm off.' He shot each of them a wry grin. '*Enjoy* the weather.'

They both answered at the same time. 'We will.'

Ackerman gave the roses a cursory glance as he left and spoke to them from the road. 'And... *I* love roses too,' he said, with a grin and a wave.

Liam watched Ackerman walk away in a cloud of smoke before standing and checking his pockets. He pulled out a twenty guilder note. 'I'll go and get you those *roses* then... shall I?'

Zita frowned at him. 'You shouldn't ask me that, Liam. You should just... just do it.' She looked away as she lowered her hands and squeezed them tight. 'Liam, action is worth a thousand thoughts. Yeah?'

CHAPTER FORTY-EIGHT

Never Can Say Goodbye

Weeks later

Liam leaned back in his favourite chair and watched Zita as she carefully picked her way between the hand-painted pots overflowing with vibrant late summer flowers that still filled much of the houseboat deck. She finished dead heading her geraniums, penstemon, rudbeckia and the last of her roses and watered the huge sunflowers before leaning against the wooden handrail and looking contentedly down the canal.

She closed her eyes and faced towards the last of the cooling afternoon sun and spoke without turning around. 'Liam, do you know that next Thursday is your birthday?'

'Is it?'

'Would you like a special birthday present - to go back to Madeira for some time?'

'Madeira?'

She turned her head and look at him.

'This time it is *our* exit route,' she said.

He smiled at her. 'Where we went to that café... in the garden...?' He reflected. 'I liked it there.' He nodded. 'Yeah - why not?'

She looked at his pale face. 'It is perfect for you. Not too hot. They say it is like eternal spring.' She paused. 'And I will take you to somewhere special...' She smiled. 'To Reid's Hotel for afternoon tea.'

Liam grinned mindlessly. He had no idea who or what it was so he innocently reached out, grabbed her hand and kissed her on the cheek. 'Nice,' he said, considerately.

When they heard the motorbike they both turned towards the sound. They watched the telegram boy as he rode slowly along the cobbled street at the side of the canal on a yellow and black livered machine. He stopped alongside their houseboat and checked the name on the envelope before turning off the engine. He walked onto the deck and spoke to Zita. 'Sigrid Obermeyer?' he asked.

She forced an exaggerated smile and nodded.

He handed her an envelope.

'Thank you,' she said.

She held it in her hand and watched as he climbed onto his motorbike and accelerated away.

Liam was in shock and mouthed her name. 'Sigrid–?'

'So now you know...' she said, exhaling heavily.

'Fuck.'

He was now totally confused and looked nervously at the envelope in her hand. 'Is that what I think it is - a telegram?'

She nodded.

'The last time I saw one of those - I was only a kid,' he said, recalling that afternoon. 'They told my mother that my father was being released.'

Zita shot him a blank look.

'Prison,' mouthed Liam.

She didn't respond and fiddled nervously with the envelope. After expelling a series of huge sighs and with heightened apprehension she opened it. As she read the one-word message all colour drained from her face.

'What is it?' asked Liam.

'They know...' She exhaled. 'They know...' She squeezed her bottom lip and tugged at it. 'They know I've broken *their* rules–'

'Who?'

She whispered her reply with a trembling breath. 'My bosses–'

'Bosses?' He swallowed hard. 'But...but you don't have a *boss.*'

'Don't I?'

'Well... do you?' He shook his head. 'Is that why they used your *real* name?'

She replied in little more than a whisper. 'Yes, of course it is.' She swallowed nervously. 'It is their signal–'

'Signal?' He tried to stand but the shock was too great and he slumped back into his seat and while he looked at her bowed head he shook. 'Fuck! What the hell is happening now?'

She looked up at him her face dejected and bewildered. 'I have a handler. And... you *never* leave them.'

'What?'

She shook her head. '*They* don't like it.' She held up the telegram and spoke as she exhaled, her voice fading to little more than a whisper. 'I broke their protocol. That is why they used my true name. They know I used their... their special...' She paused and gasped for breath. 'Their *secret* codes to hide our locations when...' Once more she struggled to catch her breath before she continued. 'When...' She paused and looked directly into Liam's eyes. 'Do you remember when I called Amsterdam and told Ribeker and Ackerman we were still in Berlin - when we weren't?' She swallowed hard. '*You know...* that each time we weren't. We were on the *De Groot's* island and... and *then* in Lisboa.'

'Oh, that,' said Liam, dismissively.

For the first time since Liam had known her, she openly displayed true fear. Still holding the telegram, she dropped the envelope and it was blown along the deck by the light breeze settling between the flower pots. She slumped into her wooden seat, grabbed at the arms and squeezed them until her knuckles, starved of blood, turned white. Her body tensed as she stared blindly ahead. She took several ragged breaths and continued. 'They will punish me and...' *She looked at the once wild Englishman now contaminated and tainted forever by the skilled ruthlessness that was second nature to her.*

She sighed with forced regret. 'And maybe...' She lowered her voice to a whisper. 'Maybe...' She sniffed as her sad eyes burnt into him. 'You too,' she said, weakly.

Zita's fear now gripped him and quickly swept throughout his body. The ensuing tension caused the scar tissue in his brutally damaged throat to tighten. He coughed hard then retched painfully and vomited onto the deck.

He turned his head and looked up at her. 'Do we deserve it?'

A beat.

Zita's head twitched uncontrollably and trembled as she looked furtively around. Once more, she released her mixed emotions with a deep shuddering sigh. She reached across and flicked the button on the CD player and after choosing the Bryan Adams 1985 song, *The Summer of '69,* she cranked up the volume.

As the music filled the deck she stood, walked unsteadily towards him and tugged gently at his hands. 'Liam... will you dance with me?'

He didn't move.

She tugged harder at his arms and reluctantly he stood.

She pulled him close to her and they hugged and moved gently, the opposite reaction of dancing enthusiastically to the pulsing rock track.

The assassin's first bullet blasted the head of the huge sunflower shredding it and spewing black and white seeds into the air and onto their heads.

Zita closed her eyes and pulled Liam tighter into her and as Bryan Adams sang "the best days of my life," she whispered in his ear. 'We have had fun... *haven't we, Li–?*'

Other titles by the author

COWBOYS AND ANGELS

Harry Clark was a soldier stationed in Cyprus where he met and married Xanthi but within weeks of the birth of his daughter he left to join the Special Forces.

His precarious life was cut short when he was shot by Malik, an Iraqi insurgent, and left for dead.

Twenty years after getting married Harry finally returned to Cyprus to fulfil his dream of opening his own restaurant. That was soon shattered when he was unwittingly dragged into the seedy world of people trafficking, and the reappearance of Malik.

Will he survive this time?

"A book for today ..."
"Another original thriller from Sclater ..."
"Things you don't imagine when you're on holiday ..."

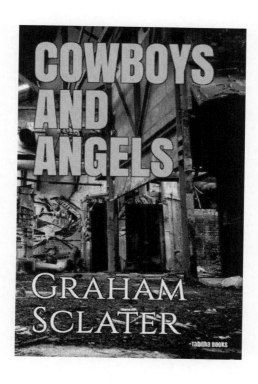

HATRED IS THE KEY

On June 18, 1812, the United States declared war on Great Britain. Almost immediately they called for an invasion of Canada. The initial American successes turned to a number of defeats resulting in English ships effectively blockading the American coastline and subjecting it to a series of hit and run raids and the capture of numerous ships.

The majority of the crew captured from the American ships were transported to Plymouth in southwest England to spend their time in notorious Dartmoor prison, constructed primarily by French Prisoners of War to house them and their countrymen.

Despite the end of the war neither country could agree who was responsible for repatriating the prisoners so they remained in jail.

"Compulsive reading"
"It felt like I was actually there"
"A story waiting to be told"

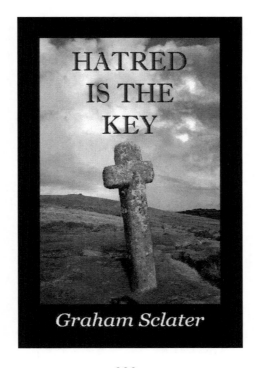

330

LOVE SHACK

A chance meeting between a young boy and Michael Collins in Macroom, a small town in County Cork, on the fateful day of his death on 22nd August 1922, affects the next three generations of the Reilly family.

Liam Reilly is an East End criminal, and alcoholic, and in 1999 he is forced to leave his home and family following a horrific episode caused by his drunkenness. He finds himself alone in Amsterdam, a city notorious for its extraordinary take on drugs and sex.

Can he finally beat his demons? Can he survive the next chapter of his pathetic life as he is immediately immersed in the seedy underworld that is the Red Light District?

"A great read that captures the very essence of this infamous part of Amsterdam"

"Sclater uncovers a world that few of us ever knew existed"

"Red light spells danger and in this book it does just that"

"Amsterdam als het wordt gezien vanaf de binnenkant"

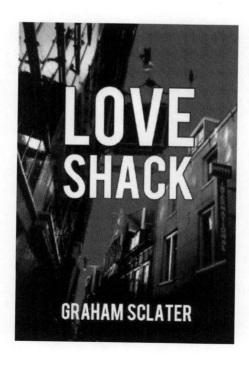

MORE THAN A WOMAN

Julian Hamilton-Lufton is a good looking, high-flying dealer at the London Stock Exchange. He can't resist a pretty woman and with his money and fast cars he finds it incredibly easy to satisfy his deep rooted lust anywhere, anytime. Alicia Fisher, a pretty woman married to Robbie who works in South Korea, is one of his many conquests, and following yet another illicit weekend with Julian at his country cottage she is racked with guilt and commits suicide.

Robbie returns from Asia for her funeral and as the truth unfolds he learns why she killed herself. The police have their suspicions but are unable to bring charges against Julian so Robbie takes things into his own hands.

He ruthlessly pursues a vendetta against Julian determined to ruin his success, business and ultimately his life in the most macabre way.

WE'RE GONNA BE FAMOUS

Young sisters Hannah and Abi are faced with a dilemma that would not be wished on anyone.

How do they help their seriously ill mother who is in desperate need of lifesaving and expensive treatment in America when all they have is their pocket money?

'Perhaps their love of music will help them but can they do anything in time?

'I cried several times while I was reading this book...sometimes with happiness.'

'A feel-good story that will make everyone smile.'

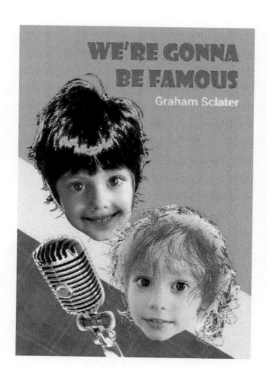

333

TOO BIG TO CRY

It's 2010 and the world is on the edge of a financial meltdown.

Brian Chapman feels the brunt of the problem as he struggles to keep his family business afloat with diminishing income and the looming financial catastrophe.

Can he survive this most challenging crisis of his life or will he lose everything?

"Sclater grabs the reader from the first chapter and tells it how it really is. . ."

"A seismic breakdown in family life. . . "

"Harrowing and shocking. . ."

"Sclater has the reader at the centre of the story. . .

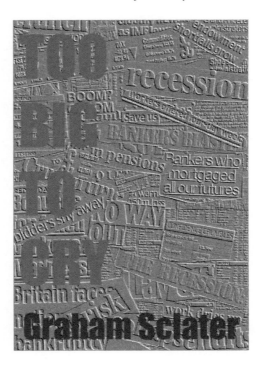

TICKET TO RIDE

'Ticket to Ride' is a satisfyingly filthy yet delightfully innocent, romp through the bars and clubs of late 60's Germany as The Cheetahs, a young band from small town southern England chase their dreams along the trail blazed by the Beatles in Hamburg. Along the way they discover the realities of life on the road in all of its...

Dirt & Glory - Sex & Drugs - Life & Death - Rock & Roll

...and it's all here in one gangster and hooker infested plate of realism, which was the Reeperbahn at that time...

Pulling no punches telling it like it was Sclater, who lived in this world himself for much of the 60s, tells us first hand through the eyes of characters based on real life kids who grew up fast faced with this in at the deep end rollercoaster ride of debauchery and ultimate demise. Not all gloom and doom though as the tale takes us beyond Hamburg, with occasional human kindness and discoveries of new loves of the strangest kind.

You'll be pulled into their world and the Horrors & Highlights befalling Reg, Jimmy, Adrian, Gerry and their leader Dave and their ever changing entourage, will keep you reading as the pace moves on just quickly enough to keep you hooked, never overblown with drama but full of the contrast between the naivety of our characters and the grittiness of events, mostly recognisable to anyone who's spent any time in the live music business, here, however, experienced in extremis. This book will leave you amazed that any of them survived, not all of them did, and there is a certain sadness to the conclusion, alien to any Hollywood version of books like this, but it's a melancholy which gives this slice of modern history the humanity it deserves. "Don't let your kids join a rock band Mrs Worthington!'

Dean G Hill

WRITE ON!

So you want to write a novel, your story, your life, your memoir, autobiography or your family history.

WRITE ON! Will help you do just that.

Graham Sclater has published seven novels in different genres and now gives creative writing talks on cruise ships, at libraries and literary festivals.

Graham said, "When I was asked to write this book I made a decision to keep it simple while at the same time aspiring to encourage you to release your potential."

Graham Sclater's book - WRITE ON! is written just for you.

Coming in 2021

STREETLIFE

People of all ages at one time or another yearn to drop out and follow their dreams in an attempt to escape from the real world of stress and the day-to-day worries, of conforming and following the system. While the majority fail, surprisingly a few do succeed, and in the strangest of ways. Talents that have lain dormant for years now become the only way to scratch a meagre living.

The beautiful and ancient cathedral city of Monkton in south west England has long been a magnet to holidaymakers, tourists and more recently travellers and buskers.

Street life and the seedier side of what the tourists don't see or imagine bubbles beneath the surface. Petty crime and drugs are an everyday occurrence in the struggle for survival, sometimes against each other but certainly against authoritarianism. Although Buskers are enjoyed by the tourists and traders, the local authorities do not make them welcome.

Buskers live in a world of their own but are able to at least scrape a living on the strength of their talents, and retain an independence of sorts.

"Sclater went busking to find out what it was really like on the streets and he was shocked at what he found."

The author in Hamburg

Printed in Poland
by Amazon Fulfillment
Poland Sp. z o.o., Wrocław

62330542R00192